BACKWOODS

The Girl in the Box, Book 47

ROBERT J. CRANE

Ostiagard Press

Backwoods

The Girl in the Box, Book 47

Robert J. Crane

copyright © 2021 Ostiagard Press

1st Edition.

This book is a work of fiction. Names, characters, places, and incidents are products of the author's imagination or are used fictitiously. Any resemblance to actual events or locales or persons, living or dead, is entirely coincidental.

The scanning, uploading, and distribution of this book via the internet or any other means without the permission of the publisher is illegal and punishable by law. Please purchase only authorized electronic editions, and do not participate in or encourage electronic piracy of copyrighted materials. Your support of the author's rights is appreciated.

No part of this publication may be reproduced in whole or in part without the written permission of the publisher. For information regarding permission, please email cyrusdavidon@gmail.com.

CHAPTER ONE

The chirps of crickets and cicadas, and all the pleasant noises of the woods, were giving way to the sound of chainsaws, bulldozers, and backhoes, and Larry Benson found he didn't much care for it all. Sure, it was his job to build, to clear the land, to make ready this site – all 2,000 acres of it, a cherry spot just outside the small burg of Fountain Run, Tennessee – for the new Waters Tech corporate headquarters.

But Larry didn't have to like it. And Larry damned sure didn't.

"Should have taken up that rehab project on the UT campus," he muttered to himself, swatting at a fly that buzzed his neck.

But he hadn't. Because this had paid more.

"You think that billionaire that hired us is really going to build out this whole place?" Elijah Torres asked. He swatted at the fly as it buzzed him, too. Weird for it to be this hot in the first week of November, but it was, and that was fine. It just gave them more time to get the clearing started to lay down the roads into the valley for the first phase of construction. This was a job that was going to be paying Larry's bills for years to come. First, clear the trees – not all, but most – and build the road into the valley. Then, the next phase, down in the valley – he was supposed to start building the HQ, then mixed use buildings with housing and commerce for the rank and file workers. Grocery store, restaurant, an ice cream shop. Then they'd start on the houses for the big shots a little farther out.

"I think he means to see it through, yes," Larry said, peering ahead. The woods were thick, and the land dropped off quick. They were at the crest of a ridge, and the vegetation was so tight there wasn't much seeing ahead. It wasn't exactly a foggy morning, but the vines and thick shrubs in these untamed woods made it difficult to see very far. "He's big on all that small town sort of flavor, that 'walkability' thing."

"Hey, boss?" Elijah called out, and Larry turned. Elijah was older, thick around the middle, didn't exactly get up and hustle these days, and he got the feeling if it wasn't impermissible, Elijah would have his hard hat in his hand.

"Yeah?"

Elijah shuffled back and forth on his feet. "I, uh...I sent Tyrese, David, and Andrew down there to get the lay of the land ahead?" He pointed into the morass of green ahead. "They been gone about an hour and ain't come back yet."

Larry frowned at that piece of news. "Well, go find 'em. They probably decided to take a nap in the woods." He mopped at his forehead with his sleeve. That certainly seemed like a good idea.

"I don't think so, chief," Elijah said. "Think you better come take a look."

Larry thought about protesting, thought about saying something along the lines of "I don't do that."

But he didn't. He obliged and followed Elijah forward, toward the thick wall of shrub and vine and trees. His skin was already crawling. Or was that the sweat trickling down it? God, why was it so hot in November?

"I got a bad feeling in here, chief," Elijah said.

Larry followed him, brushing his hand against a series of vines, pushing them back to see the crinkled, brown, long-dead leaves on the maples above. Soon, they'd be turning colors. Hell, he was amazed they hadn't begun to go bright yellow and blazing red yet. "You don't get out in the woods much, do you?" Larry cracked a smile. "David? Tyrese? Andrew? Where y'all at?"

No answer. Just the rustle of the trees and the sound of the chainsaws and earth movers going back at the site.

They walked and called, walked and called, pushing through the scrub brush, the heavy vegetation. Larry's hands were scraped within minutes. Stupid to do this without gloves. He paused, putting a hand on a pine tree's rough bark. "They must have gone in deep," he said, holding up at the crest of the ridge.

This was where the road was going to come through. Down, down into the valley, and phase one – the headquarters – was going to be built a couple hundred yards ahead. "Six weeks behind schedule already," Larry griped. Environmental surveys. Wetland assessments. Millions sunk into this project already and all they'd done was clear earth to put in a road. "I don't need this shit. We got to get back on–"

A flock of birds burst out of a nearby bush right in the middle of his griping and about scared the bejeezus out of Larry.

Elijah was holding his hand to his chest. "Thought they had me there for a second. How about you?"

"Mmhm," Larry said, stopping just below the ridgeline.

Something set his teeth to rattling just then, and it wasn't the birds. The woods ahead looked real dark as the ridgeline sloped down, the boughs overhead joining together with their neighbors like interlaced fingers, blotting out the sun. That kind of thick canopy ought to kill off the vegetation below, but–

There was a full array of bushes and vines and smaller trees all hunkered down below the treetops, a thick and seemingly impenetrable wall of vegetation beginning about ten yards in front of them. He looked at the ground and saw...

Well, nothing. Virgin, untrammeled ground. To the left, the same wall of vegetation was thick, almost too thick to pass, and damned sure too thick to pass without making a hash of the thing.

"Tyrese! Andrew! David!" Larry called.

The only sound was branches rustling in the wind. Even the hum of the cicadas had died away.

"Where did they go?" Larry asked. "Cuz they sure as hell didn't come this way." He took a knee, looking at the ground. A reasonable tracker, he'd learned over a lifetime of hunting experience how to spot the signs of animals, and there was no hint of anything but his steps and Elijah's.

"Hey, boss?" Elijah asked, "you getting kind of a bad feeling here?"

"No," Larry said, on the knee, looking at the ground, "but I ain't getting a good one, either." He stood, going for the walkie-talkie on his belt. "Let's go back and see if we can find their trail." He looked at the ground, wishing he could see a hint of something, anything coming this way. High rock formations rising up on either side made this pass the only game in town for coming into this valley...and they hadn't come this way. "Because I have no earthly idea what happened to these boys."

CHAPTER TWO

They called him Beatz, cuz he'd come to Nashville for a career in music and the beats he dropped were sick.

Also, he had a thing – well known – for smacking a bitch if need be. Cuz he started as a pimp when no one in the record business liked his beats enough to sign him.

Now Beatz had moved up in the world, thanks to the sudden vacuum in the Nashville underworld. Yesterday's pimp was today's pusher was tomorrow's kingpin.

And Beatz? The sky was the limit for a man like him.

"Yo, get the cash ready," Beatz said to Fergs as he stepped out of the BMW 530i. Brand new lease, perfectly reflective of his moving up in the world. Fergs was his right-hand man. "I'ma talk to these punks, see what they got to say."

Two of his flunkies stepped out with Beatz into the cool night, leaving behind Fergs with the money. He wouldn't come out until it was time, then his big ass would unfold out the BMW, briefcase in hand, cutting an intimidating figure just before the handoff.

Beatz knew that was where things were most likely to go

wrong in the deal. But he had plans to make sure that didn't happen.

Another car was parked opposite them, about ten yards away. Toyota Highlander, and all four doors popped open to reveal a bunch of big white dudes with no necks and silken suits. Not traditional Mafia, but some branch of it. Beatz didn't know which, because he didn't pay much attention to these things, he just knew who the guys were he needed to deal with to get his supply.

"Yo yo," Beatz said, strutting to the midway point between their cars, keeping his hand away from his waist. People were jumpy these days 'round these parts, no reason to give 'em cause. "I got the money if you got the shit."

One of the big lumpy bastards, who all looked like they ate pasta five times a day, came out in the lead. His hair was slicked back, but he talked with a southern accent. "We got the shit if you got the money, son."

"Let's make a deal, then," Beatz said, beckoning for Fergs, who popped out of the car, surprisingly spry for such a big boy. He swayed his way over and popped the case, revealing rows of crumpled bills bound together by rubber bands.

"Hold up a minute." One of the mafiosos eased forward. "You mind if my friend here does a count while your boy holds it?"

"That's fine," Beatz said, then he cracked a grin. "You don't trust me?"

The big guy standing opposite him lost all humor in that moment. "Lately, I don't trust nobody. And you'd do real well to adopt the same attitude."

Beatz nodded. "It's been a rough couple months for y'all establishment types." He popped out his lapels and grinned, revealing gold-capped teeth. "But it's been good times for us ambitious types."

Big Boy looked like he was about to twitch. "You play

loud and stupid, your turn will come." He glanced around – left, right, up. The parking lot was lit by only a couple lamps, and beyond them was an urban wasteland for a mile in every direction. A golf complex lay to the south, the river to the west, and otherwise the place was empty.

"Pfffft, I ain't afraid of Superchick," Beatz said, smirking. "I go strapped." He patted the gun he had in the small of his back. It wasn't the only one, nor would it be the one he'd draw if these fools started something. "She can throw fire. I'll throw back lead, see how she likes it."

"I hear she's out of town right now." Didn't sound as if Big Boy liked his buoyant attitude. "But yeah, you just charge in and give her hell if you run across her. I bet that'll go real well for you." He glanced at his compatriot counting the money. "We good?"

"We good."

"All right." Big Boy popped his own briefcase open to reveal a beautiful series of bags, filled with white powder. "This stuff is either ready to go if you're feeling generous, or ready to be cut further if you're wanting to make a little extra money. Your choice."

"I'm all about the extra paper," Beatz said, creeping up on it. "And it is a seller's market in Nashville at the moment." This was fact. You couldn't keep a dealer on the streets these days.

"Not all about building a reputation for quality?" Big Boy shrugged, nodded at the man who'd counted the cash. "Well, it's yours now. You do whatever you want with it."

"Thanks, I will," Beatz said, taking the briefcase with the powder and snapping it shut before he let it fall to his side. "Oh – and because this is our first time doing business, I brought you a gift. You know, to establish mutual trust and ties and shit." He snapped his fingers.

That put everyone on edge, but Fergs popped 'round to

the trunk of the BMW, keeping his hands high where everyone could see 'em. "It ain't nothing nasty," Beatz said with a big grin. "It's nice. You'll thank me later."

Fergs lifted something out of the trunk with only a little difficulty. Big fella like him, it wasn't much challenge to pick up a girl who weighed a hundred pounds soaking wet and get her on her feet.

Keeping her on her feet...well, that was a bit more trouble for him. Her dark hair was mussed from being in the trunk, and she wore a cheap low-cut, high-rise dress that would have fit real nice in the club. Which was where Beatz had picked her up with a little narcotic assistance, and added her to his stable. But he'd tired of her quickly, and these boys were too serious, clearly needing something to take their minds off their problems. Fergs brought her over on thin, swaying legs, keeping her from wiping out on the concrete.

"The hell is this?" Big Boy asked, looking at her with vague disgust.

"She's whatever you want her to be," Beatz said with a grin. "She's real...what would you call it? Pliable. Give her a needle in the arm every once in a while, and she's sweet as can be. Hell, she'll do anything for you."

That set Big Boy to thinking, eyes slitting in that big, piggy head of his. "She do laundry?"

Beatz's grin melted away. "You joking?"

Big Boy shrugged. "I got a wife and a mistress already. That's enough trouble for one guy."

"Well, give her to one of your less fortunate boys, then, if you're already knee deep," Beatz said, scoffing. "What's that old saying, though? 'Don't be looking a gift whore in the mouth.'"

"It's 'gift horse.' *Horse*. Not whores. Honestly, you guys are so stupid," announced a voice from...where the hell had that come from?

It was harsh but feminine, and it echoed between the cars. Beatz looked around, feeling a little trickle of worry run up his spine.

"Shiiiiiiiit," Big Boy said, backing away, clutching his briefcase of cash. He looked up, and his eyes locked on something. Beatz followed his gaze, looked up, too, and found–

There she was, floating down, TBI windbreaker flapping behind her as she landed. Short, thick-thighed, hair in a dark ponytail, face pale and freckled in the lamp light. Her eyes were big, but amused, and she was keeping an eye on every last one of them with a watchful gaze.

"I guess you guys haven't heard – or maybe you have, given the content of your discussion earlier – but crime is over in Nashville." She kept her hands at her sides, but one of them was already glowing softly with light. "So throw down the briefcases, put up your hands..." And now she smirked, "...because you're under arrest."

CHAPTER THREE

Sienna

I watched the drug sale turned-human-trafficking swap get real tense when I showed up, and that tension did not fade after I delivered my ultimatum about arrest. It infused the night air like humidity during the summer, and the newbie gangsters on my left with their nouveau riche BMW looked shocked-bordering-on-pissed while the old school mafiosos with the Toyota looked ready to run for it. The big guy in charge over there looked over his shoulder again and again, like he could just run away without me noticing.

No chance of that. Not only because I doubted his knees would hold up to a good run, but because I would fly him down.

"Yo, you think you can just run up in here and lay your thing down on us and we're just gonna give up?" the guy with the golden teeth asked. He really put his money where his mouth was.

I blinked a couple times, hand next to my waistband. "If you're smart...yes." I drew my pistol and had it aimed at his head so fast he took a step back in surprise. His big friend caught him before he fell over backwards. "Now...hands in the air, boys."

"I didn't do nothing," the big guy in the suit said in a southern accent, lifting his hands and dropping the money briefcase to the parking lot with a clatter. His fellows followed suit, raising their ham-like hands.

"Yeah, I'm sure you got that money from painting houses," I said.

"You gonna just bitch out like that?" Gold Tooth asked. He had his blond hair in corn rows for some reason. The man looked like a white trashier Post Malone. "She show her face and you show your belly, like a dog?" His hands were at his sides, quivering.

"Oh, come on," I said, keeping my gun lined up on his head. "You know I can drop you faster than your high school math team did, right?"

"Pfft, I ain't got that book learning," Gold Tooth said, "but I know what time it is." He looked at his rather more well-fed trading partners. "And I ain't no punk that lays down for some bitch."

"Hey, who you talking that trash to?" the big guy turned real red, real fast. "My momma didn't raise no bitch!"

I frowned. This was not going the way it needed to. "Guys, I think we're losing sight of the fact that there's a TBI agent with a gun on you telling you to—"

"Your lips are flapping it, but I don't see you reaching for your hip," Gold Tooth said. "That makes you a bitch. You old-school punks were just asking to be taken out by this girl. Y'all weak." He made a noise of clear disapproval.

"Listen, number one patient of the Midas Dentistry Practice, you're about to get taken out by 'this girl,'" I said, feeling my brow furrow.

"You want me to draw on her?" Big Boy was yelling at him now. "I don't see you drawing on her. What kind of man are you, huh? Huh?"

"If anybody draws a gun they're getting shot," I said. "Let's get that clear right now–"

"You a bitch," Gold Tooth said. "Nothing but a bitch, flapping your mouth like a bitch does, looking to get slapped–"

"I'll slap you, how about that?" Big Boy fired back. They looked like they were about to come to blows. Right here. With me pointing a gun at both of them, and them ignoring me.

"If you guys are going to have a dick measuring contest," I said, feeling my patience slip away, "I'm going to need a microscope and a pair of tweezers to officiate–"

It was then that I heard a car's tires screech, and close by. It had crept in out of the darkness with the lights off, sneaking up behind me while I was listening to these two snipe at each other. I turned my head, but didn't dare to spin around, because I was keenly aware I still had hostiles in front of me. Eight of them, to be exact.

And in behind me rolled not one, but two SUVs packed with guys with guns. They screeched to a stop and started to deploy, and I knew I'd just been pincered.

"Who's the bitch now?" Gold Tooth asked. He was grinning, showing me what he had, and next to him, Big Boy was smiling, too, because these rats could smell that the odds had just shifted in their favor.

And then they all went for their guns.

CHAPTER FOUR

There's a subtle trick to winning a gunfight that's maybe lost on the uninitiated, which is to say people who've never been in one, and it goes like this:

You need to shoot them while assiduously avoiding being shot yourself.

Profound wisdom, right?

Yeah, I'd started this one off in a bad spot for keeping that rule intact. I was stuck between four carloads of gangsters, all armed, and they had me boxed in on either side. I didn't wait for the guys behind me to get out to realize that they were rocking black rifles with large capacity mags and I was just standing here with a HK VP9 handgun, a Sig P365 as my backup gun, and a couple reload magazines for each.

Outgunned.

Outmanned.

Outmaneuvered.

"You motherf–" I started to say. I finished it in proud Samuel L. Jackson fashion.

And I opened fire.

I put two rounds in Big Boy's heart, then one in his head,

what the pros call the Mozambique drill. He'd been breaking for his gun first, and I needed to change position. I took out another of his guys, then shot forward at high speed, catching hold of the toddling party girl with the dead, drugged-out eyes and dragging her behind the Toyota as I tried to save both our lives.

The quiet night was split with a shit ton (that's a technical term) of gunfire, turning this empty parking lot down by the river into a war zone. The sound of rifles ripping up the Toyota was combined with the tinkling of glass falling on me, catching in my hair and pinging off the engine of the SUV.

I spun to my right, running another Mozambique drill on the big guy from the BMW crew who'd held the money. He looked vaguely shocked that I'd had the raw effrontery to shoot him in the heart, but his umbrage faded when his brains exited out of the back of his head on my third shot.

Looking to the swaying girl in the party dress, I said, "You need to stay down."

She burbled an answer, and I couldn't even tell if I was talking to a human being, they had her so damned strung out.

The Toyota was not going to stand up to sustained rifle fire forever, and I knew it. Dodging around the far side of the SUV, I popped the last two of the old-school gangsters with a Mozambique drill each and dropped my empty mag, one round left in the chamber. They fell over dead on the pavement, clearing that entire side of the vehicle. Not that that meant much; at any moment the riflemen could decide to come charging in from that direction.

Still, it gave me a moment's peace as I spun back around, pushing the dead-doll-eyed abductee behind me to protect her as best I could. "Stay down," I said again. Still no response. God only knew what they'd done to her.

Slapping a fresh mag back in my HK, I came slowly around the corner of the Toyota, and found Gold Tooth there waiting. He fired at me thrice, shattering the Toyota's taillight and blasting me with plastic shards. I ducked around the tailgate for cover.

"I'm gonna shoot you right in the heart – bitch," Gold Tooth called out, sheltering behind the hood of the BMW.

"Not sure that exists anymore," I said, looking at the back of the BMW – and a quick answer for how to guarantee that he wouldn't, regardless of whether my heart existed.

I shot a blast of fire, hot as I could make it, into the gas tank cap on the side of the BMW. It took a few seconds for the flames to eat through the cap and then the safety valve inside. Once they did, though...

They made their way quickly to the gas tank, which went up with a giant, flaming WHUMP!

"This way," I said, seizing hold of the dead-doll-eyed girl and dragging her around the side of the Toyota, putting it between us and the burning BMW. I could hear screaming over there, because fire was not a fun way to die, but I had other things to worry about.

Shoving the girl lightly, I watched her fall back on her ass with a thump that she barely acknowledged, she was so doped up. With her as safe as I could make her, I moved forward, crouched behind the Toyota and taking advantage of the distraction of the sudden rush of heat and noise.

I popped up and started firing as fast as I could. I dropped one guy before they turned their rifles loose on the Toyota while aiming for me, and I was forced to fling myself backward behind cover again.

I reached out with Chad Goodwin in mind, trying to push my sense of magnetics past the lead flying around and the heavy frame of the Toyota. Most of the shots were passing over my head and few enough were even hitting the Toyota at this point. These boys had gone wild, and were starting to move to flank me, which meant I needed to take some remedial action.

"You can't burn me out! And I'ma make you pay for torching my new whip!" Gold Teeth crowed from somewhere between me and the burning car, over the sound of the perpetual gunshots. I triangulated his voice to just beyond the Toyota's passenger door.

"Did he just say 'whip?'" the girl in the club dress asked. She was plopped down, staring dully straight ahead, and her voice had a dreamlike, drunken quality. "Who calls their car a 'whip' anymore?"

"Idiots," I said. "Mostly idiots." And then...

Got him.

I could feel his teeth, dotting his filthy mouth, and below that, the gun in his hand. He had a firm grip on it, and was stroking the trigger at regular intervals; I wouldn't be able to stop that for more than a second.

But I also felt the second gun in the back of his waistband, a striker-fired weapon with a polymer frame–

And no safety.

I pulled the hammer back internally (because the trigger was polymer, too) and let it rip.

An epic scream cut through the air over the rifle blasts, and Gold Teeth screamed, "Damn! I got *got!*"

The gunfire faded for a precious few seconds, during which I heard someone ask, "You okay, boss?" I could feel the guys because of their guns, poised at the ends of the Toyota, ready to encircle me in both directions, which would be – let's not mince words – bad.

"No, I am not okay!" Gold Teeth said, dancing around so strong I could feel his pistol moving with his gyrations. "Y'all shot me in my ass!"

"I didn't shoot you, boss!"

"Me, eith–"

As amusing as it would have been to listen to them assert their innocence all day, I had seconds before they remembered they were in a gunfight.

I used those seconds as wisely as I could.

Dropping to my back, hovering an inch above the parking lot, I slid up to the Toyota, planting both feet on the frame of the car as low as I could get them. I clenched my gun in my hand and looked right into the doll eyes of the girl, who stared at me blankly. "Cover your ears."

She dutifully, slowly obliged, but I was already in motion.

"Good thing I've been working my quads," I said, and, holding my body in place with my flight powers, pushed for all my thick and steely thighs were worth.

The Toyota slid sideways like it had been going fifty and hit a patch of ice. Ignoring the screams from the other side of it, I put the sights of my pistol on the nearest guy to my left who'd been about to pop out from behind the hood and drill me.

I drilled him instead. One to the head, because I was in a hurry.

The second I saw him start to drop I shifted targets, popping the next guy twice, because he didn't immediately begin to fall down. Flying along to follow the Toyota as it slid forward, I aimed right, firing at two guys who suddenly appeared at the back of the SUV as it slid away, popping them both and letting them fall like puppets with their strings cut.

The Toyota smashed hard into the burning BMW, producing a crashing, crunching noise that played well with all the screaming.

I gradually stood up, scanning with my pistol, but there was no one still alive and walking around. A couple of the guys had been dragged under the Toyota by my hard push, and I could see legs sticking out from beneath like some modern-day parody of the Wicked Witch of the East. Except their shoes were shit.

"Unnnnnh...ahhhh," Gold Teeth moaned, and I looked to find him pinned between the Toyota and the burning BMW, head visible through the Toyota's broken windows, his fancy clothing just starting to catch fire. "You don't fight...fair..." His voice drifted off. The gold teeth were stained with blood.

"True," I said, "because then I might lose." I looked around once more, counted the dead. Yep, I got 'em all. "And I don't like to lose."

The flames were creeping up his jacket, and he was grunting. "You cold, bitch! You so cold!"

"You're not, though, are you? Though I do feel like people are forgetting that," I said. "And they probably shouldn't. It seems...important. Like they should remember that before they mess with me."

"Ahhh – ahhhh – ahhhHHHHHHHH!" His voice reached a high-pitched screaming as the heat on his nerves overrode his ability to speak coherently. "Help meEEEEEEE!"

"Oh, hush up, you big baby," I said, grabbing the Toyota by the frame and pulling it back to free him. Leaping over it, I pulled him to safety. "I wasn't going to let you die." I looked at his body, which was crushed and bloody, about a half-dozen spots welling crimson. "Uhhh...of that, anyway." I cringed, because there were no good signs for his survival here.

I laid him down gently next to the doped-out girl, who watched with bleary eyes. "Unnnnnnhhhh..." he groaned. "You...killed me..."

"You tried to kill me," I said, checking him over. I pulled the gun from out of his waistband and laid it off to the side, out of his arm's reach. It clattered against the asphalt, harmonizing with the crackle of flames and the sound of sirens, which were now drawing closer. "You really thought it was going to work?"

His eyes looked dazed. "You...killed me..."

A gun fired, loud and hard, about six inches from his head, and I sent a light web flying in the direction of the flash.

The strung-out girl tipped over, her hand trapped with the gun in it, both bound to the parking lot. She struggled, once again flat on her ass, but her eyes now showed just enough life to reveal one overriding emotion–

Pure, unadulterated hatred.

The sirens drew closer as I surveyed what she'd done. Gold Teeth was definitely dead, brains scattered all over the pavement. There was no putting that genie back in the bottle, and frankly, given what I'd heard him say about her, I couldn't really find much sadness in my heart for what she'd done.

"Welp," I said as the first TBI SUVs raced into the parking lot to join us, "you sure settled his hash."

"Bitch had it coming," she said, her head swaying gently side to side.

"I believe you," I said, extracting the pistol from the light web trapping her hand with great care, so I didn't break any of her fingers. "And I'll testify to it in court, so you probably won't see any jail time." The first TBI agents were popping out of their cars on the scene now, and I waved over the nearest one. "Scene's secure. Tangos are down. This girl was a prisoner of them and shot one to get free. She needs a blood test for whatever they've got her doped up on. Maybe some narcan. Treat her gently, okay?"

"You got it," the agent said, hustling in with the rest to secure the scene.

A little farther back I could see the command SUV come rolling up. A tallish, thin man came popping out with a vest with TBI written across the chest. His deep black hair was starting to get a little longer, and it got in his eyes, forcing him to brush it back. "Holy hell, Sienna," he said with a slight Indian accent. "I thought this was going to be a simple bust?"

"It got a little complicated, okay?" I shrugged. "They started it."

"And you finished it," Chandler said, looking over the carnage. "Dead bodies, burning cars...this looks like a scene from *Mad Max*."

"Well, I am mad. Mad Sienna," I said, lifting a few inches off the ground.

"Where are you going?"

"Gotta go talk to my CI," I said. "This was not the layup I was told it would be." I felt my eyes narrow as a hint of anger escaped me. "We need to have a little chat." And I jetted into the sky, heading across the river toward the skyscrapers of downtown.

CHAPTER FIVE

I set down in the parking of the Pussycat Connection and breezed past two bouncers with nothing but a flashed badge. They were cowed, either by my sheer authority or the look on my face, but either way they stood aside and let me into the neon glow of Nashville's seediest strip club.

I ignored the riot of flesh and flashing lights, skirting my way past drunken customers and in-progress lap dances to a table at the back of the room where a short, slightly plump woman with completely straight hair sagging around her shoulders was sitting with a laptop in front of her, eyes watching me, face lit by the phosphorescent glow of her screen. No sign of worry showed itself on her face, save for a single cocked eyebrow.

Robin Hayes didn't rise to great me as I stormed up to her table. She stayed seated, upright, and pulled her fingers away from the keys. "What can I do for you, Agent Nealon?"

"I have half a mind to arrest you right here and now," I said, loud enough that half the room could hear me over the pulsating music. "You can get a damned office that's not in a strip club, for one," I said, switching to the meta-low voice register I knew couldn't be overheard by anyone without powers. And in here, under this aural atrocity of club music, that meant by no one but myself and Robin Hayes.

She kept a blank-bordering-on-steely look and said, "I think you need to have this conversation with my lawyer," so that everyone could hear. Then, below it, she said, "You really flew all this way and put on this show to complain that I'm working out of a titty bar?" She shifted in her seat. "Something go wrong on that deal I tipped you off about?"

"Parking lot full of dead guys," I said, low, then, high, "That lawyer shit holds no water with me, Hayes. I know you have your fingers in a dozen dirty pies in this town."

That caused Robin to raise an eyebrow. "How'd that happen?" she asked, just for me. Then, loud: "I don't like pies, Nealon, let alone dirty ones."

"Judging by your place of work, you don't much care for clean," I said. "I ought to have every single law enforcement agency in the state tearing this place apart – and that includes the health inspector." I let my eyes alight on the next table, where a guy was getting a lap dance but had a burger and a plate of fries right there, a little too close to a stripper's crotch for my taste. "Bet he'd find a bonanza of violations in here." Then, beneath it all: "They tried to ambush me."

"Dixie Mafia tried to ambush you?" Her eyebrow crept a little higher. Then, her voice went loud: "You can come in here and bluster all day, but I don't see you getting a warrant. And our last health inspection was a perfect 100, I'll have you know."

"Did he see your girls gyrating their snizz all around the food?" I asked, chucking a thumb at the display at the next table. Low: "I don't know. Which ones were the Dixie Mafia?"

"Guys in suits."

"They were all wearing suits."

"Big guys in suits."

"Some of the other guys were big."

Robin loosed a frustrated sigh. "I don't really know the new players, all right? The old, bigger guys in suits, okay?"

"We have to continue our argument," I said, looking around; we'd stopped playing to the crowd about five seconds ago.

"I don't know how you want me to respond to that," Robin said out loud, and I got the feeling she was speaking for both conversations here.

"I want the truth," I said, giving her a hard look.

"My girls are very clean," she said. "Clean enough to—"

I shook my head subtly, hoping only she could see it.

"I didn't set you up," she said, closing the lid of her laptop and speaking meta-low. "No one with a brain and a basic knowledge of what you're capable of would try and double-cross you, especially in what I'm guessing was a clumsy way. I mean...I'm just trying to walk the line between being a cooperative source and being a femme Whitey Bulger, okay? I'm helping. As much as I can. And look – Nashville is cleaner than it's ever been."

"You're in a dirty business," I said, not bothering to lower my voice on that.

She stared at me for a second, then seemed to realize that was for both parts of the conversation. "Just because you don't like my club doesn't mean you can come in here and insult me." Then, lower: "I told you, I cleared out of the worst parts. Per our agreement."

I searched the room with my eyes, cringing inside at the display. "I may not be able to bust you today, Hayes," I said, loud, "but I'm watching you." Then, low: "Fine. I accept your explanation. Explanations. Just got a little dodgy about getting shot at."

"They're gangsters," she said. "Surely you know they do

that sort of shit." She stood, then, quite loud, "Like I said – take your complaints up with my lawyer – and get the hell out of my club."

"Seriously, get an office," I said, looking around in revulsion. Naked bodies still bothered me in this context. And in most contexts.

"Then you might stop by more often," she said, meta-low. "And we can't have that, can we? I don't need anyone thinking I'm cooperating with the law. I need them thinking I'm the illegal last game in town, so that I can then feed the worst of them to you. Smile – you're cleaning up Nashville. Everyone says so." Her faced changed subtly. "But maybe don't smile here, unless it's an evil one."

I hardened my face into a disgusted look. It wasn't hard, because being in the presence of this much paid-for, unnatural lust and exploitation made me slightly queasy. "I'll see you again soon," I said, glaring at her.

"Yeah, try a phone call next time," she said softly. "Unless you're inviting me to a social event. Then a text will do." She raised her hand to show me the door.

"I was thinking about starting a bunco game," I said, meta-low. "You interested?"

"I might be, depending on which night of the week it is," she said, replying in kind. "Now get out."

"Probably once a month. I'll text you," I said, low. "Up yours, Hayes."

She shot me a bird. I replied with my own, then flew out the front door so fast that every patron in the place gasped in shock at the sudden wind storm. Taking a northwesterly tack, I headed back toward the parking lot where I'd left the dead, figuring I was going to spend the next several hours answering uncomfortable questions about my role in that damned, unexpected massacre.

CHAPTER SIX

About an hour and change later I landed at my house, the moon already high in the sky under a cloudless, slightly crisp night. I found the hollow rock and clawed out the key within, unlocking my door and then returning it to the place in the planter where it hid, slipping in through the basement to a quiet house.

Too quiet.

"I'm upstairs," came a male voice, familiar as hell. "No shooting me."

I floated up, not even inclined to pull my pistol. "What are you doing here?" I called back, rising above the top step and coming around the corner into the kitchen...

...To find my brother sitting in the big chair in the corner of the family room, both pups on his lap and a bottled water in his hand.

"Isabelle's out of town, remember?" Reed looked at me, one eyebrow cocked, running a hand over Cali's smooth fur, then switching to Jack's short, brown coat. Those two appeased, he then moved his hand to pet...well... "By the way...did you really need to get a kitten?"

"That's not my kitten," I said, watching him stroke the kitty's lush, baby-soft coat with practiced gentleness. "That's Cali's kitten. And her name is Emma."

That thing is not mine, Cali said. Then she lifted her head. *Unless it's dinner?*

I want it for dinner! Jack said, lifting his own head in anticipation.

"No," I said, tapping into Priscilla voice. "The kitty is a friend, not dinner."

Awwwww, Jack and Cali's disappointment was almost tangible. *But it's so small.*

Hardly a snack, Cali said.

"This is why I keep the kitty in the little cage while I'm gone," I muttered.

A jaded look flitted over my brother's face, turning amused as Cali and Jack put their heads back down on his lap. "How many pets are you going to adopt as part of this new addiction? Round to the nearest ten, please."

"I decline to answer that on advice of counsel," I said, slipping off my jacket and tossing it around the corner into the mudroom area. It landed on the floor, but who cares? I lived alone, after all.

"You didn't even consult a lawyer before answering."

"Brianna is my counsel," I said. "She says 'hi,' by the way."

"Hey," Reed said, petting the triad on his lap once more. "So...what were you up to tonight?"

"Should have listened to the police scanner," I said, tapping the one sitting on the counter as I went by. It was tied into local counties via the internet. "You'd have gotten a full account of my thrilling adventures taking on the few remaining mafiosos up in Nashville tonight."

"Uh huh," he said, seemingly unimpressed. "You know, I'm leaving for Atlanta tomorrow with Jamal."

"I hope he enjoys his trip home," I said, flying myself up

over the sofa and then landing my tush delicately upon it, probably a weird thing to watch but the sort of thing I did all the time these days. "But why are you going?"

"Taneshia needs a hand with some sneaky villain plaguing the town. Georgia asked, we answered."

"You should have sent Augustus," I said. "Maybe they could have worked out their issu–"

"He passed on it," Reed said. "So I sent him with Scott to Arizona for that energy projection case."

"Mmm," I said. "Busy boys."

"Everyone's out again right now, Sienna," Reed said, giving extra attention to the sleeping kitty on his lap. "We have more cases than we can handle."

"I know." I shrugged. "So do I, though, and someone's gotta keep the State of Tennessee happy so we can keep having a base of operations and all that."

"Uh huh," Reed said. So jaded, my brother. "Can I make an observation?"

"I'm sure you *can*. *Should* you, though?"

"You're not going to...get mad, or spiral, or start drinking again if I do, and it upsets you?"

I made a face. "I'm not making any promises, but I think it's unlikely I'm going to crawl back in the bottle just because you hurt my feelings."

"Well, I did ask if you were going to get mad."

"That's a fair possibility," I said, "and if I do, you'll know it because I'll gather up some water from the pool and douse you with it."

Cali put her head up again. *If he gonna be wet, I need know so I can leave lap. Scratches not worth bath.*

Jack lifted his head, too. *Same same.*

The kitty was sleeping, and not really capable of cute speech yet. But soon, I hoped. Soon. She slept, with a little purring action coming from her nostrils that was adorable.

"Of course if I soak him, I'll keep it off of you guys," I said in animalese.

Oh, okay, Cali said, always the ringleader. She and Jack both put their heads back down again. *Mmmm...scratches*, Cali said as Reed's hand found its way to her thickly-furred neck once more.

"All right," Reed said, apparently steeling himself for a tough conversation. "Here goes: I think you need to get out of Nashville for a while."

I looked around like I was being punked. "Um...we're not in Nashville now. This is Franklin."

"You know what I mean," Reed said, so long-suffering. "You need to get out of the metro area. Hell, you need to get out of Middle Tennessee."

"And I was just about to suggest an adjournment to Murfreesboro."

"Have you seen the crime stats from this area?" Reed asked, not letting up on the puppy/kitty petting, lucky for him. "Violent crime is down eighty-two percent since September, when we got here. Property crimes down eighty-seven percent."

"What I'm hearing you say is, 'Sienna, you need to get out of town for a while to give thieves, murderers, and rapists some room to work.'"

Reed stopped the petting for a moment to rub his forehead. "That's not what I'm saying and I think you know it."

"Kinda feels like you are."

"Then allow me to elaborate," Reed said, trying to project an aura of patience that I knew he wasn't feeling inside. Hey, I'm his little sister; I'm supposed to frustrate him. "What I'm saying is that it's a big world, and places outside Middle Tennessee could really use your help."

"I just helped New York in September, and I kindasorta helped some other places last month." I cringed involuntarily.

Reed didn't miss it. "Ah ha. Now we're getting to it."

I sighed. "Yeah."

He pointed an accusatory finger at me. "This is about the president, isn't it?"

"Mmmmmmmmmaybe."

"Sienna," he said, so very seriously, "it's not your fault President Gondry had a heart attack."

"Yeah," I said, "but it's not *not* my fault, either. And let's face it – with the election a couple days away, I kinda just want to lay low until it's over, and hope that Sarah Barbour is destroyed in a horrific landslide." I paused for comedic effect. "And also loses the election."

Reed chuckled. "Hey...I've been out there, okay? I know you and Barbour have beef or a history or something, but let me tell you – it's not like the bad old days when the feds were hunting you like a dog."

"Yet."

"And it's not like Minnesota, either," Reed went, apparently oblivious to my apocalyptic prophecies. "Steer clear of there, and everywhere else...it's pretty okay."

"I don't think Los Angeles is very pleased with me, either. In fact, we might want to call it 'Lost Angeles' for now."

"Kat works out there all the time and she says it's fine. She and Eilish are working a series of bank robberies out there right now, and everything's copacetic for them."

"Yeah, well, some women are more comfortable with pain than I am," I said with a broad shrug. "I mean, seriously, look how many of them paid major bank for candles that smelled like Gwyneth Paltrow's hoo-ha."

He shook his head slowly, a stupid grin plastered on his face. "Come on."

"I'm serious. Can you believe that shit?"

My brother looked amused and torn all at once. Tornmused, I would say. "All I'm trying to get to here, Sienna, is...don't let this town become a new box you confine yourself to. Branch out a little. Get beyond your comfort zone and live a little, you know?" He gave baby kitty Emma one last pat. "And also..." His handsome face twisted in a frown. "Stop picking up strays."

"Hey, man, don't tell me how to live my life; you're marrying an Italian."

Reed laughed. "You're just saying that because she's one of the few people who can righteously scare the shit out of you."

"Damned right," I said. "Message received, though. I'll, uh...consider it, at least."

"The sooner the better," he said. "Now...you want to play a game or something?"

"Long as it's not Magic: The Gathering," I said. "You're gonna have to stick with the boys for that one."

"I'll play anything," he said, shifting uncomfortably in the leather chair. "I just have got to get some of these fur heaters off my lap before I die of spontaneous combustion."

CHAPTER SEVEN

Deputy Director, Tennessee Bureau of Investigation. That's what the nameplate read outside Ileona Marsh's office in the TBI building in north Nashville, and I gave it a compulsive tap as I breezed in the next morning. The Memphis Belle herself was working at her desk, head down, eyes attentive to whatever she was dealing with. She barely looked up when I came in, but registered my presence with a grunt that sounded seventy percent pleased/thirty percent put out. "Nealon."

"Hey, boss," I said, inviting myself to sit down in true Karen fashion. "You read my report from last night?"

"You know I have," she said, a little reservedly. As one does when one's top agent has engaged in a gunfight in which, oh – sixteen lives? Something like that – were lost.

"I just want to say that what happened last night was only like...twenty percent...my fault."

Marsh put down her pen, laced her fingers together, and sat upright. Her coffee-brown eyes twitched slightly. "I'm very interested in the apportioning of numbers to this blame game. How do you figure?"

"I didn't shoot first," I said, shrugging, "and I didn't shoot last. If we assume that the start of a thing is like fifty percent of it, and the end is like thirty percent, then – at most – I'm responsible for twenty percent of it. And I still think the guys who were trying to kill me and that poor, trafficked girl bear some blame, more or less, for shit going down."

"Uh huh." Marsh seemed underwhelmed with my explanation. Probably as it should be. "Look – I'm not too bent out of shape about it." And she glanced back at her work, frowned, and picked up the pen to make a correction.

"Good," I said, relaxing a little in my seat. "I mean...I was just doing my best. I wasn't *trying* to go Wild West over there, I was just trying to bring the guys in. They totally set up an ambush for me, though."

"Yeah, you should probably anticipate that going forward," she said, looking up. "You've pissed off and terrified every OC group in the area. Maybe give some forethought to their possible responses in the future."

"Hey," I said, "there was no anticipating one of the factions was going to stage a quick reaction force nearby in case I showed up." My frown deepened. "Or that they'd do so with such conventional weapons and tactics."

"Maybe anticipate that changing for the worse in the future," Marsh said. "Just to spare us some trouble. Post your backup closer next time. Arm them more heavily. Bring our SWAT guys–"

"No," I said with the firmness one might ascribe to a steely wall. "I am not calling in Jackson if I can avoid it. Not if my very life depended upon it."

Marsh's eyes flashed. "What if other lives depended on it?"

"What kind of lives are we talking about here? Because if it's pedophiles, I might be okay with Jackson helping, because no matter how he effed it up, I'd be okay with the collateral damage. If it's kids and puppies? Forget it. That guy's a menace."

"Funny, he says the same about you," Marsh said, leaning back in her seat. "But I don't think it matters, because unless I'm reading these files wrong...you're just about out of actionable leads here in the area."

"Nuh uh," I said, brandishing my phone. "I've got bail jumpers I can go collect. I've got..." I pulled it up, glancing at the Time Killer app, which was, admittedly, running a little faster these days because there were just not that many felons out there I hadn't already picked up. I'd been making a diligent effort at knocking out every one of these clowns I could over the last few weeks, and boy, was it showing in the emptiness of the map for about a hundred miles in every direction around Nashville. There were like two alerts, and I clicked on them both in turn. "...uh...a failure to appear for a child support case and another for a traffic citation." My face fell. "Okay. Point taken."

"Face it, Sienna," Marsh said, folding her slim but well-defined arms across her chest. "You've done an outstanding job. Criminals are terrified to show their faces in the greater Nashville area. You've waged a more-or-less one-woman war against crime and won it here. That's good."

"So should I, like, take a day or something?"

"Well, if you want to be a lazy-ass slacker, sure," Marsh said with a glint of amusement. "Otherwise...Tennessee is a long state, and there are two other sectors: West and East. Pick a direction, and go clean them up, will you? Put fear of the goddess in the criminal elements of Knoxville, Chattanooga, and Memphis."

I made a face. "It sounds mocking when you say it."

"No mocking intended," Marsh said. "They're quaking in their boots around here. Now...follow the concept of the Prayer of Jabez and expand your territory." She shrugged.

"Just tell me which direction you want to go and I'll let the offices in the area know you're coming."

"It's so far, though," I whined, only half meaning it.

She raised an eyebrow again. "Pretty sure you can fly Tennessee from end to end in about forty-five minutes without breaking the sound barrier. That means you could work in Bristol and still make it home at night in half an hour. Less with Memphis. That's a normal commute for most folks. Welcome to the working class. Now..." she made a shooing gesture, "...go find a case or chase a criminal. But elsewhere. I need things to simmer down here for a minute."

I pulled myself out of the chair and sulked my way to the door. I wasn't really sure how to feel about any of this.

"Hey," Marsh called right before I exited. "The agency caught a missing persons case out of East Tennessee this morning if you're looking for something fun and different." She nudged a folder on her desk. "Three, technically."

"Three people went missing?" I asked, taking a few tentative steps back to pick up the folder.

"Yep," she said. "Three construction workers vanished into thin air off a major construction project about seventy miles outside Knoxville. Small town called Fountain Run." She glanced at me. "You should look into it. It'll get you out of the city for a bit, maybe let you work outdoors, put some color in those vampiric cheeks."

"That's the Irish in me," I said, thumbing through the folder. "All right. Missing persons. East Tennessee. I'll take it." With a glance. "Let 'em know I'm coming?"

"You driving or flying?"

I thought about it a second. "This sounds like conventional criminals, and these sort of cases always take me longer to unravel with all the legwork. I'll probably need my car."

"You mean you'll need that arsenal you tote around in the back of your Explorer?"

I totally did, but I couldn't say that. I'd just been involved in a gunfight where sixteen people had died. Or so. I couldn't really remember. "No...I just want to listen to the radio while I travel." An extra three and a half hours. I wondered if she'd be offended if just flew with a bunch of guns slung over my shoulder. The answer to that was: probably.

"They have these things called earpods now," Marsh said. "Also...your Explorer only has a police radio." She smiled. "Stay out of trouble, will you? I'll let the agent in charge know you're coming."

CHAPTER EIGHT

I followed my car's GPS east out of Nashville in the middle of the day, along I-40 and past towns called Lebanon, Cookeville, and Crossville, which I'd heard was the meth'd out, shithole center of Tennessee's hard drug culture. I didn't stop to find out. Maybe on the way back. I went up and down the green and forested hills, past the open stretches of farmland that already lay fallow for the winter. The sun beat down on my car, and I traveled part of the way with my windows down.

Before long, I went through the heart of Knoxville, with its decaying glass tower from a World's Fair long before I was born. Let it fall down, guys, I thought. It's over. I wondered if maybe someday in the future I could take a case there, and knock the eyesore down. Would they love me or hate me for that, I wondered?

Then I realized it was Knoxville, and I didn't care. God, intrastate rivalries spring up fast. Or maybe it's that I'm just always looking for a target for snark, and Knoxville seemed like it could handle it.

Outside Knoxville, I hit Interstate 81, and the character

of the land started to change. Gone was the hilly terrain of Middle Tennessee, giving way to genuine (if small, compared to the Rockies) mountains. I took an exit that didn't have so much as a gas station off it, then followed a winding road to another winding road, to a place where the road gave way to dirt, and pretty soon my Explorer was kicking up gravel. The clangs, bangs, and thumps might have alarmed me if I weren't well nigh invulnerable.

I came to the end of the road and a shocking amount of deforestation as the sun was going down. The dirt path opened up, wide, and to one side lumber trucks sat, being loaded with countless logs. Earth movers were pushing dirt all over the place, and I drove past them all, following the path of this attempt at breaking nature to the will of man and carving a road where nothing had been before.

Someone was waving at me to stop, so I triggered my flashing lights and let the siren rip one good squeal, and they waved me on. I kept going until I came to a patch of dirt and clay that looked like it had been cleared very recently, the stumps of trees still sticking out of the ground where they hadn't been fully ripped from the earth.

I pulled up next to a couple of local law enforcement cars with their lights flashing and a Ford Explorer that was not unlike my own. TBI was on the scene, it appeared.

Stepping out of my vehicle, I stretched my legs and waved to a couple of the local uniforms. I could tell by the looks they were giving me that they were not super excited about my presence. Which was fair, I thought.

"Ms. Nealon?" A dark-haired woman with a careful braid draped over her pantsuit sauntered up, followed by a dude in a khaki law enforcement uniform. "I'm Ashley Aylin, TBI."

"Hey, good to meet you," I said with a sisterly handshake, then moved on to the big burly sheriff. "And you are?"

"Fred Miles," he said. "Fountain Run Sheriff."

"Kinda guessed that by your uniform," I said, and came at last to the final guy, who'd crept up quite demurely in the wake of them both. "And you must be the man in charge."

"I'm the construction project manager," he said, and boy was this guy in the middle of an ocean of regret. Every pore of his body screamed that he didn't want to be here, and his almost halting delivery only added to it. "Larry Benson." He did not offer his hands, either of them, because both were clenched on one of those extended blueprints construction managers worked from, and it was damp, crushed and limp in the middle, like really al dente pasta.

"So it's your guys that went missing?" I asked.

Larry twisted his hands around the center of the blueprint. "Yeah."

"Uh huh," I said, surveying the scene. Sheriff Miles was watching me closely, but the lady TBI agent was all eyes on Larry. "And you have no idea where they went?"

Larry shook his head slowly, but his eyes were anchored on the ground. "I tried to track 'em, but their trail just sort of disappeared up ahead at the start of that thicket."

"Mmmhmm," I said, looking at the wall of heavy greenery ahead, a marked contrast to the tilled dark earth and dead stumps sticking up around here. I could smell the musk of the ground, and it was rich. "What is all this, anyway?"

"It's the road to the new Waters Tech corporate headquarters," Larry said, almost miserably. "Relocating a bunch of workers here from San Fran, LA, New York, and Connecticut."

"Big project, I'm guessing?"

Larry nodded again. "A dozen corporate office buildings to start. All the roads and infrastructure. Two dozen apartments and condo buildings. Plus a neighborhood of luxury homes."

"Huh," I said, looking around for no particular reason. "Kinda out in the boonies, though, isn't it?"

"I'm just building the thing," Larry said, quite pained. "I didn't pick the site."

"Okay," I said, because there was something else going on here and I didn't know quite what. I could sense that my eastern TBI counterpart – whose name I'd already forgotten – was picking it up, too, though.

I didn't have time to explore it, though, because the sound of a chopper in the distance started to get louder and louder, the volume blaring as it popped up over a hilltop nearby.

The helicopter was a civilian model, a kind I wasn't familiar with, but it looked super fancy. The words Waters Tech were written in an elegant text along the side.

The TBI lady sidled up to me. "You know who owns that company?"

"Don't believe I do," I said. "Who is it?"

"His name's Wil Waters," she said, raising her voice to accommodate the chopper noise as it touched down and some lackey immediately opened the door and stepped out, "and unless I miss my guess...I think you're about to meet him."

CHAPTER NINE

Wil Waters stepped out of the chopper, looking nothing like I would have expected a big-shot CEO to look. I'd met a few in my time, and they often conformed, in part or in full, to the stereotype you might expect, at least during working hours: suit, dress shirt, excellent and expensive shoes.

This guy was not wearing a suit, was not wearing a dress shirt, but he did have expensive – if not excellent – shoes.

He came springing out of the helicopter in tight-fitting bicycle shorts and top, bright green, white, and black. He was thin and lithe, the figure of a man who'd eschewed carbs and enjoying life in favor of being able to wear tight-fitting clothing without shame. With a half-smile, he said something to the lackey in the suit who'd opened the door for him. Though he was taller than me, I would have bet I could have broken him over my knee in a fight even if I'd been darted.

His hair was short and slightly moussed, and his smile was very punchable, as smiles went. This was a man who was used to getting what he wanted. As he drew closer to our little quartet, I caught a hint of dried sweat, suggesting he'd jumped off his bike and straight into the helo for the flight without a shower. I tried not to cringe; I'd smelled worse.

"I see they already called in the experts," Waters said as he walked up. He offered me a hand and I took it, getting mine pumped good a few times. "Wil Waters. And you're—"

"Sienna Nealon," we chorused together. I hate it when people finish my sentences for me or with me. Unless they're cute. And I found no part of Waters cute, except maybe his wallet. "Did you fly down from New York?"

"As soon as I heard," he said. "Didn't take long on the private jet, and until we put an airstrip out here, it's a quick jaunt right to Greeneville. We've already got a helicopter stationed there, so..." He shrugged, then made his introductions with the sheriff and the TBI agent, whose name was spoken and immediately vanished again from my brain. Whoops. He didn't so much as acknowledge Larry, though, which I found interesting. "What's the word, officers?"

"The sun's about to go down," Sheriff Miles said with that thick southern accent. "Now, we could go bumbling around those woods in the dark, but as you presumably know, this is a valley that's got some impressive geographic features. Sudden drops, rock faces, fast-moving river running right through the middle, and thick vegetation. We send in search parties tonight, there might well be some injuries, and I don't just mean turned ankles."

"We're thinking we wait until daybreak," the TBI lady said. "These men were last seen around ten o'clock this morning. The worst thing in these woods are bears and bobcats, and it's improbable that something like that killed three of them. They're probably just lost down in the valley. We wait until the morning and go in, we'll spare ourselves a heck of a lot of trouble, and the possibility of getting people real lost, real turned around or, like the sheriff said, badly injured."

"Have you tried using a helicopter yet?" I asked, chucking a thumb at Waters's helo. "For search and rescue?"

"We actually called in a local drone pilot," the sheriff said. "Used a quadcopter to scout ahead some. Because fall is so damned tardy this year, the canopy is still full through the whole valley, so he couldn't get much of a view of the forest floor." He made a face. "I got to warn y'all, cuz I think most of you are city folk – this here is a primordial forest. Nature at about her meanest, at least that you can find in Tennessee. It's old, it's thick, and it don't take kindly to intruders."

"Uh huh," I said, filing that one into the 'skeptical' column. "How big a tract of land are we talking here?"

The sheriff looked over at Waters, who grinned broadly. "Two thousand acres. That back up to Cherokee National Forest."

That landed with a dull thud in my head. "National forest? That's not small, is it?"

The sheriff shook his head. "Over 650,000 acres. Over a thousand square miles."

I cringed. "So that means, these guys could have wandered through here and into the national forest, which gives us a search radius of—"

"It's the size of the state of Rhode Island," the sheriff said. And in that moment, I got a feeling that our missing persons case had just turned into a search for survivors with a hell of a big search footprint.

CHAPTER TEN

"Well, that's not great news," I said, taking another look at the forest in the distance. A thick wall of green broken by hints of brown tree trunks, it looked like an impenetrable wall, made even more foreboding by the falling sun.

The sheriff shook his head. "I'm not one to try and stick his head in the sand and hope a problem solves itself, but it'd be real nice if these boys found their own way out before we have to mount a search, because it's going to be a hell of an undertaking, lemme tell ya."

He wasn't kidding.

"Well, let me see if I can nip this in the bud before it gets started," I said, and lifted a couple feet off the ground. "I can overfly the zone and scout." I turned an eye to the west, where I'd come from, and saw the sun already threatening to sink below the horizon. "You got a bullhorn I could borrow, Sheriff?"

He nodded and shuffled off, not as light on his feet as I imagined he was thirty years or so ago. That left me alone with Larry, who'd gone just about catatonic, my eastern TBI counterpart, and Waters, who apparently couldn't keep himself from grinning like an idiot.

"We've got a mutual acquaintance, you know," he said, leaning a little closer toward me. He smelled of sweat and whatever silken material his bike pants and shirt were made of. The same stuff as yoga pants, I suspected.

"Is it someone I've put in prison?" I asked.

He laughed. "No, it's Cam Wittman."

"Ah, yes," I said. "Last time I saw Cam he just about put me through a wall with his meta powers. How's he doing?"

"That doesn't...really sound like Cam," Waters said, frowning. "But I guess he does aggressively protect his interests." He shrugged, but I felt like he was making a mental note. "I don't know how he's doing. I haven't seen him in months myself. He's on the board of one of my smaller acquisitions. Probably due to talk to him soon."

"Give him my best when you do," I said, only slightly serious. Sheriff Miles was hustling back over about as fast as he could, brandishing a bullhorn. "Thanks." And with that, I lifted off.

"You gonna be back before sundown?" Miles asked.

"Why, you want your bullhorn back before you pack it in tonight?" I asked, letting myself drift up about thirty feet. Now I could see the impressive, thickly grown forest that Larry and his cronies had been systematically demolishing to put their road through.

"Nah, it ain't that – but I do, though," Sheriff said. Then he kicked at the ground. "Gonna need it to direct rescue ops tomorrow. But I guess we'll see you when we see you," he added, a little too quickly for my comfort. Someone else holding something back.

"Probably," I said, and headed for the forest at a leisurely thirty or so miles per hour. I left them behind in the sandy, dust-strewn area of deforestation and headed out into the wild, open greenery of the valley.

CHAPTER ELEVEN

"Anybody out there?" I called, bullhorn turned to max volume, listening to the electronic squeal of my voice magnified and projected over the seemingly endless treetops that made up the hills and lows of the valley.

I swept low over the contour of the trees, the leaves rustling beneath me in the warm wind blowing off the high ridge to my left. I had lost all track of direction until I remembered that the sun was setting behind me, just a big orange orb in a burning sky, and it dipped below the horizon as I took a sudden drop, following the trees into the natural contours of the valley.

Water rushed somewhere in the distance, trickling over rocks. The boughs creaked and cracked between my calls of, "Anybody out there? Anybody?" through my megaphone. Birds burst forth into flight out of treetops intermittently, probably a fraction of what could be found here in summer. It had been a warm fall, and my view was still mostly green with a little brown and a few dashes of red and gold and orange filling the treetops. I was sure back home in Minnesota –

well, back in Minnesota, anyway — the leaves were already fully turned, and probably on the ground.

But here nature was taking her time putting on her fall colors, and the cool breeze coming out of the east suggested that she would continue to do so for at least a little longer.

"Whoa!" I almost caught a branch to the face while I was thinking and babbling, avoiding it only at the last minute. Taking myself a little higher off the treetops, I called down again, listening to my voice echo over the valley and crackle through the trees. The wind decided to take a break, and I heard an animal, then multiple animals, break into a run on the forest floor below. The heavy canopy blocked my view of the ground, and there was not so much as a clearing anywhere in sight.

"It's like the freaking East Tennessee rainforest out here," I mumbled, going a little higher. Miles and miles of undifferentiated woods, rising to the peaks of the ridges that fenced in the valley. If the workers had gone in here, they were going to have a hell of a time getting out any way but the one they came in. To my right, a couple of cliffs peeked out from behind a facade of trees hiding their sheer, limestone faces.

Another rustling beneath me caught my attention, and I knew it was more than just the wind, which had fallen silent. I was churning above the treetops at about thirty miles per hour, which was probably a little too fast for a reasonable search.

"Anybody down there?" I called, probably to a spooked deer. Taking a quick U-turn, I came back as the trees went silent. I crept along the canopy of the treetops, belly almost brushing the branches and leaves. "Anybody? Anybody?" I paused, trying to see into the darkness beyond.

"Bueller!" someone shouted from just below. A rustling in the branches there surprised the hell out of me, and a dirty face launched out of the boughs, slamming into me in a rush of earthen scent mingled with sweat. A skinny arm wrapped around my neck, and a sudden weight dragged me down into the leaves and branches. My flight powers cut out in my surprise as a choking force ratcheted down on my larynx.

I fell down, down into the trees with someone wringing the life out of me with every foot I dropped.

CHAPTER TWELVE

The arm was wrapped around my throat in just the wrong place, and my flight powers had cut out from the sheer distraction of a human – a dirty, earthy, slightly smelly human – throwing themselves out of the branches of the East Tennessee forest I'd been flying over and catching me in a perfect choke hold.

Now I was tumbling down into the woods, spinning all the way. I could feel the branches whipping at my ribs, my chest, my arms and legs as someone – heavy, but not absurdly so – rode my back, trying to choke me out.

The small branches whipped at me like miniature chain flails, but the bigger ones hit like clubs, and I bounced, catching one in the ribs on my right side, losing all the breath my attacker hadn't already taken from me, and then continuing my fall in graceless fashion.

I tried to twist, to position my attacker so they would take a hit or two, but no sooner had I got them angled down to absorb either the next tree branch or the ground impact than they hit one and daintily flipped us right back over, so that I had a clear view of the ground coming up at me.

"Yeeeeeehawww!" shouted a distinctly female voice in my ear.

That jarred me out of my surprise, and I remembered Aleksandr Gavrikov. We stopped inches above the forest floor.

Hanging there for a second, skinny forearm in my damned trachea, I heard my attacker say, "Well, ain't that a barrel of beans."

I forced my chin down hard, bone against bone, biting into her arm, and heard her scream. She punched me in the back of the head, twice, and it was not gentle. My world rocked, and got hazy, the darkness of being beneath the canopy lit by lightning flashes as I suffered surprise head trauma.

That didn't stop me, though. I rocketed forward, taking advantage of the lightning-flash, negative view of the forest before me as everything dark turned light and vice versa for a moment. Ahead, a tree branch presented itself, about as thick as a broom handle.

I flew low beneath the branch, intending to scrape my attacker off, headfirst.

Somehow, though...she avoided it.

"You ain't cheatin' me out of my ride that easy," she cackled in my ear. "Come into my home, you gonna get it, y'hear? Ain't just flying away all scot free—"

I flipped us over and went low, scraping the ground and stirring up dirt. Dead leaves flew up into the air and clouds of dust blew up as we went shredding into the earth. I heard my attacker hit rocks: "Ow! Ow! OW OW OW—"

Gripping my chin into her arm even tighter, I heard a snapping noise in her arm as I removed the pressure from my throat. "You can let go anytime," I said, getting in my first breath in about thirty seconds.

"I ain't done with you yet!" she shouted, and blasted me with another punch to the head that sent me sideways.

We crashed into the ground, and I caught a stone about the size of a fist in the face. I heard teeth crack before I felt them, but the feeling came pretty fast after the noise and it was none too pleasant. That lightning-flash sensation of the world going negative returned, and the edges of my vision started to get hazy, like sundown was preceding, but mostly from the outside of my range of sight and moving inward toward the center.

In the dark of the woods, I could hear creatures skittering and fleeing at the sound of our struggle. I caught another blow behind my right ear, and then another, and warm blood ran down the back of my neck.

"God, you're a fighting one, ain'tcha?" she asked, and gave me another just for good measure. My neck caught at a strange angle, and I felt her shove off me, grunting in pain as she did so.

She was standing up, I realized dimly, my eyes fluttering in the dark. She gave me a hard kick in the ribs, and I felt them splinter and crack, a weak fire starting in my side.

"Well, you fought a good fight," she announced, and I heard her moving. "But I reckon I've had about enough of you, and I need to go set this arm, so let's go ahead and wrap this shit up." And I heard her stance shift, her foot leave the ground beside me, and I knew what was coming from the sound of her lifting her leg–

She was going to stomp me right on the back of my neck, killing me.

And once it was done...I was pretty sure it wasn't going to be something I could heal

CHAPTER THIRTEEN

My hands were at rest at my sides, knuckles in the dirt, palms facing skyward toward the canopied treetops. Dark, peaty earth pushed up against my nose, and my body felt dully on fire, pain permeating through the sluggish torpor caused by the blunt force trauma my attacker – ambusher – had laid on me while beating me to a pulp.

I was halfway to unconsciousness, and ready to go the rest of the distance. She was lifting her leg even now, though, to deliver the killing blow, to send me into the darkness for good, just feet away...

The leaves rustled beneath the foot she was balancing on as she prepared to bring down the other on the back of my neck. I had a flash, a vision of the vertebrae shattering across the back of my neck.

Think of Eve, Brianna said.

"Eve," I whispered, and a vision of faerie wings catching the light fluttered through my mind.

I blasted light webs out of both palms, my panic giving my power added urgency. I heard my attacker catch them and go flying into a nearby tree.

"Wolfe," I muttered in my head, and felt some of the pain recede. Flipping over onto my side, I looked up, trying to find my assailant.

It took a few seconds, but I did finally find her.

She was struggling against the light webs, planted to the wide trunk of a nearby maple. Her every move seemed to bring down a torrent of loose leaves, and she was moving quite a lot.

I shook the cobwebs out as my vision cleared and that pain in my sides and neck started to recede. "You know, you're lucky I didn't burst into flames and just cook you to a crisp." I rubbed my side, feeling the ribs setting themselves back into an even row. I lifted my shirt and watched a nasty bruise recede, fading back to the normal pale color.

"I'm hearing a lot of big talk out of someone who was getting her ass kicked until a second ago," my assailant piped up, still fighting against the light bonds. She was having some meager success, the webs cutting against the tree trunk. Her hands were more or less free, but she was bound at the elbow on one side and mid-wrist on the other, which kept her from sticking them out of the web more than about a half-foot. "Come on, lemme down and I'll show you what 'cooked' looks like."

Taking a hand and stretching it over my head, then cranking my neck a few degrees to the left, I heard something pop into place that my healing hadn't fixed. "Why am I not surprised you're a cannibal, too?"

Her dirty face registered surprise. "Eww, gross, it's just a figure of speech."

"Sure it is," I said, crunching leaves as I stepped closer. Snagging the cuffs off my belt, I held them behind me. "What's your name?"

She paused, looking at me. She had dark hair, or at least it was so dirty it was dark. It was hard to tell much else about her in the shadow of all these trees, but her clothes had a real worn look, like they'd been through a literal wringer. "Come on over here and I'll whisper it in your ear."

"Oh, okay," I said, stepping closer.

A wide grin split her face as I got close, and right about the time I sensed she was going to try something, she did, snapping a hand out to grab me—

And I slapped the cuff on her wrist.

"Whut the hell—?" she started.

I dissipated the light web and jerked as hard as I could on the handcuffs, ripping her down from the tree trunk and slamming her into the earth. I pounced onto her back, landing a knee in her kidney. The scream of pain was satisfying, if a bit cruel. I yanked her cuffed hand behind her, prompting another scream, and said, "Give me your other hand or I'll make you wish you were never born."

"This is a hate crime! RAPE! RAPE!" she screamed.

"There's no one out here, dumbass," I said, and punched her in the kidney again. Her other hand bounced up and she moved, instinctively, to touch and protect the area I'd just hit. At which time I grabbed her other wrist and cuffed it, binding those suckers tight because this chick was no joke in the strength department. Meta, I was pretty damned sure. "Which begs the question: what are you doing out here?"

"Minding my own business," she huffed, clearly in pain, "'til you came along begging for someone to shout 'Bueller' at your dumb ass, Ben Stein."

"Ben Stein is quite a bright guy, actually," I said, cranking the cuffs as I dragged her to her feet. "And last I checked, quoting lines from *Ferris Bueller's Day Off* isn't an offense we ambush and murder people for." I jerked her around to keep her off balance while I tried to decide what to do with her. "We reserve that for people who quote *Mortal Kombat: Annihilation*."

"You think you're so funny, don'tcha?" she said, trying to keep her balance while I tried to keep her off it.

"I think I'm not in handcuffs and you are," I said. "You're under arrest for assaulting a state agent."

"Let me out of these things and I'll do more than assault you."

"Tell you what, honey badger," I said, shoving her to the ground and grabbing her by the ankles before she knew what was happening, "why don't you gnaw your way out of them and then try and keep your promise. Til then – maybe talk less, smile more?" And I lifted off, taking us up through the canopy of the forest as swiftly as possible.

"Don't you tell me to smile," she said once we were up in the air. She didn't seem particularly upset by being flown, upside down, toward the fading red light in the western sky. "I'll smile when you're dead."

"You and a whole lot of other people," I said, looking at the blood still dripping down my shirt. I didn't even know where the sheriff's megaphone had gone, and I wasn't about to try and retrieve it now. Not with this feral savage struggling against my hold on her ankles. "Of course, you'll have to outlive me if you want to see that day."

She stopped struggling and clammed up. Ahead, I could see the end of the woods and the last light of day falling on the construction equipment and the gravel parking lot. I heaved a sigh of relief, knowing only that I couldn't wait to ditch this particular poison pill and maybe get back to what I'd actually come here for. Probably.

CHAPTER FOURTEEN

I saw Wil Waters, the sheriff, and that lady TBI agent all waiting in a rough triad when I came flying back over the last of the trees, feeling the breeze of evening wash over me and rustling the leaves behind me. I came down to fifteen, twenty feet, and made ready to loose my now-silent cargo–

When she reared back and tried to kick me. So I just let her go about fifteen feet above the earth.

She didn't even scream; she twisted her body in midair and came around perfectly, landing in a crouch, hands still fastened behind her. She tried to turn, to look up at me so she could assess the danger coming her way–

But I blasted her to the ground with another light web, ripping her legs from beneath her and sending her face into the dirt.

"What in the hell...?" Sheriff Miles asked, first to the fallen, webbed-up problem I'd brought back with me.

I settled down next to him just as the lady TBI agent came running up, gun in hand. "What happened?" she asked.

I looked up at her. "I'm sorry...what was your name again?"

She blinked at me.

"Whatever," I said. "Later. I was flying over the woods and this absolute psychopath launched herself at me, grabbing me like a spider monkey, dragging me to the earth and beating the shit out of me," I said, pointing at my collar. The girl, not my clothes' collar.

"You was asking for it," the girl said, still struggling against her bonds, madder than a cat trying to avoid the bath.

"God, you sound like a date rapist, just stop," I said, looking back up at the TBI agent. "So...sorry...name?"

"Ashley," she said slowly. "Ashley Aylor."

"Okay, that's a lot for me to remember right now," I said, sitting, rather heavily, on my pain in the ass, writhing suspect, who grunted at my sudden weight on top of her. "I'm just gonna call you AA, because there's a really good chance I'll remember that. For obvious reasons."

"Cuz you're an alky, that's why," the girl underneath my ass taunted.

"Clearly you know who I am," I said, "which is more than I can say for you." I nodded at Aylor. "Cuff her legs, will you? And give me suppressant, if you've got it."

"Don't go medically experimenting on me! I don't want your drugs!"

"Bet that's the first time you've ever said that phrase, Holly High-a-lot," I said, taking Aylor's suppressant gun. Jamming it in the girl's neck, I gave it a pull, and the resultant pop sounded a little like a balloon getting stepped on hard.

"Sonofabitch!" the girl screamed, writhing even harder against the cuffs, the light web, and my weight. "You'll pay for that, Patty Fatass!"

"How? I'm guessing you're not set up for Visa or Mastercard, and I'm fresh out of cash." I lifted my weight for a second, then landed it back on her with a little more gusto.

Aylor — or AA, as I was already thinking of her, had gotten

the cuff around one of the girl's ankles. They were thin, thin enough to fit easily around. But she was struggling with the second.

That big burly sheriff set a knee down right on the girl's ribs, prompting a squeal. "Go help her, will you? I'll keep her down."

"The only thing you can keep down, you pig, is the whole buffet at the local Chinese joint," the girl shouted at him.

I cuffed her legs, then took an additional set of cuffs from the sheriff and locked those around between her ankle cuffs and the ones on her wrist, trussing her up like the pig she'd just accused him of being.

That done, the sheriff, AA, and I all stepped back to admire our handiwork.

"I see y'all looking at me like I'm a piece of meat," the girl said with enough hate to fuel the world's power grid for the next two thousand years or so. "Especially tubby tub tub here," she nodded at the sheriff. "Don't you leave me alone with him."

"Why?" I asked. "Because you're a delicate flower?"

"Do I look delicate to you, active-bitch-face?" she shot back. "No, it's because he doesn't look like he could satisfy a hamster with what he's packing, and I doubt he'd remember my safeword. When I needed to pee, not because I think he has a chance in hell of making me ache in any way."

"Damn, she's got a mouth on her," the sheriff pronounced, knocking his hat back.

"Really creepy you're already talking about my mouth," she said. "I'll let you know if I need your dick to floss with later, because that's the only reason I'd ever put it in there."

"Good God," AA said, cringing.

"Where the hell did she come from?" the sheriff asked.

"Launched herself out of the frigging trees like she was sitting in a catapult waiting for me," I said, rubbing a few of the spots where she'd torn and messed up my clothing. "I'm not ashamed to say she's as mean with a punch as she is with her words."

"Maybe you're just soft all the way around, Patty Fatass," the girl said. "Cut out the carb-loading and put some muscle mass on and maybe you won't be so delicate."

This is like Guy Friday's angrier, smaller sister, Brianna said.

"You think she's the one that took our guys?" AA asked.

"She's got the killer instinct for it," I said, rubbing the back of my head. "And she made a cannibal reference, so it's possible she murdered them and ate them or something."

She stopped in her struggles for a moment. "I ain't killed no one, and I told your slow ass the cannibal thing was a joke. Sorry you're too stupid to understand sarcasm, I'll talk slower next time, maybe put it in a tone that's unambiguous. And I ain't seen nobody but you all damned day." She slowed her struggle for a second. "Or ever, really."

"What, you're telling me you live out in that valley?" I asked, pointing down where the road was going to go, to the dark treeline that already looked like a foreboding, shadowy ocean on the horizon.

"Damned right I do," she said, "And you were trespassing. That's why I came at you." She locked her hateful eyes on me, beneath the mask of dirt that had gotten so much worse during our struggles. "You came looking for trouble where you didn't belong, and, well, you found it."

"What's your name?" I asked, easing a little closer.

She looked up at me, glare a little less hateful. "Alannah. Alannah Greene."

"Well, guess what, Alannah Greene?" I settled my hand on the chain of the cuff that linked the ones on her hands and the one on her feet together. "That land isn't yours." I nodded to Wil Waters, who was standing at a distance, watching this whole thing unfold with a skeptical eye. "It's his. And you're under arrest for assaulting me—"

"Lot of people do that, you soft-ass sister, what you singling me out for?"

"—for suspicion of kidnapping – and maybe murder and cannibalism, I dunno—"

"I didn't kill nobody and I definitely didn't eat 'em! You stop your lyin' ass mouth—"

"Can we get a gag bag for her?" I asked as she spit like a camel at me once again. It shot past my ear and landed on AA's right lapel, drawing a look of disgust from the TBI agent.

"Ayup," the sheriff said, and hustled off to retrieve one.

"You have the right to remain silent," I said. "And I really, really wish you'd take advantage of that."

"I bet you do!" she said. "With every fiber of your soft-hearted, cholesterol-laden, fat-ass being. Can't even take a frigging punch. Except fruit punch. Bet you take a lot of that. Washed down with lard—"

AA got at the girl's other elbow and helped me lift her. Less for strength, more for balance, because I could carry her, even struggling, with relative ease. "You really think she killed those guys?"

"Honestly, at this point," I said, listening to growingly incoherent streams of abuse issuing forth from the girl's mouth, "I just want her to shut up."

"Because I'm hurting your pillow-soft feelings?" the girl jeered.

"Because you're wasting the oxygen I could be breathing," I said, carrying her about as delicately as AA and I could manage to the back of the nearby police cruiser where the sheriff put the bag over her head to a cavalcade of screams and curses of our very beings, our names, our persons, and all the excess cellulite we might carry upon our bodies.

CHAPTER FIFTEEN

"Ms. Nealon?" Wil Waters caught me before I made it back to my car, my clothes squishing with all the blood Alannah Greene had drawn in her mad dash to beat my ass to death. The sun had set, the night air was starting to get that peaceful quiet around it, especially with a lot of the construction guys clearing out. Some local cops were standing around lighting rigs, spotlights flaring into the wall of woods that waited ahead, a beacon for the missing workers.

"Yeah?" I said, stopping myself to give him a moment to speak his mind. I didn't know much about this particular billionaire douche, but I knew the type, and they were the Karens of the male world, except instead of speaking to my manager they'd probably bitch directly to President Barbour. Sure, there wasn't much she could do to eff with me directly via my job, being a Tennessee state employee, but there were a lot of things she could still do to make my life miserable.

Which I was expecting any minute, frankly.

Waters sauntered over in his biker shorts, lowering his voice and coming closer, but not too close. I was always thankful when a man respected my boundaries, and annoyed when he didn't. "Thank you for going in there after my workers. I–"

"I didn't know you owned the construction company," I said.

"I don't," he said. "But I still think of them as one of the family, given that they're working on my project." He had a serious look on his face. "Do you really think that girl killed them?"

"My gut?" I paused, really thinking it over. "Probably not."

His face evinced a hint of befuddlement. "But you arrested her."

"Because she beat the living hell out of me," I said, raising an eyebrow at him, and one which I could feel the blood encrusted in. "Look, she's violent and all, but I think I was a target of opportunity. Still, she says she lives out there, so odds are good she's got some idea of where your guys either could have gotten to, or who might have messed with them to make them go missing." I brushed flakes of drying blood from my hairline. "Also…I don't know about you, but when I get the shit kicked out of me, I like the kicker to pay some."

Waters smiled, and it was the slyest, most arrogant thing I'd seen since the last billionaire I dealt with. "I wouldn't know."

"I never would have guessed," I said, firing one of those arrogant smiles right back at him. "Getting your ass kicked can be a thoroughly humbling experience. You should try it sometime."

His smile vanished. "I don't have any interest in losing."

I started to walk away. "If you change your mind, I can put you in touch with a Silicon Valley fight club. They're not bad. Give you a real opportunity to feel the pain – but sorta controlled. Make you feel alive."

There was a flicker of something behind his eyes, like he

was considering new information. "What are you going to do with the girl?"

"Prosecute her," I said, dabbing at some still-wet blood at the corner of my mouth. My shirt was a total write-off beneath my TBI blazer. Idiot. What did he think happened in these situations? "Why? What would you like to see happen to her?"

His eyes were like dark spots in the dusk, his face shadowed by the bright spotlights shining into the woods behind him. "I just don't want to see a young girl suffer for something stupid she did in the heat of the moment."

"Really? That's your concern?" I paused in my walk.

"Yes," he said. "Why? What would you do? Lock her up and throw away the key?"

"Near enough," I said. "I don't know; I guess you and I just have different philosophies about what should happen to someone who proves themselves a murderous psychopath by attacking a total stranger out of nowhere."

"I'm sure it was just an accident."

"Well, then I hope you don't go having any accidents in your life," I said, tossing him a small salute as I finally reached my vehicle. "Because her 'accident' would have killed anyone but me. Have a good evening, Mr. Waters." I got in my car and slammed the door, starting it up before I had to deal with one more asinine statement from a man who'd clearly never taken a punch in his life.

CHAPTER SIXTEEN

I managed to clean myself up in the bathroom of the Fountain Run sheriff's department while Sheriff Miles and AA were getting Alannah Greene processed. I had a date with her in an interrogation room once they were finished, but I wanted to clean up first, and sort of hoped they'd do the same for her, given that even before our fight her cheeks were dirty enough to grow crops on.

About halfway through a well-practiced, bathroom-mirror grooming routine that I'd developed over many years and many ass-kickings, the door swung open and AA walked in, shoes clicking on the aged and stained white tile. The sheriff's department was a functional, squat brick building off a state highway with almost nothing around, and it reflected the utter lack of budget or interest in architecture that seemed to come with municipal buildings that were not in a town center.

"She got you pretty good," AA said, washing her hands diligently after hitting up a toilet stall and doing her business. She looked into the mirror back at me.

"Let me tell you something about Alannah Greene," I

said, dabbing at blood that had crusted just below my hairline. "That girl is not the type to take prisoners. I've met dogs that are less territorial."

"Hmm," AA said, thinking. "You really think she believes that she owns that land out there?"

"I have no idea what she believes," I said, "other than that murder is a good time and that dancing on the spines of her foes is the highest form of entertainment. I'm just glad I stopped her before she performed the coup de grace, because I hear it takes the brain several minutes to die once the neck is broken, and I have a feeling she was going to pull out a banjo and dance once I was dead."

AA smiled tightly in the mirror. "So, you, uh...hate banjos?"

I paused in the middle of dabbing my face. "I actually don't. But it was a convenient and funny thing to say, so I said it."

"That your metric for saying stuff?"

"Convenient and funny? Probably. Why?"

"I'm from around here, originally," AA said. "Two counties over. Lifelong Tennessee hillbilly. Just get tired of hearing the jokes after a while, y'know? Backwoods, inbred, banjos – yawn." She feigned one.

"Interesting," I said, deadpan. "I never would have guessed. You have all your teeth and everything."

She rolled her eyes. "I missed that one in my list."

"Tell me something. Did you eat squirrel every night–"

"Okay," she said, looking a little pained. "Let's just talk business. You want to handle the interrogation?"

"No, let's talk about the all-squirrel diet," I said, really rolling along.

AA turned away from the mirror to face me. "Okay. Yes, I ate a lot of squirrel growing up. A lot of rabbit, too. You know why?"

"Because they were there?" I fired back, taking more interest in my collar, which had a decent spotting of blood, than what she was saying.

"Short answer: yes," AA said, "and they were free, while chicken, beef, and pork all cost money." She was looking at me with great significance, waiting to see if I got it.

I did, stopping mid-scrub. "Oh. Sorry."

"You don't have to apologize for me being dirt poor," she said, "unless you were the one who came in the middle of the night in 1984 and stole our meager life savings from under my parents' bed."

"I doubt I'd use my time travel powers to go back and do that," I said, feeling a burning in my cheeks.

Her brow furrowed. "Your...*what?*"

"Just a joke," I said, waving a hand at her. "Trying to distract you from the foot I have buried neatly in my mouth all the way up to my luscious thigh."

The corner of her mouth twisted up into a smile. "This is the first time you've met someone who grew up country and poor?"

"No," I said, "but it doesn't happen often enough for me to be on guard in my insults. Clearly, this is an area of my repertoire I need to think on."

AA shrugged. "I don't know that I'd bother. Most of us hillbillies have bigger problems to worry about than some city yahoo insulting us." She balled up a paper towel and made a perfect free throw into the trash can. "But I will tell you...squirrel gravy is good stuff. Chicken of the trees. That's what we call 'em."

"I'm probably going to have to take your word for that," I said, brushing off the last little flecks of blood. "Seeing as I am unlikely to have any offered to me anytime soon."

"The girl's ready when you are," AA said. "That's what I came to tell you."

I gave myself one last look over. This was as good as it got after an ass-beating. Most of my makeup was gone, and while I'd rebound my hair in a ponytail, it still looked fiercely mussed. "Well, then," I said, not exactly pleased with the results, but satisfied given what I'd had to work with, "let's go give this little asshat a serious talking to."

CHAPTER SEVENTEEN

"I've got her set up in the interrogation room," Sheriff Miles said as we walked out of the bathroom. The sheriff's station was not large, comprised of a small public waiting area, a section behind the desk large enough to accommodate about five or so workers, and a jail area behind a metal gate.

A jail which had one prisoner.

"You want to be good cop or bad cop?" AA asked with extra gusto.

I looked at her blankly. "You really have to ask?"

"Right," she said. "I'll be good cop, then."

"I dunno," I said, looking at the steel door to the interrogation room, "I'm not sure the better play here isn't 'Bad Cop, Worse Cop,' but I suppose we can try it your way and see what happens."

"Hey, if you need the worse cop, I'm happy to tag in," Miles said. "You ought to see what that little heathen did to the back of my car on the way over here. She sat kicking the cage the whole ride, even with that damned bag on her head. Sang like a drunk, too."

I could barely hold in my smile, mostly because I didn't try very hard. "How was her voice?"

"She ain't going to be making a living in Nashville anytime soon," he said, shaking his head.

"Good to know," I said, and went for the door. Miles scrambled to unlock it for us with a big key ring, fumbling until he got to the right one. "Y'all just call out when you're ready to get out, and I'll come a-running."

I nodded, falling into silence as AA and I entered the small interrogation room. It was bigger than the cell, but not by much. A heavy steel table sat in the center of the room, and Alannah Greene was behind it. She was no longer hogtied in handcuffs, but she'd had her chains run through an eyelet on the table, which was bolted to the concrete floor. Her face had also been cleaned up, and I found myself looking at a girl who was probably in the vicinity of twenty, but could have been younger or older a couple years in either direction.

"Oh, good, here comes the lesbian reboot of *Dumb and Dumber*," she said, looking away for the moment.

"You are really just a vicious, hateful person, aren't you?" AA asked. "What a childhood you must have had."

"Yeah, it was great," Alannah said. "I went to Mass every Sunday, screwed every parish priest every chance I got. Just like your momma taught me."

"If this is how you're going to be," I said, "we can leave for a little bit. Like, say, overnight. Come back tomorrow once you've had a chance to simmer down."

She stuck out her tongue at me. "Do I seem like the type to simmer down? And don't get excited by the sight of my tongue, it's meant as a sign of disrespect, not a come on. Since now I know you're into that sort of thing."

AA exclaimed softly under her breath, but I ignored the crack. "So, you want to talk?" I asked. "Or do you need some time to rest up, compose yourself?"

Greene hesitated, clearly wanting to say something snarky, but also actually considering the consequences. If we left, she'd be alone for the night, at least based on my threat. "Y'all can stay and talk, so long as you promise not to start making out in front of me."

"Because it'd turn your homophobic stomach?" I asked, smirking, really leaning into it.

"Because maybe I'd want to join in and it's awfully wrong of y'all powerful cops to molest a prisoner," she shot back. "I'm really just looking out for you here." She sat back in her chair as far as the chains would allow, looking sullenly at each of us. "What do you want to talk about? The weather?"

"Cloudy with a chance of obfuscation," AA muttered under her breath.

"Why don't we talk about what happened out there?" I asked, not bothering to take the seat across from her. "You launching yourself out of the trees like a shark at me?"

"What's there to say about it?" She shrugged. "You got hit and went down like a fat kid on a seesaw."

"How is this teenage girl the single most casually offensive person I've ever met?" AA muttered.

"Because she's trying to be," I said, and saw a flicker of surprise in Alannah's eyes. I smiled at her. "Desperately, in fact. If she was trying any harder, she might sprain something."

"Well, I wouldn't want to sprain anything," Greene said, lowering her head sullenly. "You already done plenty of that cuffing my ass."

"I cuffed your arms, not your ass," I said, wishing I had a file to casually peruse. Instead I leaned against the wall, arms crossed over my chest. "I can see how you might get confused, though, given you do all your thinking with your...I don't even know what."

"It's called a brain, dumbass," Greene said. "Though if I'd

been you, I would have said 'twat.'" She sat up again. "Hey – did you know you can remove like ninety-five percent of a cat's brain and it'll be pretty much fine?"

That did raise my eyebrow. "Know this from your own experimentation, do you?"

She ignored that dig. "No, I read it in a book, not that you know what those are. It's true, though – you take out basically everything but the hypothalamus, and as long as you keep it confined, the cat'd be more or less okay."

"That's...nice," AA said, her face revealing that it was anything but. "Now–"

Alannah sat back in her chair, the hook baited, a look of satisfaction on her face. She was the teacher here, or the fisherman, about to reel us in, and I saw it coming. "You know what happens if they don't contain it, though?"

"It attacks you in the woods then batters you with endless factoids about debrained cats?" I asked.

She chuckled. "No. It becomes what they call...hyperexploratory. It wants to see everything. Can't help itself, even. It'd jump right in a lion's cage trying to see what's in there, or leap in front of a car if it saw something interesting in the way. You might even say–"

I grunted in disapproval, annoyance, and general malaise, because I had a feeling I knew where she was going with this. "So help me, if this is just a windup for you to get to 'Curiosity kills the cat,' I'm gonna frigging lose it."

She paused for a second, then grinned. "Well, I was just talking, but thanks for bringing it around to a solid point for me."

"What the hell were you doing in the woods?" I asked, sick of talking around things.

"I live there. What were you doing?"

"Searching for three missing construction workers," I said. "Did you see anyone other than me today?"

"I already said no," she said, in that same snotty tone she used for every word she spoke. "Did you *see* anyone other than her today? Naked, I mean?" She inclined her head rather violently toward AA.

"Where in the woods do you live?" AA asked. She had a small notebook and a pen out, ready to write. I was unconvinced we were going to get enough out of Alannah to be worth writing down. Other than maybe some choice insults, because the girl had those to spare.

"Hey, I know my rights," Alannah said, suddenly annoyed. "Ain't you supposed to give me a–?"

I knew what she was about to say, so I cut her off before she could get it out. "Sure, you can have a lawyer," I said. "But we're not even talking about the crime that you're going to be charged with. We're just talking about the missing guys. Which you say you had nothing to do with."

She reddened beneath the layer of residual dirt, and for the first time, I realized she didn't even have shoes on, just dirty, near-black-soled bare feet, stretched out beneath the table. They were so dirty that I'd cuffed her legs and never realized she didn't have any shoes on. "I didn't have nothing to do with those boys you're talking about. Didn't see 'em. Don't know 'em. Don't care about 'em."

"Mmhm," I said, making it clear that I believed her about as much as I believed a smooth-talking guy on a first date telling me I was the most beautiful woman he'd ever seen, and definitely the kind he could see himself spending the rest of his life with. "So...where do you live in those woods?"

"In a hollow tree trunk," she said with dripping disdain. "Right next to this cardinal nest. Great location. Awesome view."

"Because you can see the river from there?" AA asked, clearly trying to get in on the sarcasm action.

"Only thing I can see from there is your mama's fat ass,"

Alannah said. "'Course, everyone can see that from anywhere on the planet, it's so damned big."

"You must be getting tired if you're having to resort to 'yo mama' jokes," I said.

"Not as tired as 'yo mama' was after me," she said without missing a beat.

"Yeah, this is super awkward, cuz my mom's dead," I said. "You must be really into necrophilia."

"Your mom's not dead, she's back at my house," she said. "That's just something she made up to get away from you."

I chuckled. "I doubt you know the first thing about my mom. But I can see this isn't going anywhere–"

"Hell of a lawman, your mom," Alannah said. "Or is it lawwoman? What's the proper word these days? Though she didn't exactly chart the same path as you, did she?"

"Awwww," I sighed. "Someone read one of my biographies. Or an article on the internet. Or my Wikipedia page–"

"Sierra Nealon was a real mean bitch," Alannah said. "But I hear her sister was crazier – and her mom was maybe worse." She cocked her head. "Whatever happened to ol' Lethe, anyway? Burned to death, was it?"

I felt my blood slow a little. My grandmother's name – her real name, anyway, the ancient one – was not widely known. "Yes."

"Yeah, she's alive, too," Alannah said, so casually. "Just wanted you to think she was dead."

I laughed, but it was so forced and pained I couldn't help but feel even a casual observer would recognize that. "Sure. I bet she's back with my mother at your place, too."

"Saw 'em both this afternoon, gave it to 'em good," Alannah said, and finally I felt a rush of relief.

"A 'your grandma' joke?" AA said, her mouth slightly agape. "You really push the boundaries of good taste."

"Yeah, speaking of 'good taste,' you want to keep talking about your mom and grandma?" Alannah looked right at me.

"Nah," I said, trying to keep as casual as I could. "I can see this isn't going anywhere. You can just spend the night here–"

"Alone? Well, that's a shame, because with your mom and grandma off waiting for me–"

"Oh, shut up already," I said, rolling my eyes. "Nobody gives a shit about your stupid infantile jokes." I kept my voice level, uncaring, almost bored. "I'll be back tomorrow, and we'll talk about what we're charging you with."

Greene sat up urgently in her chair. "Wait."

"No," I said, and hammered the door. "You just sit here and think about what you've said, how you are, that giant burr up your twat – and we can talk again tomorrow...afternoon." I smirked as the lock clicked and Sheriff Miles threw the door open, holding it wide for me and AA.

"Wait, no," Alannah said, rising to her feet but catching the chains halfway up. She got stuck, unable to get to her feet, and it threw her back down with a thump. I grimaced, because she made a pained expression, and I knew she'd caught her tailbone hard. "Awwwwwwww," she moaned.

"Yeah, you go ahead and sit on that for a bit," I said. "We'll talk again...not soon." And I saluted her as she loosed a tirade of profanities on me which weren't quite blotted out by the slamming of the door.

CHAPTER EIGHTEEN

"That seemed about as productive as spreading shit on your morning bagel," Miles said as we trudged back out to the video system. Alannah was visible on the screen, yelling to the heavens and rattling her handcuffs furiously, trying the strength of the table and failing.

"Think I might prefer the shit," AA said, watching the girl in the cell go nuts on the small monitor. She flipped her braid back over her shoulder.

"Surely you've heard worse?" I asked. Alannah was absolutely losing her shit on the screen, but fortunately the sheriff had it muted.

AA looked right at me. "Look, we were rural and poor growing up, but we had manners, okay? So, no, I haven't had much occasion to hear worse than the steady stream of abuse she just dealt out." She shook her head. "Most hardened criminals I've dealt with aren't as offensive as she is."

"She's just trying to shock you. That's why she switched from calling us lesbians as an insult to, once she realized it didn't bother us, going in the opposite direction as hard as she could." I cocked my head at her. "You must deal with a better class of criminal than I do. Because the one's I've dealt with? Will say anything to get under your skin."

"I've mostly been dealing with white collar criminals," AA said.

I nodded. "Yep. That's a different ballgame. Welcome to the big leagues."

"It was just supposed to be a missing persons case," she said softly.

"Well, don't look like it's just that anymore," the sheriff said. "Figure we'll get started tomorrow morning 'round daybreak, if y'all want to participate in the search."

I nodded. "I'll be there. Might park my car overnight, fly home for the evening because it's pretty close for me. You gonna take the girl down to the county lockup?"

He looked torn, but only briefly. "I mean…she could sleep in the interrogation room if you want to make her uncomfortable. We gotta pop in through the night and dose her anyway, we'll just say the interrogation is still underway."

"Yeah, let's do that," I said. "Any issues with her age?"

He shrugged. "Told us she was sixty-four."

"That's…*probably* not true," I said, uncertainly. "But it could be. Under those layers of dirt, and the fact she's a meta…God knows she's mean enough to have been born in another age. You know how to be careful about her, right? With the suppressant?"

He gave me a nod. "Took the class, so did all my deputies. Administer every four hours, just to be safe."

"That's best practice," I agreed. "Call me if you need me. I'm only a few minutes' flight away."

He hesitated. "How many?"

"I dunno – about twenty?"

That prompted a cringe. "There's a motel just down the highway. I'd feel a lot better if you were closer, y'know?"

I started to protest but stopped myself. A night away from Cali, Jack, and Emma wouldn't be the end of the world. Chandler enjoyed coming down to the house to feed the fur babies and hang out, anyway. "Sure," I said, because why not?

CHAPTER NINETEEN

I found out why not when I pulled into the parking lot of a no-tell motel off a county highway a few minutes later. The place looked like time had not only forgotten it, but had turned its back savagely and angrily, leaving this place open only for the sort of clandestine rendezvous that would produce a furious and scorned spouse or the kind that resulted in an hourly charge, or, perhaps, both.

In any case, I didn't run a black light over the bed before I conked out (thankfully), and I awoke to trucks downshifting on the highway the next morning. Getting myself together, I stepped out into the morning dusk, found the nearest gas station and got a giant cup of coffee, then made my way to the site.

By the time I pulled up, dawn was on its way and my headlights were illuminating almost nothing. A thin, patchy fog had settled in at the edges of the horizon, making visibility a problem. But I could see the sheriff as I drove up, as well as AA, who looked only slightly better for the wear than I probably did. Stepping out into the humid morning chill, I made sure I snagged my coffee before getting out.

"Any progress during the night?" I asked, shuffling my way over to AA and the sheriff, the cup steaming out of the plastic drinking hole in the disposable lid. The Styrofoam was warm between my fingers. "Or anything from the girl?"

"Just a stream of insults that were as creative as they were unprintable," Sheriff Miles said, sipping his own coffee out of an Arctic mug. It smelled good, but black and cheap. "She stopped calling me fat right before I left and started talking about how my wife was cuckolding me with the local janitors every chance she got. Little did she know that that would be fine with me, so long as I can go fishing instead of taking care of that business."

I ignored that, and looked to AA. "Sleep well?"

"No." AA's coffee smelled a little better, but not much, and her eyes were only half open. A night owl. "Why did you want to meet out here this morning instead of talking to the girl first thing? Catch her early, maybe she'll be less ornery."

"You could catch her right after she got the best laying of her life, plus a million bucks in the lottery, and I'm guessing she'd still be ornery as hell," I said, taking a sip of my coffee. "No, I think it's better to make her wait. Maybe her bravado will melt once she realizes that the inside of a cell is her new normal."

"If you say so," AA said, and I could tell she was skeptical because I wasn't a total moron.

"We got some volunteers for the search," the sheriff said, pointing to clusters of people around the site who were equipped with flashlights and water. "Say, you don't have my megaphone, do you?"

"Sadly, Alannah Greene knocked it out of my hand during the scuffle, and I have no idea where it went," I said. "I thought about trying to find it, but given how much trouble she'd already given me I just flew her out."

"Damned shame," the sheriff said. "Guess I'll do it the old-fashioned way. Hey, y'all!" he shouted.

The searchers shuffled closer, moving together as a group – or rather, a cluster of disparate groups. All sorts seemed to be represented among them – the reasonably well dressed and straight out of *Deliverance* types. Men and women, though the emphasis was heavier on guys. Beards dominated, but there were a few clean-shaven sorts as well. All of them clustered together to listen to the sheriff as a heavy wind rustled through the distant trees in the pre-dawn quiet.

"Listen up," the sheriff said. "Y'all know why we're here, and we sure do appreciate you coming out today to help. These three fellers are construction guys from the Knoxville area, and what we know about 'em is–"

My skin prickled as I stood behind the sheriff, listening to him warm up the crowd before sending them off. The air was just a little chilly, more reminiscent of September or October weather than the first week of November, but here we were. The trees were still rustling, though the wind seemed have stopped near me.

And stayed stopped.

"What the hell?" AA muttered, catching the same thing I had. The trees were going nuts, branches rattling and rustling.

Something was coming. Something...loud.

"What's that?" Miles asked, stopping his talk because it had become obvious to everyone with a functioning brain and sense of hearing and touch that something was badly amiss.

I zipped into the air, readying fire in my left hand, getting prepared to draw my gun with my right.

It felt a little like a moment out of *Jurassic Park* with a T-rex coming, where the trees were being parted in order to make room for something large and scary. The sound of the rustling was loud and violent, and it reached the edge of the woods as the boughs of the smaller trees and the vines burst aside to reveal–

A woman. A little taller than me, a little thinner than me, a whole lot grungier, but dark-haired, and–

Well…a reasonable amount angrier than me.

"What the hell," she said, her voice carrying in the still of the early morning, "have you done with my daughter?"

CHAPTER TWENTY

"Hoo boy," I said, coming forward farther, trying to put distance between me and the crowd in case this woman went full nuts. Given that – just connecting the dots – it seemed she was mother to Alannah Greene, the local psychopath, I didn't think that was out of the realm of possibility. "Ms. Greene?"

She snapped her head around to look right at me, where before she'd been distracted by the crowd of men and not the woman hovering in front of them. Typical. Her eyes got slitted and narrowed, like a snake. "I know you. What the hell are you doing here?"

"Looking for some missing construction workers," I said. "But I take it you're Alannah's mother?"

She bristled and tilted her head forward, scowling, her dark hair blossoming out around her shoulders like a cobra's hood. It didn't look like she'd done it intentionally, as if she was a Medusa; more like that was just what her hair did when she bent her head that way. "How do you know my daughter?"

"Well, see, I was flying over the valley last night," I said, "looking for the aforementioned missing workers? When your daughter decided to try and murder the shit out of me for no particular reason. So...she's in jail right now."

Greene stared at me, and her hate did not decrease. If anything, it went up a few notches. "You arrested my Alannah?"

"Yes," I said, keeping that fire burning in my left hand, and my right on the butt of my HK VP9. I didn't know what kind of powers this woman possessed, but I knew based on my encounter with Alannah that I didn't want to get caught out on the wrong side of them, because I'd likely be dead before I got a chance to remedy that error. "She's in the local jail."

She brought her head back, and I recognized a decision being made as she relaxed her body somewhat. "Take me to her."

The sheriff cleared his throat. "Ma'am, your daughter's being held until her preliminary hearing later today. She's not going to be able to have visitors until we get her in front of a judge—"

"My daughter is seventeen years old," Ms. Greene said with a fury as cold as dry ice. "She's a minor. If you have questioned her without counsel or myself present, you've already made a hell of a mess for yourselves."

"She told us she was...older." I held in my grimace. She wasn't wrong. Annoyingly well informed about our legal system, which told me something about her, but...not wrong. "Why don't we take you to see her now?" I offered, because boy had we stepped on a rake.

"Yeah, why don't you do that," Ms. Greene said in a snotty tone, heading right for the sheriff. "You give me a ride, big boy. I don't have a car."

"Sure," Sheriff Miles said. "You mind riding in the back?" He gave me a questioning look, like, "Should I do this?"

"I'll be right behind you," I said. Which wouldn't save his

life if she decided to kill his ass, but I'd be Janey-on-the-spot to avenge him. I gave him an encouraging smile, though, because he didn't need to know that.

Besides, what were the odds she'd go full psycho and decide to murder him without warning?

That made me cringe, too, as I headed for my car. Because if the apple hadn't fallen far from the tree…they were better than I would have liked.

CHAPTER TWENTY-ONE

At the sheriff's station we marched straight past the guy on watch, who greeted us with, "Just gave her the morning injection. She was asking for breakfast."

"We'll get something going for her in a minute," Sheriff Miles said, his face red. I knew he hadn't had any plans to feed her anytime soon, and given what I'd already seen from her, that didn't bother me much. "Right this way, Ms. Greene."

We'd left the search party behind, and they were out combing the woods already. Personally, I'd have rather been there, overflying the place, but I had a bad feeling about Ms. Greene here, and I needed to get some info from her hellcat daughter in any case, so it seemed like the time to get some questions answered.

"Do you have kitchen facilities here?" Ms. Greene asked, looking around the station. They certainly had a kitchenette, complete with a refrigerator that looked vintage, right out of the 1950's. But nothing other than a microwave to prepare anything.

"Oh, I wouldn't worry about that," the sheriff said

breezily. "We'd make sure she got fed. There's a McD's right down the road."

Ms. Greene's eyes slitted again. "She's a kosher vegan and requires a very specialized diet."

AA and I exchanged a look behind Ms. Greene's back, and AA mouthed, "Kosher vegan?" I just shook my head, because I doubted that it was a thing, and furthermore that even if it was, that Alannah Green was one.

"Before I let you in, I need to see some ID," the sheriff said, pausing just outside the door.

Ms. Greene paused, shooting him a spiteful look. She seemed to be gauging whether this was a fight she could bull her way to victory on. Apparently, she realized she couldn't, so she reached into the back pocket of her torn and scuffed-up jeans, which had about ten or fifteen slits all over them to reveal tanned flesh peeking out from within, and came up with a faded driver's license. "This do?"

The sheriff looked at the license. "Out of date a bit." He looked at the picture, then at her. "But it looks like you, so...it'll work. Brenda Greene? Born August 18, 1965?"

"That's what it says, don't it?" There was enough ire in this lady to burn through the door.

"You just don't look fifty-five is all," he said. "I'll go ahead and let you in." He started leafing through his keys.

While she was focused on that, I sent a quick text to Chandler: *Brenda Greene, born 8/18/1965, TN driver's license now expired. Run her through the databases for me?* I didn't wait for an answer, putting my phone away as Brenda got bored and turned to look at me. When her eyes met mine there was a moment of electrical anger flashing through her green irises and tightening the lids.

Then she glanced at AA and that look faded just a bit, and by then the sheriff had gotten the door unlocked. "Wake up," he announced, throwing open the door. "Got a visitor, Greene."

"Oh, good," Alannah said, "I was getting bored after banging your deputies all night. Could you not find a man in this county hung any better than a damned otter? Or is it just the guys who become cops naturally have teeny peckers?"

Her mother paused at the door, and I could feel the heat coming off her. "You got a mouth like an outhouse, girl."

"Wonder who I learned that from?" Alannah shot back. She was giving her mother a look only marginally less acidic than any of those she gave me.

"The damned internet, I imagine," Brenda said, stepping further into the room. "Giving you that phone was the worst mistake I ever made. Ever since, you been a real prissy bitch with your Socialite and Instaphoto and Tumbler and Tinder–"

"Yeah, I'm not really on Tinder," Alannah said. "Cuz it's based on distance, see? And the only entries that come up are like three goats in the next valley over, and, sure, they're hung better than his deputies, but still, a girl has to have some standards."

Brenda took two steps forward and slammed her hand down on the steel table with enough force that it rattled Alannah's chains. "You think this is funny?"

"I think *I'm* funny," Alannah said. "The situation's just mediocre, I'm mining it for all the comedy I can, but spinning straw into gold ain't a thing–"

Brenda jutted a finger into her face. "Shut. Up. They give you the right to remain silent, you know? Only an idiot wouldn't take advantage of it." She spun on us. "Where's her lawyer?"

"She never asked for one," I said, "and she didn't tell us she was a minor."

Brenda looked back at her daughter, and appeared to be

verging on apoplexy. Swallowing a bitter bunch of emotions, she choked out, "Well, she is. And we want one."

"Sure," I said. "But we want to talk to her about the missing–"

"We don't know nothing about them," Brenda said, keeping her eyes fixed on her daughter, as if willing her to keep quiet. "We're private people. We keep to ourselves, and stay on our own land."

I chuckled. "Yeah, that doesn't fly with me. Your daughter attacked me, and not in a quiet or private sort of way."

"I wouldn't attack you in a private sort of way if you were the last person on earth, succubus," Alannah said.

"Why?" I asked, verging on chuckling again. "You don't have a soul to worry about."

Alannah started to erupt but Brenda silenced her with a look and a single upheld finger. (The index, not the middle, just to be clear.) She looked to the sheriff and said, "This is who's alleging my daughter attacked her? Clearly anything she says is prejudicial."

"Yeah, I do tend to form a bad opinion of people who leap out and try to stomp my brains out of my skull," I said. "I wouldn't say I pre-judged her, though. It definitely happened 'post' her trying to murder me."

"You know her history," Brenda said, appealing to the sheriff again. "Everything she's accusing my daughter of is something she herself has done." She nodded at me. "Why, she'd probably unplug my daughter's life support if she had a chance."

"I'd unplug her mouth, that's for sure," I said. "But I'd only unplug her life support for something really important – like brewing a cup of coffee." AA blinked at me, and I took advantage of the silence to add another layer to the joke. "But in fairness, I'd do that to a lot of people. Not because I dislike them, but because I love coffee so much."

"You can tell all this to the judge," the sheriff said. "She'll be up in front of him about three or so this afternoon, if his usual schedule holds."

"Fan-tastic," Alannah said. "Can't wait to meet him. Is he hung any better than your itty-bitty deputies? Because if I'm gonna get screwed by the legal system, I'd sure like to at least *feel* it." And she spat on the floor.

"You keep your damned mouth shut while I go find you a lawyer, you hear me?" Brenda said, leaning far over the table to look her daughter right in the eyes. Then she pushed off lithely, with the easy power of a meta. "And you—" she pointed at the sheriff, then AA, and finally came to rest on me. "You don't talk to her again without a lawyer present, or I'm gonna sue your asses so hard you'll think your dead momma will feel it."

CHAPTER TWENTY-TWO

Brenda stormed out in a bit of a huff after that, leaving me, AA, and the sheriff in the anteroom of the station, the silence of two slamming doors – the cell door and the front, as Brenda blew through it – ringing in our ears.

"Well," AA said, completely deadpan, a slightly soured look upon her face, "that went well."

Couldn't help but agree. Looking to the sheriff, I asked, "How are the judges around here? We gonna get dinged for interrogating a minor without a parent or lawyer present?"

"Depends on the judge," he said, running fingers through his thinning hair. "Could go either way. Some are reasonable. Some...not so much. We likely have a more favorable proportion on the 'law and order' side of the equation than you'd find in Nashville." He brightened a tic. "On the plus side, I expect after dealing with young Ms. Greene for about five minutes, he might come around to our way of thinking."

"She does have a winning personality, doesn't she?" I asked. "If the prize you were looking to win was a Claymore mine, detonated directly in your face."

AA chuckled. "I would have equated her to wearing a pair of barbwire-crotch panties on a five-mile run."

That hurt me just thinking about it. "Welp, we're stuck on talking to the angry young badger girl about our missing workers. Any news from the site?"

The sheriff checked his phone, then shook his head. "Not a peep. I told 'em to call me if they found anything."

"Hmph," I said, thinking. "Hey, did we ever figure out where Brenda and Alannah live?"

"Why?" Miles took a few steps over to the sign-in book and popped it open.

"Because she said something about me trespassing, right?" I followed him over, and AA shadowed me. The lone sheriff's deputy on duty was talking quietly into the phone across the room, taking down details of someone's lost cow, if you can believe it. Kind of a cute soundtrack to our devastating reversal on the interrogation. "How she lived where I was searching?"

"Yeah, but that's all Waters's land," the sheriff said, flipping open the sign-in book and peering at the page. "Or his company's, at least. Don't see how they could be living on it – unless they're squatters." He made kind of a face as he peered at the logbook. "Huh. Well, her driver's license did list her address as 1404 Millwright Road, which…" He glanced up at me. "That's the closest road to the valley. But there ain't no mailbox out there for that."

"That doesn't make any sense, though, does it?" I asked. "Her living on Waters's land."

The sheriff shrugged. "Not to me, but I'm just a cog in this-here machine."

"Was she the previous owner?" AA asked.

"Don't know," the sheriff said with an expansive shrug. "Long as I can remember, that land was owned by a timber concern or something. Not that I really get over to that area much; nothing really happens there, see."

"Isn't that a little weird?" I asked. The sheriff stared at me blankly. "You have that much wooded area, you don't get hikers going through, getting lost? Hunters poaching or something? Keg parties in the forest? Anything?"

"Lots of places to have a kegger that are more accessible," he said. "Same goes for the hiking. You saw that place. The undergrowth is prodigious, the trees are tightly packed. I reckon it'd make sense someone might try and poach out there, probably some big old bucks hiding in the back country, but..." He shrugged again. "...I don't know. It's difficult to get out there. Reckon no one's ever bothered to go that deep."

"We should look up the property records," I said. "See if Brenda Greene actually has any connection to this place." My phone started buzzing, and I paused to answer. It was Chandler. "Hey. You got that info I asked for?"

"You could at least start with a hello," he said, sounding very focused on something. "Small talk. Build up to what you want me to do."

"I could," I said, "but I have this feeling you're going to be watching a movie in my theater room this evening, with two dogs and a pretty little kitty on your lap and, frankly, that's as much thanks as I can give you."

"Yeah, I wish you hadn't gotten the kitten," Chandler said. "I'm mildly allergic."

"It's Cali's kitten, not mine. And you're going to love Emma."

"I'm going to sneeze my frigging head off while watching the *300*. I can't shake the feeling that King Leonidas is going to be gutting some poor Persian and look up and be like, Dude. You need a tissue? You're distracting me from killing these guys."

"Probably wouldn't he look up and kill you? Not saying you're Persian, but their empire did stretch to parts of India."

"Yes, thank you for that bit of historical accuracy and killing my dreams of donning a red cape and Spartan helmet so as to give my life in a glorious cause. Anyway – I *do* have something for you."

"Oh, are we done with the small talk already?"

"Hah. Brenda Greene?"

"Yep," I said, glancing around. AA was watching me, but the sheriff had gone to the kitchenette to fill his coffee cup. I could hear and smell it pouring, and I was undecided whether I wanted to drink some or use it to clean my gun. "What about her?"

"We do have a record," Chandler said. "Last known address 1404 Millwright Road in Fountain Run, TN. Apparently she did ten years in a federal prison out in Arizona."

"I find that completely unsurprising," I said.

It felt like I could almost hear him frowning over the phone. "Never even heard of that prison. Must have closed. Anyway, looks like she did time...well, it was in the eighties. Meta?" Chandler asked.

"Seems so."

"Weird. You run out there for a standard missing persons case and run into a meta?"

"Two of them, so far," I said. "What other details do you have about her arrest, her conviction?"

"Uhm, it's a bit spotty," Chandler said. "Looks like...accessory to bank robbery, maybe? All it's got is what looks like a plea deal, no trial info. Maybe if I look at...huh?" There was a pause, then his tone changed significantly. "Oh."

"'Oh' what?" I asked, really hanging on the rentorhooks.

"I think I just figured out why this file is so limited," Chandler said. "It's not really an FBI file at all."

"Then what the hell is it?" I asked, frowning. The smell of

the sheriff's foul coffee was starting to get to me, and I was itching to either drink it or to have my question answered.

"Something else entirely," Chandler said. "Because listen to this – the arresting officer? Is about the only piece of information on this file – and it's someone you know."

"Who?" I asked, figuring it might be Andrew Phillips, or Heather Chalke, or someone like that. Someone from my past, someone with a history in the bureau.

Which is why the real answer clubbed me nearly insensate.

"The arresting officer's listed as 'Sierra Nealon,'" Chandler said. "Looks like your mom's the one who put Brenda Greene away, back when she worked for the US government's metahuman agency."

CHAPTER TWENTY-THREE

"Son of a bitch," I said the moment I got off the phone with Chandler. There wasn't much else to be said after he'd delivered his bombshell, after all. "I am feeling about as clueless as Alicia Silverstone in that one movie."

"...*Clueless?*" AA looked at me funny.

"No, *Batman and Robin*," I said. "She was great in *Clueless*. Turns out Brenda did a stretch in the federal pen, and my mom is the one who put her there."

"She was looking at you pretty angrily," the sheriff said. "I just figured it was because of you arresting her daughter."

"Family history is repeating itself," I said.

"So Greene's definitely a meta, then?" AA asked.

"As if her entrance back at the site wasn't evidence enough?" Sheriff Miles asked. He lifted his hat and brushed back graying strands of hair.

"She was arrested by my mom, and it sounds like she did her time in the old agency prison in Arizona," I said. "That's pretty compelling evidence." I clicked my tongue against my teeth, thinking. "I want to get back to this property business, though."

"Oh," the sheriff said. He was in front of a computer of his own. "I was looking it up while you were talking but then your conversation got juicy and I lost focus." He squinted at the screen. "The property was sold to Waters's company by the county about a year ago."

"Wait," AA said, wearing a frown of her own, "the county sold him the property that the Greenes live on? How does that work?"

A slow dawning of comprehension ran over me. "*Kelo v. New London,* all over again."

The sheriff looked up at me. "Yep. Property was condemned and purchased by Fountain Run County via eminent domain."

AA looked at me blankly. "Wait. I thought eminent domain was when a government, state, local, whatever – buys your property to put in a road or a school or something."

I shook my head. "That's what it's supposed to be for. But that's not always how it's used. In *Kelo v. New London*, a case decided by the Supreme Court, the city of New London, Connecticut used eminent domain to buy up some houses to turn them into a corporate park. The court decided that yes, the government can buy your property and kick you off of it to give it to a corporation."

"That's a little outside your normal purview, ain't it?" the sheriff asked. "How do you know so much about this?"

"My brother gets really agitated by stories like this," I said. "The big versus the little. Most people get hung up on sides – are you in favor of the big corporations or the big government? Well, I can tell you from personal experience – either one can do its level best to kill you and ruin your life. *Kelo* was a case of the two working together, hand in glove, kind of a nightmarish worst-of-both-worlds for those of us suspicious of large concentrations of humans exercising power." I made a mental note not to tell Reed about this. It'd just give him heartburn.

"You think that's what happened here?" AA asked.

"You tell me," I said, looking at the sheriff. "The county works out some kind of deal to entice Wil Waters to build a corporate HQ here, then proceeds to condemn the land necessary to furnish him with it."

"Boy, they really rolled out the red carpet for him," AA said.

"I need to talk to Waters about this," I said, checking my phone. "The hearing is this afternoon, right?"

"Two o'clock," the sheriff said. He shifted back and forth on his feet, glancing at the computer.

"Any idea where Waters is staying?" I asked.

The sheriff grinned. "You mean he's not in the same motel as you?"

"I didn't notice a Rolls Royce parked out front, no."

"Then he's probably staying in Knoxville," Miles said. "That'd be the nicest accommodations he could find around here, and he's got that helicopter, remember."

"If you're going to talk with him, mind if I go with you?" AA asked.

"You starting to get interested in this eminent domain business?" I asked.

"Maybe," AA said. "It does have some of the aura of corruption I've come to expect from the white-collar crimes I deal with. A county buying up a property and then turning around and selling it to a corporation?" She shook her head slowly. "Kinda stinks."

"Ride along," I said, beckoning her. "Let us know if anything goes wrong and I'll zip right back, sheriff."

"Hopefully we can handle Cupcake in there until this afternoon," he said. "Surely her momma wouldn't try and spring her without waiting for the hearing?"

"You know the recidivism rates as well as I do, and let's face it," I said, heading for the door. "a one-time loser like Brenda is only separated from a second round by opportunity."

CHAPTER TWENTY-FOUR

I managed to get routed through Wil Waters's corporate switchboard to his secretary after about twenty minutes of solid effort, and squeezed a meeting with the man himself in Knoxville. Once we had confirmation, AA and I found ourselves westbound and down, heading to Knoxville and hitting the eastern suburbs as rush hour was starting to really kick in gear.

Green exit signs proclaimed destinations such as Asheville Highway and Louisville, but I ignored them and headed for downtown, which just required riding Interstate 40 past a million and a half trees until the skyline appeared on the horizon.

"What do you think of Tennessee so far?" AA asked as I fixated on that golden dome atop the mirrored central tower, the old World's Fair landmark from 1984. Would today be my day to "accidentally" destroy it? One could only hope.

"Which part?" I asked, looking at Knoxville's skyline, which felt anemic next to Nashville's.

AA blinked a little. "Uhh...in general, I guess? Figured there'd be a contrast to Minnesota."

"Yeah, there's a contrast, all right," I said. "Here the government gives me a gun to go shoot at bad guys. Back there, the government took their guns and shot at me."

AA chuckled, a dry sound. "There must be more than that."

I frowned, really thinking it over. "I've had occasion to get around Tennessee a little bit thus far. Been to Memphis once. Now I've been to Knoxville. Of course I live outside Nashville. If I'm struggling with the question, it's because things are totally different from city to city."

"How so?"

I shrugged. "Tennessee's one of the oldest states, and kind of on a...growth trajectory or something? Not sure how to describe it, but it kinda goes like this: Knoxville is the oldest big-gish city in Tennessee...but it's not very big. It's got UT. Memphis was *the* big city of Tennessee, still the most populous, barely. And Nashville...I don't know what it was like thirty years ago, but I get the feeling because it's blowing up right now that it must have been kind of a flyspeck, comparatively. So I view it like those cities were three sisters."

AA put her head back against the passenger headrest. "Three...sisters?"

"Yeah, like three sisters of a southern great old family with a tradition of cotillions and coming out parties," I said. "Knoxville's the oldest sister. She's important. Got the university, you know. But she's aged kinda poorly. I guess you could say she's the sister that never was. She almost made it, just...flamed out, hit the crack pipe, and now she's sort of a wreck but also trying to put her life together. Some people are still interested, but mostly not.

"Then there's Memphis," I went on, "she was the youngest sister, the belle of the ball, always got everyone's attention, right on the river. But she went too far, went too hard, got addicted to meth, really lost her looks, kinda went to shit. Now people avoid the hell out of her."

"Wow," AA said.

"Then there's Nashville," I said. "The middle sister. Always felt left out, although she had an important function in the family. State capital, all that. Thing is, she hit forty, and suddenly she's got a dynamite new stylist, maybe had a little work done, has grown into her look, and she's suddenly the knockout turning everyone's head. A hundred people a day are moving into Nashville. She's in demand, the name on everyone's lips, and I think Memphis is sort of pissed and Knoxville is just resigned to always being overlooked for her younger sisters."

AA's lips quirked, a smile threatening to break out. "What about Chattanooga? Where does she fit in all this?"

"Chatta-who?" I asked with a smile of my own. "Chattanooga is the sister that got pulled off the stage with one of those long, hooked sticks because no one liked her."

AA laughed. "Ouch. My condolences to the people of Chattanooga. What about–"

"Don't say Murfreesboro. She's living in Nashville's shadow at least for a while longer."

"I can tell you've put a lot of thought into this," AA said as we hit the downtown exit. I hit the lock button for the doors – a little obviously.

"I try to put thought into everything," I said, hiding my smile as we headed toward a towering hotel that already stood out on the Knoxville skyline. Waters was waiting.

CHAPTER TWENTY-FIVE

"Come in, come in," Wil Waters called as one of his assistants, a nameless, near-faceless woman in glasses and a blouse and skirt ushered us into his hotel suite. A commanding view of the Knoxville skyline loomed behind the seated Waters, who was on a couch with a yellowish tinge that looked more opulent than anything I'd seen in any hotel room I'd ever stayed in. Other, similar furniture stood before the floor-to-ceiling glass windows in the suite's open living room, and the air had a musk of some kind of citrus smell that I realized was emanating from Waters's cup. "Can I get you anything to drink?"

"Coffee?" AA asked, and Waters nodded to his assistant.

"I'm fine, thanks," I said, really not wanting to be beholden to him for anything and preferring to get this over with. "Mr. Waters, we're here because—"

"Hey, before we get into that," Waters said, standing up. He gave his slacks a quick brush-off, and I could see the crumbs of breakfast still upon them, "let me ask you something. Do you and Cam Wittman have a rough history or something?"

I had a momentary flashback to the last time I'd actually spoken with Cameron Wittman, CEO of his very own venture capital fund. He'd blasted me with his – shocking, at the time – metahuman powers and then told me to get out of his office.

In fairness to him, I'd exceeded my government mandate and thrown my weight around, grabbing for him. I hadn't been drunk on anything but power, but what he'd done had stung.

Still, I didn't hold a grudge. To Waters, I gave a broad shrug and said, "We had a conflict last time we worked together. I don't know how he feels about it, but I don't have any ill will."

Waters rested his fingers on his chin, miming contemplation. "Interesting. I think he might be carrying some for you."

"Then he can join the club," I said. "Now, about the–"

"So," Waters said, a little grin playing across his face, "did you really kill Jaime Chapman?"

I avoided sagging, annoyed, because I sensed Waters was baiting me. Instead, I stayed absolutely still, and said, "I was in DC, in the White House, when Chapman died – at the hands of lethal, illegal booby traps he'd set in his own office. So no, I did not kill him. He killed his own dumbass self, and rather spectacularly, I hear."

Waters surveyed me with piercing eyes, a kind of humor playing behind them, as if deciding whether to believe me or not. "So you can't mind control people at that distance?"

"Clearly not," I said, "or else I'd be mind controlling you at this distance so I can get on with the questions I want to ask instead of letting you spin me in circles all day while you test if I'm flappable."

Waters smiled. "How am I doing?"

"You gotta work a little harder," I said. "I've been shot, beaten, stabbed – questions don't really do it to me anymore."

"Hmmm," he said, stroking his chin. "All right. What did you want to know?"

AA beat me to the punch. "Did you enter into an arrangement with Fountain Run County to buy the property for your corporate HQ?"

Waters's smile vanished. "Of course. I needed a parcel, they arranged it. Pretty straightforward stuff."

"What about the previous owner?" I asked.

"They were absentee," Waters said, seating himself back on the yellowy sofa. Most yellow couches looked like piss. This one was more goldenrod, and you could tell by looking at it, the texture, the stitching, that it was expensive. "That's one of the reasons the county got involved. Requests for a sale sent to the address the property tax bills were sent to went unanswered, both by me and the county. When they surveyed it, they couldn't find any dwellings on it." He shrugged. "So they made it happen. Why do you ask?"

"Just trying to figure some things out," I said. "That girl who tried to beat the hell out of me? She says she lives there."

"That's a lie," Waters said, frowning. "It's my property. No one lives there."

"The mother of the girl – her driver's license has an address that's on the property," AA said. "We think they might actually be living out there."

"What, with no power, no water?" Waters said, his face shifting into something irritable. "On my land?"

"It was their land before it was yours," AA said, and I sensed a crackle in her voice. "And yes, people can live without power. And there's plenty of well water out there."

"Ridiculous," Waters said, leaning forward. "They're lying to you. We checked to make sure. No one is living there."

"How hard did you check?" I asked.

A flash of annoyance crossed Waters's face. "What does that mean?"

"Well, it's rather difficult to access," I said. "Cliffs, dense forests, rocky edges and no roads and all that–"

"Look, we complied with doing our due diligence as required by county, state, and federal law," Waters said. "I can put you in touch with my lawyers if you want to know more." He settled back in his seat, putting his arms out, hands wrapping the back of the couch. "Frankly, this purchase was a gift to the county. We could have gone anywhere."

I caught a flash of irritation from AA before she got her face under control. Ignoring it, I said, "Why choose here, then?"

"Because they made me a great offer," Waters said, but there was definitely a catch in his voice. "If there are people still living on that land, they're squatters. I'm going to need that to get taken care of. Who do I talk to about that?"

"Uhm...your lawyers?" I stared at him. "Not sure why you're looking at me. I don't do evictions."

"The girl's a meta, isn't she?" Waters put a hard look on me. "The one that beat you up? I'm guessing if she responded like that to you, she's not going to take an eviction notice from a local sheriff with any grace." He gripped the back of the couch, white-knuckling it, and forced a smile. "Just trying to think ahead, here. Read the road. Anticipate obstacles coming."

"Yeah, that's not my obstacle," I said.

"Yet," Waters said tightly. Then he smiled. "I am curious why you're asking about all this? Because I thought you were here for the missing workers."

"I can work multiple cases at the same time," I said. "This one's related to my assault at the hands of Alannah Greene."

Waters seemed to take this in with a shrug. "Fair enough."

"So you picked this corner of Tennessee because of the

county," AA said, and there was a strain in her voice that was new. "Why pick Tennessee at all?"

Waters seemed to relax. "I know, right? Tennessee, of all places? Backwoods, backwards – like synonyms for the name of the state. But let's face it: Silicon Valley, NYC, LA – they're all overplayed, overbuilt. With broadband, you can work from anywhere. And it's not like Central Park is really 'nature' anymore, you know? I wanted a place where we could build bike trails through actual woods. Where I could walk out my office door and be under the sun, grass beneath my feet, leaves rustling by in seconds. No competitors nearby trying to steal the energy of my workers – there are advantages, you know?"

AA had a dark look in her eyes that I hadn't recognized before, and a robotic tone to her voice. "Sounds like you're still making some real sacrifices, though."

"That's mostly my workers," Waters said with a shrug. "I'll jet up to NY or LA or SF anytime I need to or want to. The real challenge is going to be bringing the amenities, the restaurants, the night life to them. Which we're set to do. I'm making a huge investment in the area, basically building a new town – but walkable, nice, with natural splendor close at hand. Some tradeoffs, sure, but...hey, it beats the shit out of the valleys of trailers out here now." He grinned. "We're bringing the light of civilization to this ass-end corner of the country – and I think the county is grateful for it." He reached up and adjusted his shirt, unbuttoning one to reveal much less in the way of pecs than most guys would have if they could afford all the personal trainers in the world. "As they should be."

AA's lips were a tight line, and there was an angry but triumphant look in her eyes. She started to open her mouth, and I sensed where it was going and clamped a hand on her arm just as my phone buzzed. Hers must have gone off, too, because after giving my grasping hand a look, she reached for her phone as I checked mine. "Shit," she muttered.

I knew what she was talking about, of course. A text message from the sheriff to both of us:

Hearing moved up to 12:30. Hurry back if you want to see it.

CHAPTER TWENTY-SIX

"I was fine in there, by the way," AA said once we were back in my Explorer, heading east. She was hunched over in her seat, staring straight ahead. Not the posture of someone who was fine, then or now.

Interstate 40 was already blazing past, and I had my lights on, getting people to move out of the way. It was highly unlikely I'd be needed at the hearing, but I wanted to be there nonetheless. Sure, I could have flown, but I didn't know AA well enough to abandon her in Knoxville with the keys to my car. Besides, it was 11:39. We could make it in time, even by car.

"That was only 'fine' in the sense that a woman means that other murder-worthy offenses are 'fine,'" I said.

She laughed under her breath. "Maybe."

"Something about Waters set your kettle on boil," I said. "What was it? All that stuff about Tennessee being backwards?"

"Yeah, he's talking about my family when he says that, you know," she said, swallowing audibly. "He doesn't know it. Maybe he'd apologize if he did, but that's who he's talking about. My mom and dad, sisters, cousins, aunts, uncles, grandparents – that's who he's calling 'backwoods, backwards.'" She looked sullenly at the Explorer's dash. "Shouldn't be surprised. I bet he's never even met anyone from out there. Thinks we're all rubes. Probably didn't even realize I'm from Appalachia unless I grinned at him with three or five teeth missing."

"I mean…you're probably not wrong in his thinking," I said, "but you've got to be used to it by now. Sneering dicks like Waters are a dime a dozen. You meet 'em everywhere."

"No, I don't, actually," AA said. "I see them on TV and in movies a lot. But I don't meet them myself very often." She looked down again. "You know what's so shocking about Alannah Greene?"

I paused, considering, my hands locked on the wheel. "The sheer amount of dirt she was wearing as a face mask? The lack of shoes…?"

"Conversationally," AA said, "she was willing to casually cross a lot of lines we'd consider to be off-limits, and in a really mean kind of way. Making fun of people because of their weight. Their sexuality. She couldn't have been much more shocking to our current sensibilities without dropping a racial epithet."

"Which I could totally have seen her doing. Girl seems a real edgelord. Edgelady? Whatever."

"As we evolved as a society, we've fenced off making fun of people for certain inherent qualities," AA said. "Which I think is generally a good thing. If you're making fun of people for things they can't control, and they haven't earned that—"

"Whew, I'm glad you added that disclaimer. Because I mock my villains constantly, with whatever opening I'm given."

"—then you're really just being a prick," she said, warming up to the subject. "I've thought it was a good thing that we were being more decent and less insulting to large groups of people. But that's not what we were doing." She looked out the window. "Because humanity doesn't change in our need to belittle others. So we went from insulting based on race and weight to insulting them based on other disfavored, uncontrolled characteristics like being a rural person, or not having a college degree. We didn't stop, we just changed targets."

"If you think that's bad," I said with excess cheer, "you should hear what they say about me on the internet – and occasionally to my face – for not having a high school diploma."

"I bet it's really searing," AA said.

"Can be," I said. "But in my case, if I couldn't take it, I probably shouldn't be dishing it out." And, boy did I love to dish it out. I thought back to something else she had said in the midst of her tirade. "Say...you didn't mention 'brothers' in your kinda rant."

She shook her head. "I only have sisters. I'm the oldest of the four."

"So...did your dad do the squirrel hunting in your house, then?"

AA looked straight ahead, out the front window. "No. He was busy working. I was the squirrel hunter in the family. From the time I got old enough to hold a rifle, they'd send me out in the woods." She pressed her lips together, and they turned a little pale. "If I didn't kill something...we didn't eat much that night." The look in her eyes hardened. "So you better believe I killed something, pretty much always."

"I believe it," I said, nodding slowly. "Kinda explains why you took exception to what Waters said."

She made a scoffing noise deep in her throat. "If I have a problem with Waters it's because someone who was raised like him – nannies and gardeners and tutors and private schools in the right neighborhood of Manhattan – doesn't think a thing of what my upbringing was like before he casually slurs my entire family as white trash. I have more in common with the people I met in college from the real bad neighborhoods than I do with Wil Waters." She looked out the window again. "Which is why it stings to get insulted by him. The man wouldn't know a real problem if it walked up and slapped him across those lily-white cheeks."

"He'd probably faint dead away from the shock of being touched like that." I got her to chuckle, but it didn't dissolve all the tension. And we drove eastward, hurrying, in silence.

CHAPTER TWENTY-SEVEN

AA gave me the directions to the Fountain Run County courthouse, and we pulled up about five minutes late. It was a pretty building, one of those Depression-era edifices built back when America took pride in its governmental architecture. It towered above the town square, the first few turning leaves of fall already showing red and yellow on the trees scattered all around. The grass in the center of the square was starting to lose some of its green luster, and the hustle and bustle of the surrounding businesses – the ones that were still open and not boarded up, gone – was that of people hurrying inside because the air had taken a brisk chill.

"Can you believe the election is tomorrow?" AA asked as we hustled up the steps into the courthouse.

"I actually voted already," I said.

"Me too," AA said. "I know it's not polite to ask, so feel free not to answer, but–?"

"Charlotte Mitchell," I said, tossing her a look as we stepped into the tile-lined entry. "It's not politics, though. I've had some issues – personally – with Sarah Barbour."

"I am not a fan of Barbour, either," AA said. "But mine are politics, not personal. Other than I just don't like her."

"Mitchell kind of impressed me during that last debate," I said. "I figured after Gondry had dropped out, y'know, she'd pull her punches, but man, she went after Barbour *hard*." Because she had, pinning the former VP in place verbally on the debate stage and absolute battering her about her record as Oregon's senator and the HHS Secretary.

"Barbour definitely got the worst of the last debate," AA said, and pointed toward a hallway at the left side of the building with a placard on a stand out front: Courtrooms. "She did fair on the one before. I just don't like her personality." She made a face. "Seemed kinda snaky, you know?"

"Can confirm. She once tried to walk me into a deadly trap at the White House," I said, "so yes...snaky." I sighed. "I guess we'll find out tomorrow who wins, though. Hopefully."

"The polling has just been a mess," AA said. "No one seems to know anything."

"Well, in fairness to the pollsters," I said, hustling down the side hall, "when the president nearly drops dead of a heart attack less than a month from the election, it probably doesn't make their job easier."

The doors to one of the courtrooms were cracking open just as we approached, and I saw Sheriff Miles come strolling out, a sour look on his face. He caught my eye as I walked up, huffing a little, and said, "No hurry now. It's already done."

"Already done?" I checked my cell phone. It was 12:38. "How?"

"We started early," he said with a shrug. "The judge and the lawyers were all there, so..."

"What happened?" I asked

But before there could be any answer, the door to the courtroom popped open to belch forth Alannah Greene, uncuffed and walking beside her mom, still not wearing any shoes. A tidy man in a suit followed a couple paces behind them.

When she saw me, Alannah broke into a wide grin. "What's up?" And she flashed me her bare wrists...and two extended middle fingers. "Guess who got released on her own recognizance? Recognize, bitches!" And she laughed, walking right past us, her mother in tow, heading for the courthouse exit.

Free as a frigging bird.

CHAPTER TWENTY-EIGHT

"I guess they don't take attempted murder of a state agent seriously in this county," I said, dry as a damned bone.

"Actually, it was the interrogating her underage thing that screwed us," Sheriff Miles said, watching Greene cackle as she walked around the corner, middle fingers still extended skyward. "The judge was put out about that little mixup."

"She didn't have ID, she didn't cooperate in telling us her age," I said, nonplussed. "What did he want us to do, check the tea leaves?"

"Extend the benefit of the doubt to her, I reckon," the sheriff said, shaking his head sadly. "The DA is assembling the case against her. I took some pictures of how you looked once you got out of the woods, but..." he shrugged. "It's your word against hers, other than that."

"Because nothing she said in the talks we've had is admissible, right?" AA asked.

"That's right," the sheriff said. "Any of her humbragging about kicking your ass is useless."

"Great," I said and turned on my heel, and started heading back the way I'd come.

"Where to, now?" the sheriff called after me. AA seemed to be hesitating to follow.

"I don't know," I said. "Probably back to the site to look for the guys." I gave him a look. "Any word from there?"

He shook his head. "Last update I heard, there was no progress to speak of."

"That's fine," I said. "Maybe I'll help them make some progress. AA?"

AA looked up, then frowned. "Still haven't gotten used to being called that. I want to dig into this property matter a little deeper, so I'll go back to the station with the sheriff – if you're heading that way?" She looked at the sheriff, who nodded.

"Sounds good," I said, throwing them a thumbs up. "We'll catch up later."

I made my way out of the courthouse and into the cool air. The breeze was just kicking up as I reached the top of the steps and froze. Brenda and Alannah Greene were down on the sidewalk, talking in (extremely) hushed voices. It reminded me of a thousand angry discussions I'd had with my own mother – though it had obviously been a while.

"Shhh – shhh!" Brenda said to her daughter as I walked down, heading for my Explorer.

"Oh, don't let me get in the way of a little mother-daughter brawl," I said.

"We're getting along just fine, thanks," Brenda said with a forced smile.

I could tell by the sour look on Alannah's face that this was a lie. "Yeah. You look like you're getting along about as well with your daughter as you got along with my mom."

Brenda seemed to have missed what I said at first, but then she let out a slow breath and said, "God, you are smug, aren't you? Got a smart-ass mouth just like your momma. Just like all of them, really." And she shook her head.

"Like all of who?" I asked. "Because if you're gonna toss an insult my way, it needs to be...y'know...comprehensible."

Brenda smirked. "Like all of *them*. Your smugass family line. Your momma–"

"Hehe, *your momma*," Alannah said, clearly triggered to giggles by the possibility of a 'your mom' joke.

"–your crazy auntie Charlie," Brenda said, as if speaking to an idiot. "Oh – and your bitchass grandma, Lisa. God, she was maybe the worst of the bunch."

"Wait." I raised an eyebrow. "You actually knew Lisa Nealon?"

"I knew your whole piece of shit family branch," Brenda said smugly. "It's how I know you're a piece of shit, too."

A car pulled up seconds later, and I saw the tidy man in the suit wave to Brenda. She walked over to the passenger door and opened it. "I can take you as far as my office," the lawyer said. "After that, you're on your own."

"You can't go a little out of the way to drop us off?" Brenda asked. She sounded a little put out about it.

"I have to get to an appointment in Sevierville in an hour," he said. "Sorry."

"You're sorry?" Alannah sneered. "I'm gonna have to walk fifteen miles on the pavement, barefoot. These tender tootsies of mine are gonna need a good soak in the creek when I get home tonight."

I paused. Sighed. Debated.

And opened my stupid mouth.

"I'm heading back to the search," I said warily, jarring both Alannah and Brenda into looking at me suspiciously. "I can give you a ride – if you think you can avoid killing me for twenty minutes while I'm driving."

"I ain't making that promise," Alannah said.

"Hush, you." Brenda snapped her on the shoulder, causing her daughter to jerk in surprise or pain, or some combo of both. Brenda squinted at me, and I could see the gears turning in her head. "This ain't some plan to entrap us, is it?"

"It's not a plan to," I said, "but if you commit a crime while you're riding with me, I will arrest you. Think you can just behave yourselves on the ride? If not, maybe walking is your best bet. Or a rideshare."

"Dumbass, there is like one rideshare in this town, and it's probably Steve-o," Alannah said, causing her mother to look at her in alarm. "And Steve-o don't start driving til like six at night cuz he's always drinking the afternoon away." She mimed drinking.

"How would you know that?" Brenda asked, looking daggers at her. "You been leaving the property?"

"Other than to get arrested?" Alannah scoffed. "You learn these things being around. Steve-o posts it on his profile." Trying to shake her mother's suspicions, she added, "I don't have a credit card, how I would be using a rideshare? Answer me that."

Brenda appeared soothed by that one, and looked at her attorney. "Can she entrap us if we take a ride with her?"

He leaned his skinny, bow-tied face out to look at me. "You're not going to talk to my clients about the case at all, are you?"

"I don't want a mistrial or charges dismissed, so no," I said. "Just..." I rolled my eyes. "...trying to be...something."

Alannah cracked a nasty grin. "Nice? You trying to be nice?"

"Maybe," I said, and jerked my head toward the Explorer. "If you want a ride, get in, otherwise...whatever. I'm leaving."

I heard the quiet chatter between them as I headed for my car, and sure enough, as I paused to unlock my car, I saw them coming.

Yippee.

Now I was the rideshare.

Except unlike Steve-o, I wasn't going to get to spend my afternoon getting blitzed.

But, oh, how I wished I could have.

CHAPTER TWENTY-NINE

I had to roll the windows down because, confined in the back of my Explorer, Alannah was a lot more fragrant than I remembered. It was her breath, it was her body odor, it was the general scent of someone who hadn't showered in a day or two, and I started to worry it wouldn't come out of my upholstery when I dropped them off.

"So..." I said into the silence, about three minutes after we'd started moving, "...what kind of meta are you? Uh, youse." I paused, could feel their eyes on me. "Fine...*y'all.*"

Alannah cackled. "Boy, you went real hard out of your way to avoid that one. What's a matter? Don't want to be associated with us backwoods folk?"

"You, specifically? Maybe a little," I said quickly. "But that has more to do with the lack of shower and toothbrush for the last day than anything else."

"Bitch, that's your fault," Alannah said. "I had a shower yesterday. Not my fault some claim-jumper showed up and I had to fight her off."

"You had no idea why I was there," I said. "Don't give me this 'claim jumper' crap."

"But you are," Alannah said. "I heard 'em talking about this construction project. I know what's going on."

"Girl, you don't know nothing. Shut up," Brenda said, then leaned forward to me. "What do you know, though? How'd these people end up with this claim to our land?"

I shrugged. "They bought it, I guess."

"I didn't sell it, so how'd they buy it?" Brenda asked.

"Eminent domain," I said. "Same way the government buys anything."

"But they ain't the government," Alannah said. "You are. So you saying you stole it, and then they bought it from you?"

I blew air noiselessly through my lips as I followed the announcement of my GPS to turn left. "I may be *with* the government of Tennessee, but I had zero to do with whatever the Fountain Run County government did to seize your land. But...I can look into it, if you want." Because I was kinda planning to anyway.

"Yeah, why don't you do that," Alannah said, "but don't expect me to just forget you locked me up without giving me my lawyer. Made me smell like the inside of your shoes." She sniffed at herself, then made a face I caught in the rearview. "Maybe worse."

"You look into that, then," Brenda said, without much feeling, as she settled herself into the back seat. "And me, I'll take a look 'round my property, see if I can find your missing boys."

I raised an eyebrow. "Really?"

She gave me a smoky look in the rearview. "Yeah. I'll put about as much effort into my search as I bet you put into yours."

"I'm genuinely looking into your problem," I said, brow furrowing.

"Then you ain't got nothing to worry about, do you?" Alannah sniped.

I shook that one off. Let them believe I wasn't going to put any effort into this. I could feel this turning into a real case, and I was determined not to let the murk that seemed to surround me go unquestioned. "Not gonna tell me what your powers are?" I asked.

"None of your biz-snatch," Alannah said.

I gave her a little smile in the rearview. "Such a charmer."

She leaned forward, sticking her fingers between the links of the car's cage. "Boy, you got ice water in your veins nowadays, don'tcha?"

"What do you mean?".

"I've seen the videos of you," she said. "Remember in that cafe in New York when that earthquake guy who was trying to rob the Federal Reserve piped off to a waitress, asking her whether she wanted a big tip–"

"'Or the whole thing,'" I said, staring straight ahead, a little tingly feeling running up the back of my neck from the memory.

"You knocked his ass into next week, handcuffs and all," Alannah said, almost crowing.

"And I was then demoted from Director of Metahuman Law Enforcement and my agency got folded into the FBI," I said. "Where it has since become a real shitshow. Moral of the story: don't beat the shit out of a prisoner for making a nasty comment to a waitress."

"That's a dumbass lesson," Alannah said. "Sounds to me like you lost your nerve."

I chuckled. The chutzpah of this girl. "Sure. My nerve. Like I haven't thrown myself into about a billion fights since then."

"Lady with your strength," Brenda said, piping up, "doesn't take much effort to get into a fight."

"No, but the risks are a little higher when I get into a fight than the average person," I said. I could see the turn ahead as the GPS started telling me to take it. This was where the pavement ended, and the dirt road began, trees giving way to bare gravel roads. "People can get hurt, people can get killed–"

"People do that anyway," Alannah scoffed. "My question is – did they lady-castrate you? Or did you just become a robot? Because I kinda liked that girl who'd knock a prick across a room for exhibiting his dick in public like that. Not like this corporate shill sitting in front of me. I mean, do you feel anything at all anymore?"

"You'd have to hit me a lot harder than you did in our scuffle to make me feel something," I said, feeling surprisingly amused. "But hey, it's not your fault. Some metas are just weak–"

"Bitch, I'll knock those pretty teeth right out of your mouth, you diss me that way–" Alannah had her fingers locked around the joints of the cage and looked ready to rip it out. I slowed the Explorer, watching to see if she'd go the last mile.

Her mom was all over it, though, grabbing her by the back of the neck. "Shut up, you, you got yourself in enough trouble already." She dragged her back – or Alannah allowed herself to be – and thrust her into the seat. "Now pipe down."

I chuckled theatrically. "It's all right, Brenda. We both know she's just mad because the only thing she feels is herself at night after you go to sleep."

"Spoiler alert," Alannah said spitefully, "I don't wait for her to go to sleep, I start flicking the hell out of that bean anytime I damned well feel like it."

"God, you are a breath of sewer air, aren't you?" I asked, almost laughing. "I can see it's going to carry you far. Probably like it did your mom – all the way to prison."

Brenda's face twisted in the rearview as we started to pass

the first of the cars of volunteers come to search for the missing men. "That was your mom that did that to me."

"Oh, I know," I said. "But it was well earned, I'm sure."

"Don't be so sure," Brenda said, and she was surprisingly calm. Unlike, obviously, her daughter. "Your mother Gitmo'd me. I didn't do what she said I did."

"Yes," I said, nodding, "everyone who goes to prison is innocent. I saw *Shawshank Redemption*. Oh, and also I've worked with criminals pretty much since I was your daughter's age, so...I'm aware of how things go."

"There's plenty of guilty people on the inside, but I wasn't one of them." Brenda leaned up to the cage. "And your mom took everything from me. You might want to look into that, too."

"Yeah, I'll put just as much effort into that as you do looking for those missing men," I said as I pulled in at the head of the queue of parked cars, avoiding looking at her but through the mirror.

Brenda Greene stared into my eyes through the reflection, then she nodded slightly. "Come on, girl," she said, nudging Alannah. "Let's get on home."

I let them out and watched them walk away, no more words spoken. They disappeared into the treeline a few moments later, into the darkness between the trunks.

CHAPTER THIRTY

I got a status update about the search – it was going poorly – and hung around the site for a couple hours before I decided to get something to eat, which I did at a local greasy spoon back in town. A half-decent Reuben coupled with crisp fries was my reward and I ate it in the late-afternoon silence, absorbing the clinking sounds of dishes being washed coming from the kitchen, and the scent of coffee that had gone stale.

All that done, I headed back to the motel where I'd spent last night. A run-down place on the side of the road that looked like it had never really seen days much better than this, it had nonetheless provided a moderately comfortable mattress free of bedbugs, and four walls. The wood paneling looked like it had been there since the seventies, and the brass fixtures had the sharp aroma of cleaning solution caked into them, telling me that however long they'd been here, they'd at least been well cared-for in their tenure.

I wandered up to the office, wondering if they'd kept my room for me. I'd checked in for one night and told them I might need an extension. Now, as the bell rang and I came inside from the slight chill developing, I found the older lady who had run the desk last night standing on a step stool, a paper turkey in her hand that looked like it had been made by a four-year-old.

"Oh, you're back," she said, sounding vaguely pleased to see me. Since my car was the only one in the lot, this was an interesting reaction. The office was a smallish space, and behind it I could see a door that opened into what looked like a living room. A TV was blaring some *Judge Judy* style show, which she appeared to be ignoring as she decorated.

"Yeah," I said, feeling a little weary and a little wary. I rubbed my eyes; usually it took me a couple days on a case before I started to feeling the fatigue set in, but it felt like I'd been up late last night and running around all morning, and a little rest didn't seem unwarranted. I checked my cell phone compulsively just to make sure I hadn't missed something, then shifted my attention back to the lady. "Did you keep my room open for another night?"

"We sure did," she said, getting down from the step stool. She had to be pushing seventy, with a gray, close-cropped haircut, and a white, laced-around-the edges top. "Figured you might be back."

"Oh?" I suppressed a yawn. "What made you think that?"

"Well, I know they haven't found those men yet," she said, trudging back behind the counter.

"Right you are," I said. "Better give me another night."

"Same credit card I have on file?" she asked, and brushed aside about ten other Thanksgiving decorations that looked to be made by someone with a similar skill level as the infantile construction-paper turkey. I nodded, and she said, "Just making sure." She clicked the keys of an ancient keyboard. "There. Checked in for another night. You have your key?"

"Sure do." I patted my front pocket. They hadn't upgraded to key cards out here yet. I turned to leave.

"Please be gentle with the furniture," she called after me. "And the fixtures."

"Why?" I asked, my fatigue giving my question a snarky edge. Or maybe just my personality did that. "Are they vintage?"

She blinked at me. "No. We just aren't made of money and can't afford to replace them."

I froze, my back against the office door, ready to push out into sunlight and warmth from the musty office. "...Huh?"

"Well, we aren't a hotel chain, and we aren't wealthy," she said, looking into my eyes with her own, surprisingly earnest ones. "You go turning this place into a shootout like you did in that parking lot over in Nashville, and we might have to close down." She rubbed one wrinkled hand over the other. "This is a small business. We don't make much. Certainly not enough to have the place torn down around our ears."

"I'm not planning to destroy your motel," I said, brow furrowing as I answered her. The flaw in my logic was easily spotted: of course I never *planned* to thrust myself into mass chaos and destruction; it happened because I was Sienna Nealon, and chaos and destruction was my business.

"Oh, well, good," she said, and seemed reassured by this. With a nod, I left her to her decorating and stepped back into the light of day.

I trudged slowly across the parking lot toward my room, which was on the far end of the motel. It was an L-shaped design, with the office anchoring the top of the letter and my room as far away from that as you could get.

With a jangling of keys, I opened my door and felt the smell of aged wood paneling hit me, the slightly musty aroma of a room that had been shut up for some time – probably weeks – until I'd opened the door late last night.

"Honey, I'm home," I muttered to myself, feeling strangely at odds more than I ever did walking into my own home. Probably because I was missing the dogs. Yeah, that must be it.

I smelled the faintest whiff of an aroma that wasn't my own; a sweet-smelling deodorant that permeated the air and made me pause a step past the door. Had it blown in with me? Had the cleaning lady come in after all?

The question was answered a moment later as forearm greeted my throat, bone against my larynx, crushing it along with all the wind from my body.

I was being choked.

Again.

CHAPTER THIRTY-ONE

Someone was choking me and I had no safe word, no defense against the hard pressure on my throat. Strong arms wrapped me up as my attacker fell back, pulling me to the ground and snugging their legs around my abdomen. It was the strangest feeling, like being squeezed by a cobra. It was almost like what Alannah had done to me; and yet different. I wasn't flying out of control, my mind panicking at the imminent crash, and instead felt the tight grip of an arm trying to squeeze the life out of me slowly, not quickly.

Life seemed to pause as I was pulled down, a few possibilities flashing in my head:

Fly high and blast through the roof, then shuck this murderous interloper off my back like dead weight. Let them greet the earth in a grand and destructive crash, like Katherine Heigl's career.

But no. I'd just told that nice old lady in the office I would try not to destroy her motel.

Scream? I could bring this Dom right to their knees with a good Brance scream, making them claw for their ears, popping the drums, making them bleed profusely from their skull.

That'd break the windows, though. And lightbulbs. Which would probably be damaging to the motel and their thin bottom line.

Lift my gun with my magnetic powers? Turn it around, pump four or five rounds through my assailant's ribcage?

There'd be blood everywhere. And other bodily tissues, probably. Messy. Plus bullets in the wall.

"Making my life difficult," I muttered, but it was almost certainly inaudible because when you can't breathe, you can't speak.

I felt strangely calm about this whole thing, as though people choked me out all the time. They did, funnily enough, but this time felt different. It wasn't like I'd been held immediately below the water, feeling it rush into my nostrils, panicked bursts of air escaping my lips as I fought for life.

This person had grabbed me from behind swiftly but with surprising grace, trying to choke me out quietly but as fast as possible. Still, it had taken a second or so to snug in their choke hold, and in that moment I'd had what felt like an eternity to slow down, think it through...

Which was why I had just enough time to realize that I needed to use my magnetic powers to catch the door knob and throw it back open.

And I did.

The door squeaked on its hinges, causing my assailant to turn their head in surprise as a shaft of daylight flooded into the room, spearing us both and casting a long shadow over the bed. My attacker turned to look, losing just a little balance in the abruptness of the motion.

Which was less than I needed, really.

I flung us both backward at supersonic speed across the parking lot. I used my assailant as a shield against the rough, pebbled surface of the asphalt and heard a distinct cry of pain as we ripped across it at a hundred miles an hour.

Well, *she* ripped across it. I could tell from the scream. Also, when she loosened her grip, I pummeled her in the side and found her to be much narrower than your average guy.

We shot across the highway to the blaring of a horn, leaving a trail of blood across the rough surface. I'd partially skinned my assailant, and delivered another hammering hit to her side as I let loose.

With a flip I broke her grip and dismounted, leaving her to skid to a stop in the ditch. Which she did, her entire back bare and covered with vicious road rash. "So," I said, hovering over her torn and bloody self, "how are you feeling about your idea to attack me from behind?"

She looked up at me from within a ski mask like Friday's, save her mouth was visible. Her voice was tiny, like a squeak, when it came. She looked short, but swole, and I knew I was dealing with a Hercules. "Not so good," she said, just dripping pain. "Any chance I can get a do-over?"

"To kill me?" I kept myself carefully out of her reach, but raised my eyebrow at that one. "I don't think so."

"Damn." She stood, brushing herself off, scattering small clouds of dust off her black, stretchy pants. "Can't blame me for asking, can you?" Her voice seemed like it might have been high-pitched but rough, like she was trying to disguise her voice. It was working inasmuch as I didn't recognize it, if I'd ever heard it before. "Where does that leave us, then?"

I kept my hand carefully flexed, ready to unleash hellfire on her if she tried anything. "Pretty sure it leaves you shit outta l–"

She leapt without warning and with way more speed and strength than I would have thought her capable of. I tried to get away, but she managed to snag my left leg and haul herself up my body in one quick, gymnastic maneuver. In a second she was on my back again, arm locked around my throat. "About that do-over," she said.

I'd reached the end of my patience, so I didn't answer.

At least...not in words.

I went hot, covering my entire upper body in flames that burned instantly through my clothing, billowing out in a puff of pure fire. I heard a squeal of pain and surprise from her as she cast herself off of my burning body. She did it with some real strength, and flew for some distance, probably thirty, forty feet. Crashing into the woods, she disappeared behind the bough of some trees and I heard her thump as she hit the ground, out of sight.

"How'd you like your do-over?" I called out, heading up another twenty feet, above the trees so that I'd be out of her reach. My body was still wreathed in flames, my clothes burning in a pile back by the roadside.

"Can I get a do-over, over?" she asked weakly, and I homed in on her voice. "Don't know what you'd call that. A Mulligan?"

"I'd call it 'unlikely,'" I said. "Fool me once and twice and all that. Third time–" I was coming around a tree, and caught sight of her on the ground, kneeling, half her body hidden. She looked pretty bloody and scuffed up, plus she was still smoking from the flames.

Then...I saw it.

In her hand lay the broken trunk of a sapling which she held like a spear. Before I could even fully process the sight, she loosed it at me like a javelin.

It had been aimed right at my heart. I swerved, bucking sideways, my head coming forward–

And it caught me directly in the left eye.

Six inches of tree drove through my eye socket, pulping the eyeball instantly and ramming into my brain. The world got cloudy and dark, but didn't entirely blip out.

"Gotcha," I heard the Hercules say below me, though I didn't understand the words at the time.

Go, Brianna whispered in my head, and bereft of thoughts of my own other than *Ow, that hurts*, I listened.

I shot backward at a few hundred miles an hour, skimming the tree tops, and landed somewhere, the sun already going down in my damaged brain.

When I hit the ground, I barely felt it at all.

CHAPTER THIRTY-TWO

I awoke naked in the woods, my body pressed against the warm dirt, a cool breeze tingling my skin into gooseflesh.

And there was a giant lump of sapling sticking out of my frigging skull.

"Ungghhhh..." I muttered, landing a weary, weakened hand upon it. Tightening my grip on the rough pine bark, I gave it a hell of a pull and it ripped free, thinking of Wolfe all the while.

If you weren't a meta, you'd desperately need some antibiotics right now, Brianna said.

"And if I hadn't just ripped a small tree out of my brain, I'd be dumb as Shia LaBeouf. What's your point?" I sat up and felt the clinging blood on my face, dry and crusty. I didn't know how long I'd been out, but I knew it had been a minute. Checking the position of the sun told me it was afternoon, presumably on the same day. I'd lost my cell phone when I'd burned my clothes off. "What the hell was that all about?"

I can't say for sure, but I'm going to go out on a limb and guess it has something to do with either Wil Waters being a rich enough dick to hire metahuman mercs to put a hurting on you...or...

"Or what?" I pulled a small amount of water out of the air; enough to splash on my face to aid the cleaning and then give myself a drink. "Come on, I just regrew a not-small portion of my brain. Do my thinking for me while I recover."

...Or Alannah Greene just took another shot at you.

I paused, giving that some thought. The Hercules nature of the meta's build skewed things, but what I'd seen of my attacker didn't rule the girl out. "Maybe," I said, hesitant to jump to that conclusion. "If she's a Hercules, why didn't she use those powers the last time she tried to kill me?"

Maybe she did. It's not like you could see her every second of the fight.

"A reasonable point." I shook my head, trying to clear the cobwebs. "Let's keep those theories going. Why do you think Waters would make the jump to wanting me dead, though?"

I don't know that he does. But he's the richest guy around, and if someone hired someone to kill you...

"Takes money. Can't argue with that. But I will put forth a third possibility: someone else wants to kill me."

That's pretty evergreen, as statements go.

"Yeah," I said, lifting off into the air, above the trees. I set my body on fire, because flying naked was probably frowned upon here even for TBI agents. Peering into the distance, I tried to figure out which direction I'd come from. Rising higher into the sky made it easier, and eventually I could see the cut in the woods where the road wound past the lonely motel.

I headed in that direction, making it back in about thirty seconds of sustained, not-too-hard flight. The motel parking lot was swarming with sheriff's cars and another, unmarked vehicle. As I came in for a landing I recognized Sheriff Miles and AA both standing just outside the office, talking to the grandma who ran the place.

With flames covering me over, I descended beside them,

giving each a nod in turn. "You guys looking for another missing person? Cuz I think I found her. A little worse for the wear, but still." None of them spoke, just regarded me with something shy of awe, so I added, "What brought you all out here, actually?"

"Uh, the sonic boom that rocked the town?" the sheriff said, brow lined deeply.

"Oh, and I called 911," Grandma said. "After I saw you wrestling with that big girl. Plus the sonic boom." She cringed, holding a hand up to her ear. "Rattled the windows."

"Sorry," I said. "If it makes you feel better, she ambushed me in my room, but I managed to get her outside immediately without damaging a thing."

"Oh, I know," she said with a little twinkle in her eye. "I checked while I was waiting for them to show up." She flashed me a thumbs up.

"Who attacked you?" the sheriff asked, eyes dark with concern. "Was it Greene again?"

"Can't say for sure," I said. "She was wearing a mask and disguising her voice. Maybe."

"You've been attacked twice in the last twenty-four hours," AA said. "Is that normal? People trying to kill you?"

"Pretty much," I said.

"Glad you're okay," AA said. "I was beginning to worry we were going to have to send out another round of search parties."

I shook my head, and I could have sworn I felt something rattle in there. "No. I got lost but I found myself." I lifted off the ground once more. "Need to go check on something, though."

"Um...shouldn't one of us come with you?" AA asked. "Seeing as you were just bushwhacked?"

I shook my head. "Nah. Besides, where I'm going, you'd

only slow me down." And I headed off to the east, sure of what I needed to do next to stamp out my own doubts.

Or get myself killed. Either or.

CHAPTER THIRTY-THREE

I swooped over the construction site with its empty volumes of dirt and endless rows of searchers' cars. A few people waved, specks of color on the reddish earth below. Then I was over the trees, the piney boughs with their needles that didn't sting – unless you landed at a hundred miles an hour, which I had before, quite against my will.

Onto the disputed lands of the Greenes – or Wil Waters – I went, trying to stay high above the branches to avoid the homicidal psycho teenager lurking somewhere below. The smell of mountain air was brisk and fresh, and afternoon had turned warm, taking some of the bite out of the morning chill. The November sun was beating down like it was still October, and I had no complaints because this was my idea of the perfect temperature.

I flew over the valley fast, listening to the crash of search parties moving through thick underbrush and calling the names of the missing men. It faded into the babbling of a creek running through the center of the valley, and below I heard the faint sound of someone...

Whistling.

I overflew it at first, and looped around, coming back to make sure I'd heard what I thought I'd heard. Getting close again, over the sound of the running water, I confirmed it. A pleasant enough, kinda high female voice putting her efforts into...well...

"Bang Bang" by Jessie J, Ariana Grande, and Nicki Minaj.

She'd just gotten to the chorus when I parted the trees and came down on the riverbank to find Alannah Greene, shoes off, pants rolled up to her ankles, wading in the creek as she sang. She clocked me as I came in for a landing about thirty feet away, but showed no sign of springing on me like last time. Instead, she gave me a vague nod and stopped her singing. "'Sup, bitch? You coming to find me? Cuz my lawyer might have something to say 'bout that."

"Is there a reason I might need to find you?" I asked, my bare feet touching the leaf-covered ground, crunching them as I walked.

"Well, you got no clothes on," Alannah said, providing me with a toothy grin. "Looking like Jennifer Lawrence's dress in *The Hunger Games*, 'cept it's just hugging you, and I'll be honest – you need to cut out the late night Haagen-Daz runs. Look like you got some rolls of fire going on there."

"It's Hattie Jane's Creamery runs, thanks," I said snarkily. They were a local brand, and beat the shit out of the national stuff. "And you're about the last person who ought to be criticizing anyone's physical appearance, being as you look like you just stepped out of a high school production of a Charles Dickens play. You know, where the costumer decided their talents lay elsewhere and really phoned it in by putting everything in the mud for a while. Plus maybe a little cow shit."

Alannah chuckled roughly. "All right. You ain't here to arrest me. You just searching for those lost boys?"

"It's the job," I said, deciding how I wanted to approach this prickly pain in the ass for maximum effect.

"Well, you could do it with some clothes on, that's all I'm saying." She shrugged, turning back to splashing her feet in the creek. "I've never had a job myself, but I imagine if I showed up naked, it'd probably affect my performance reviews."

"Don't sell yourself short," I said. "I can think of a job you'd be wonderful for that requires no clothes. You gotta be okay with body glitter, though."

"Hey, strippers make bank," Alannah said, cheeks reddening slightly. "Probably more than you, *bureaucrat*." The way she said it made it sound like the lowest form of life, maybe even below cockroaches. "Though I guess they ain't living in some sugar daddy's mansion."

I laughed out loud. "It's my uncle's place, thanks. I know you'd probably date your uncle in a heartbeat, but that's not really how I roll."

She flushed a deeper red. "Backwoods hillbilly, I must be into incest, huh?"

"That and sodomizing innocent river rafters passing through."

That actually made her crack a smile. "So...you just stop by to trade trite insults? Or are you looking for a fight?"

"Not really, no," I said, keeping my distance but pacing the opposite bank of the creek slowly. "Someone just tried to kill me."

She matched my slow stroll, feet in the water. "Clearly they sucked at it, then, cuz here you are."

"Does that mean you suck at it, since you tried and I'm still here?" I tried to keep from smirking, but not that hard.

"Hey, I came close, awright?" She shrugged. "Even you'd have to admit that's not bad for a rookie."

"What, was that your first fight?" I asked, pausing as a twig crackled under my bare foot. In order to keep from setting the woods on fire, my flame pants were now capris.

"Yep, first ever," she said proudly. "Don't get me wrong, Momma and I have tussled some. It's where I learned. And I've gone at it with some animals 'round here when they proved a problem. But that was my first fight with an actual person."

I tried to imagine what kind of animals she'd battled. "Have you wrestled a bear?"

"You're damned right I did," she said proudly. "Beat his ass, too. Ain't gonna be getting into my apple trees no more, I sent his sorry self running back over the hills."

Glancing behind me at the high ridge that defined the valley, I had to wonder: "Is that really just a hill? Seems more mountain-y."

"I don't know." She shrugged laconically. "I hear the Rockies are higher than the Appalachians, but I reckon this is plenty enough for me to climb." She got a kind of sparkle in her eye. "Are they?"

"Enough for you to climb? I assume so based on what you just told me."

Impatience flashed over her face. "No, stupid. Are the Rockies bigger? You've seen 'em. I know you have."

"Lots of people have seen the Rocky Mountains," I said, realizing at last what I was dealing with here. A total shut-in. Except...outdoors. Like a free-range Sienna Nealon. "And yeah...they're mighty. Question for you – how does your mom keep you here?"

Now Alannah's face darkened, and not just because of the dirt smudges. "None of your damned business."

"Ah," I said, glancing around. "Was just curious why a rebellious sort like yourself would put up with being trapped, even on so large a game preserve such as this."

Alannah's suspicious eyes found me. "Because she knows there's dangerous people out there. People who might be keen to hurt a delicate flower like me."

It only took me a second to get that. "She's worried about *me?*"

"She had a bad experience with your mom," Alannah said.

"Join the club."

"Yeah, you look like you're really hurting from your upbringing," Alannah said. "Famous hero, living in a mansion. Let me carve out a whole tiny orchestra to play for you." She looked out over the landscape, the wall of trees around us. "Your mom met my mom last time, and she took everything from her."

I pursed my lips. "How so?"

Alannah glanced at me quizzically. "You really don't know?"

"Let's just say there was a lot my mom didn't tell me," I said. "I grew up thinking she was a radiologist. And the FBI file? I don't have full access to it. Just the record that says your mom went to prison and mine was the arresting officer. That's literally all I know."

"Hmmm," Alannah said, pensive. "I could see how that might be. Moms do keep things from their daughters. Surprising, though."

"What's surprising about it?"

"Well," she said, almost chortling, "my whole life I've heard about how 'Sierra Nealon done us wrong, we'd have so much more if not for her.' And then after you came on the scene, well...let's just say I'm surprised my momma was as civil to you today as she was. Figured she woulda clubbed you to death given half the chance I had."

"What the hell did *I* do to her?" I asked, furrowing my brow.

"Nothing," Alannah said with a broad shrug. "But you're the daughter of someone who screwed her over hard, and that leaves a mark."

"I get it, my mom sent her to prison," I said. "But I'm

guessing she deserved it, and she's clearly out now and doing – well, sort of fine–"

"Oh, it ain't that simple," Alannah said. "My momma harbored the guy she was dating at her family's farm in Ohio after he pulled a bank job. That's legit. She copped a plea on it, that's why she only served three years. Turned state's evidence against him, gave him and his whole meta gang up." She shook her head slowly. "The time served ain't what pissed my momma off. It's what happened *after* that."

I felt like I was being set up. "What happened after that?"

"Your mother came in with the full force of the government and their civil asset forfeiture laws," Alannah said, a hint of malice in her delivery, like she was punching me all over again, "and had them seize and sell off my momma's farm that had been in our family for almost *two hundred years*."

CHAPTER THIRTY-FOUR

I rubbed my forehead as I stood in the warm woods next to the creek bed, listening to it burble past. Birds chirped in the trees overhead, and beads of sweat were already forming at my hairline and the small of my back. "So what you're saying is," I repeated to Alannah Greene, who stood barefoot, pants rolled up to her knees in a babbling brook, "my mother used the law to take away your mom's family farm? That's why she doesn't like her?" I cocked my head. "And why you launched yourself out of the trees at me like a crazed squirrel yesterday?"

"Well, yeah," Alannah said, faintly scowling. "Didn't realize you were looking for missing construction guys. I just figured you were coming to take everything else you could from us."

"Hm," I said, trudging a little farther from her before slipping into the stream with my own bare feet. "No, I'm not much for civil asset forfeiture myself. I tend to prefer sending people to prison over seizing their stuff. I mean, if it's a yacht and it's being used for murders and corpse disposal, sure, but a family farm? For someone who made a bad call and harbored a fugitive?" I shrugged. "I feel like the prison time would suffice."

"I guess your mother didn't," Alannah said with surprisingly good cheer, "cuz she came for it, and bam, my momma got out of prison with nothing but the money her dad left her from inheritance. Which she used to buy all this." She waved a hand around. "Which now the government wants to take from us again."

"I'm not a lawyer and I don't play one on TV," I said, "but it seems to me that if you never received word of the sale of the property, you might have a case to fight it out."

"Yeah, lemme tell you what my momma already said to that: 'I can barely afford the lawyer to spring your dumb ass out of jail and now I'm gonna have to fight to keep my property against some rich bitch city boy?'" She shrugged again. "I don't know how much money it'd take to put the law on our side on this one, but I'm guessing we ain't got it lying around."

"Your mom really had no idea they were coming for your land?" I asked, trying to gauge through that smoky, jaded, cynical facade whether the girl was BS-ing me.

"Nah," Alannah said. "We're just out here minding our own business. Didn't know some rich asshole was deciding to come for our home." Her eyes flashed. "Don't expect him to get it easy, though. We ain't just gonna lay down and die."

"I'd be shocked if you did," I said. "Try to stay on the right side of the law, though, will you?"

"Because you don't want to have to come out here and tangle with me?" Alannah asked.

"Yeah, I don't go looking around for fights, that's true," I said.

"Pffft," she scoffed. "I read the stories about what happened when those men came to your house for the first time – you beat the holy hell out of them."

"But I didn't try and kill them," I said. "Kind of an important distinction, don't you think?"

"Oh, yeah, you didn't get to your 'stone cold killer' phase until later." She wore a wide smile.

"Wow, look at you, reading all about me on that phone of yours," I said. "Just keep in mind – half of what you read is lies."

"Well, they did say you were tough." Alannah smirked. "Seems like a lie now."

"Yeah, you must have ended up in cuffs cuz I'm a real marshmallow," I said, lifting off and leaving the rippling stream behind me. "Stay out of trouble, will you?"

"Hey, like you, I ain't looking for trouble," Alannah said, watching me slowly drift up into the sky, "but this is our land. And if trouble wants to come up on it to bulldoze our trees and tear down our house, well…" She slapped a fist hard into her palm. "…You tell me – what do you think I'll do about it?"

"Something unwise, I'm sure." And I took off before she could answer, because I was starting to get a bad feeling about what would happen when that particular clash came to a head. Maybe I could solve this one and get out of town before it happened.

CHAPTER THIRTY-FIVE

I headed back to the scene of the attack and found AA waiting with Sheriff Miles. Landing, I asked, "Hey, did anyone find my cell phone?"

"Got it right here," she said, fishing in a pocket and coming up with a slightly dinged, slightly singed but quite familiar phone.

The sheriff sauntered over as I took it out of her hand. "Do I need to go clean up a body? Maybe of a slightly sarcastic teenager who had it coming?"

"No bodies," I said, clutching my phone in my hand. "She pleaded innocence."

AA frowned. "You weren't supposed to talk to her without a lawyer."

"I only mentioned it," I said. "She told me she didn't do it all on her own, voluntarily. Since I received no incriminating evidence—"

"You're free and clear on having it be inadmissible." AA's scowl deepened. "But that's not the point. What were you going to do if she confessed right there?"

"Kick her ass," I said. "Possibly to death, since she'd just tried to do the same to me."

"I wish you had," Miles said. "Save us all a lot of trouble."

"I know you're not exactly a 'by the book' type," AA said, "but that's really pushing the line."

"Well," I said, waving at my flame unitard, "I think you might be underselling it saying I'm not 'by the book.' Now – I'm going to fly home real quick and get some clothes. Because in my genius, I somehow thought I'd have solved this thing before I needed a fresh blouse. How silly of me to think a simple missing persons case could turn out, y'know...simple."

AA just shook her head. "Hurry back," the sheriff called as I jetted into the air, turning west and heading for Nashville – and home.

CHAPTER THIRTY-SIX

The flight was short, but I decided to cut the boredom by making a quick call en route. The trilling noise of the ring halted as a smooth voice answered, "Didn't expect to hear from you just now."

"Catch you at a bad time?" I asked.

"No. Just about to board a flight from Orlando back to Odessa. So I've got nothing but time for the next, oh, thirty minutes or so. Speaking of West Texas, though–"

"Yes, yes, I know," I said. "I need to come out there and visit Mimaw. Been a little busy. I did call her last week."

I could hear my grandmother's smile over the open line. "That's not nothing, but it's not a visit. Come on – you can fly at supersonic speeds."

"I can, but I'm not allowed to go supersonic over the continental US. Hell, I'm probably going to get that privilege rescinded, too, given who's in charge of the government now." I already missed Richard Gondry, who'd retired to New England to live a more sedate life.

"Probably don't push it, then," Lethe said. "So...to what

do I owe the honor of this call? I hear air rushing behind you, so you must be flying somewhere."

"We have that in common. I'm just heading home from East Tennessee to pick up a change of clothes."

There was a pause. "The ones you were wearing were presumably destroyed in some sort of attack?"

"Yup."

"Figures," Lethe muttered. "You know, your high-violence lifestyle was a lot easier for me to tolerate back when I knew you were going to survive. Because I'd met you in the future, see."

"Yes, I figured that one out all on my own."

"Nowadays, seeing your exploits on the news, or the internet? They scare the hell out of me, Sienna."

"Well, I'm not stopping, so...sorry?" I paused, thinking. "Wait, you're in Orlando?"

"Yeah," she said, sounding even more pained. "I came in to visit Dad and...an old friend."

"You're hanging out with Odin," I crowed. "Catching up with your old...pal? Old boss? How would you define that relationship?"

"I don't know that I'd try in a modern context," Lethe said. "I'm not sure the words exist. Deeper than friends. Less than lovers, obviously, in the past–"

"Yes, I heard he still has his life and soul."

"Listen, whippersnapper, being a succubus was really a lot more difficult before the invention of latex, especially if you wanted to have kids. Sometimes I think you have no appreciation for how good you've got it."

"Not to cut off the 'kids these days' rant before it really gets going," I said, "but how's Hades doing?"

"Good," Lethe said. "You forcing him to give up his schemes and control and just retire may be the best thing anyone's ever done for the old coot. Still–"

"He misses being part of the action."

"Yes. How'd you know?"

"I called him a few weeks ago," I said, my eye catching Cookeville on the right as I shot east. I'd be in the Nashville area very soon, and it was probably time to start slowing down. "Between crime scenes or arrests or something. You could hear it in his voice when he talked about golf and whatnot."

"Hm," Lethe said. "I knew you'd talked to him. Didn't realize you knew him well enough to suss that out."

"I know him well enough," I said. "I only called him because Reed told me he was...different now."

"He is."

"...Trustworthy?"

"I'd be careful on that," Lethe said. "The answer yes – up to a point. Where that point is, though..."

"Right. Don't trust him with anything that matters to him." I nodded to myself in the air. "That's kind of what I figured, too."

"Anyway," Lethe said. "Thank you for letting me know about Odin. It was a good visit."

"Did you hearken back to the times when you mad Vikings pillaged and plundered?"

Lethe sighed. "Okay, see, this is a language issue I have with the modern world. We were not *vikings*. When we went raiding, it was called going *a-viking*."

"And here I thought you were all just Vikings."

"They were Norse, I was Greek. We would go *a-viking*. Get it straight in your head."

"Oh, the places you'd go...a-viking," I singsonged. "So, did you guys make a top ten list of the most awesome places you looted and plundered and slaughtered? Top ten skulls you split?"

There was a deeply discomfortable pause on the other

end of the line. "We mostly stuck to reminiscing about the more pleasant parts of our adventures, sort of eliding over the societally acceptable slaughtering sections for some reason."

"Because it'd make your Blood Orange Martini seem a little too actual-bloody for your taste?"

"Are you needling me for a specific reason?" Lethe asked. She wasn't squirming, exactly, but I could tell she was uncomfortable with this topic of conversation.

I held my breath for a second. "I got told today that I'm not feeling anything anymore."

"…And? Who told you this?"

"Some random girl who tried to kill me," I said. "Thing is…I'm not sure she's wrong."

"You prodded me on the whole slaughter and pillage thing because you were uncomfortable getting to this, didn't you?"

I felt a sting of shame. "Well, yes. But also because you slaughtered and pillaged and maybe you need a reminder every now and again."

"Trust me, I don't need to be reminded. I still wake up with screams in my ears sometimes." She paused, took a ragged breath. "Look, Sienna…it's okay to be emotionally detached, especially after the year you've had."

"And we're squarely in the middle of an election, because by golly I needed to cap this year off with a bang, y'know?"

"You started the year in government service, under the thumb of the Network, and now you're about to wrap it up somewhere new after being kicked out of your home state. Hell, it was barely more than a year ago the whole Revelen thing unfolded and you basically went through a small-scale war."

"Ended my fugitive-hood, came home in a blaze of glory. Yeah, I know the timeline."

"But does it feel real to you?" she asked, and I could hear her moving around. Ahead, Lebanon, TN sprang into sight, an obvious strip of commerce strip right off I-40. I swung southwest in my heading. I'd be home in a minute or less. "That much happening over that short a period?"

"The years of my life have tended to be rather eventful, so...sort of?"

"My point is this – coming out of all that, coming off that burst of enthusiastic alcoholism you experienced–"

"Chose. I chose it. And now I choose differently. Choice is important."

"Right. In any case, coming out of all that...is it really a surprise if you're...numb?"

"Maybe not," I said, feeling that in my bones. "It's just...when she said it, I *felt* it, you know? Cut me right to the quick. I knew she was right the moment she spoke the words. Like...I've been on emotional mute the last few missions. I don't respond as much to easy bait, verbally, don't feel the highs and lows."

"Like you're going through life with a thin latex film over everything?"

I frowned. "You've got latex on your mind for some reason, and I really don't want to know what that reason is."

"I – uh–"

"NO," I said. "No sharing. I'm calling to dump this on you. I do not want to know – anything – at all – ever – about why you're thinking of latex."

Another long pause. "Fine."

"Fine," I said. "And...yes. Life feels muted. Last month when I was chasing after a sexy supervillain my boss was crushing on I felt..." A pained expression came to my face. "...almost nothing. Like I was hollow inside. Empty."

"...Like you needed to be filled up?"

I closed my eyes. "Stop. Just...stop. I should have called Mimaw about this."

"You think she would understand?"

"She was married to Hades, I think she understands numbness. Probably better than either of us."

My grandmother laughed. "Point."

"No, it wasn't like...that," I said, shuddering at all the clues she was handing me. Enough that even Friday at his most swole could have picked them up and assembled the puzzle. "It was more like I felt nothing at all, and I was fine with it. Like I'm walking a rote path to the end of this case and any others they put in front of me, but...emptily. If that makes sense."

"Absolutely it makes sense," Lethe said. "You should talk to your sponsor about it, but I think you'll find that it's pretty normal to feel...numb. Not alive. After giving up drink. That's one of the reasons people are drawn to it. It lets the strait-laced cut loose, gives the emotionally stunted a chance to feel more."

"That's the problem," I said, "and the key reason I was an alcoholic. It took drinking to feel normal. And now I'm without and...I didn't even realize I don't feel 'normal' anymore. I don't feel anything, really, other than punches and kicks and blunt force trauma and burns and the like."

"Give yourself some time," Lethe said soothingly. In the background, a gate agent announced that early boarding would commence in moments.

"I should let you go," I said. My house was ahead, sprawling on its mighty acreage, surrounded by trees. "I gotta get these clothes and head back to the...job site or whatever."

"Take care of yourself, Sienna."

"You know I will."

I hung up and started my landing, breathing deep...

...And still kind of feeling nothing.

CHAPTER THIRTY-SEVEN

I put on clothes and fed the dogs and the kitten, all of whom responded as though they hadn't seen food in years. Emma, in particular, gave me much playful love as I let her out of her little cage to play around for a bit while I threw a couple changes of clothes in a backpack. The smell of the house was familiar and had been missed after a day away, the lingering scent of the genuine hardwood floors triggering a wistful sense in me that...

...This place had somehow become home.

That made me pause. Living with Ariadne had been...homey, I suppose, but I'd been too drunk to appreciate the gift of a place to hang my hat in Minnesota since my own home had been destroyed, my property seized and sold off. Before that I'd spent a trio of months in New York and DC each, respectively, neither of which felt remotely home-like. Before that...

...Well, I'd been on the run for a couple years. Before that, it'd been my house, and the Directorate/Agency, and my house again. That was the sum total of my living experiences.

And of all of them...my house was the only place I'd really felt at home.

Maybe until now.

It still didn't feel quite right; the smell of the dogs helped, and Cali softly licking my face as I knelt down to fill her bowl, Jack sniffing at my haunches as I put down his water dish, and Emma nuzzling against my hand as I made sure she got her pats in after she ate...

...That felt...home-y.

"All right, kiddos," I said, putting Emma back in her little cage as I slipped my backpack over my shoulder. "I gotta go for another day or two. Chandler will be by to feed you."

Cali barked, reminding me that I had to bring Priscilla to mind before speaking, because her bark was just a bark without it. I slipped into the animal mindset and repeated myself.

But who will feed us? Cali asked. Of course.

"Chandler," I said, even though I'd said it twice now, at least once where I knew she could understand me.

What's a Chandler? Jack asked.

He is the one with a mane like a horse, Cali said.

I frowned, thinking that over. "No...that's Reed. My brother."

What is brother? Jack asked. His tail paused its wag.

Same mom, Cali said.

"No," I said. "Same dad."

Oh, Jack said. *I have many brothers, then. All in cages, back on farm—*

"Given the stories I've heard about puppy mills, I'm a little afraid of where that tale goes from there," I said, holding tight to my backpack strap. Emma was up nuzzling against the bars of her cage, and I checked her water level again. It was fine.

A lock clicked across the house, and I heard the door

open, the alarm announcing it. I looked out the laundry room door down the long hall that bisected the home, and there, crossing the foyer, was the man himself. "Hey, Chandler," I called.

Chandler almost jumped out of his skin. He was carrying a brown bag of the sort winos used to hide their prize from public sight as they swigged away. In his case, though, when he freaked out in surprise, a few Blu-Rays launched out of the bag and clattered all over my nice, lovely-scented wood floors. He landed on his feet, fortunately, but shoved a hand right to his heart, staring down the long hallway at me. "You scared the hell out of me!" He stooped and retrieved a couple fallen disc holders. "I thought you were in East Tennessee."

"Someone tried to kill me," I said. "So I needed a change of clothes."

"Because of blood on your clothes?" He picked up the last of his fallen spoils and slowly clomped his way down the hall.

"Fire, this time," I said. "Had to burn them off to save myself." I took a couple minutes and gave him the rundown while he listened patiently and the dogs nipped around his heels, begging him to feed them. He petted their heads idly with one hand while clutching his brown bag of Blu-Rays in the other and listening intently. "So anyway, I said, it's been an interesting couple days."

"This Alannah Greene tried to kill you twice?" Chandler asked.

"Once, for sure," I said. "Not a hundred percent certain about the second time."

"Wow," Chandler said.

"'Wow' what?"

"Well," he said, pausing to scratch his own head, "only you could take a normal, run of the mill missing persons case and turn it into an opportunity for murdering a TBI agent."

"That is flatly false and possibly slanderous," I said.

"Clearly other TBI agents have died in a wide variety of cases over the agency's history."

Chandler cracked a smile. "Yeah, but...usually the opportunity doesn't come up twice during the same case, and with possibly different perpetrators."

"Superpowers are a game-changer," I said, a touch defensively. "And speaking of the missing persons..." My phone was buzzing, a 423 area code. East Tennessee. "Let me take this real quick. Hello?" I answered it.

"Hey, Agent Nealon, it's Sheriff Miles," Miles's cool voice came on the line.

"What's up?" I asked.

"Got some breaking news," Miles said. "And good, for once. They found those missing workers at a bar in Johnson City." He chuckled. "Guess they just needed a drink and had enough of working on that particular job site, so..." I could almost hear the smile in his voice. "...The case is over. You can go on home."

CHAPTER THIRTY-EIGHT

I hung up after the sheriff's bombshell, a frown tugging my mouth down, an inexorable pull upon my brow lining it as I mulled over what I'd just heard.

"Oh, no," Chandler asked, peering at my dark countenance. "Did someone die? Are there bodies on the ground now?"

"Quite the opposite, actually," I said, still clutching my phone. "They found the missing workers. In a bar."

"Okay." That caused Chandler to frown, too. "But what do you mean the case is over?"

"They found the guys, so the case is over," I said, shrugging as I pocketed my phone. I wasn't sure how to feel about this. Good, right? I was supposed to feel good that no one was dead. "Closed. Case closed. All's well that ends well."

"But – but–" Chandler sputtered, his own brow as furrowed as mine. "Someone tried to kill you! Maybe two someones!"

"People are always trying to kill me," I said, shrugging. "Guess I should go get my car and drive it back here."

"No – hold," Chandler said, thrusting a hand up. "Maybe

living in the meta world has skewed your perspective. Killing people is not a normal response to average stimuli, ordinary events, okay? Now maybe this crazed girl in the woods–"

"A different kind of box."

"–tried to kill you because of a family feud. Okay. That's not out of whack for East Tennessee," Chandler said. "I was raised there. I get it, there's a whole body of academic research explaining the culture of honor and all that. But–" And he held up a lone finger. "You seemed to indicate that your conversation by the creek with her didn't degenerate into murder attempts again. Why, it was positively civil."

"Close. Probably by her standards, it was civil."

"I don't think she tried to kill you the second time," Chandler said. "And that means you've got a second person out there willing to stalk you back to your hotel and engage in murder over a case that's apparently reached its conclusion. Why?" His eyes were wild. "Who is willing to commit premeditated murder, a capital crime in Tennessee, for which we happily and eagerly apply the death penalty, over three guys who went AWOL from a construction site in order to go drinking in Knoxville or somewhere like?"

"Wasn't Knoxville," I said. "It was Johnson City."

Chandler's whole demeanor changed. "That's so much worse. They must really hate themselves to go drinking there."

I chuckled. "I take your point. You're saying that there's something deeper here."

Chandler nodded. "You don't kill people all willy-nilly." Then he froze. "Well, maybe *you* do. But the ordinary person does not."

"Which means," I said, nodding along with him, "there's something else going on over there. Something someone doesn't want me to dig into."

"I think so, yeah," Chandler said. "Otherwise why send someone to your hotel to kill you?"

"But who is it?" I asked. "If not Alannah Greene?"

"See, that one's on you to detangle," Chandler said. "I'd like to help, but I'm assigned to a full caseload here. But my guess is that either Momma Greene is really mad, or the other interested party in this case has got things going on he doesn't want you to know about."

"Wil Waters," I murmured. "It wasn't *him* in the hotel room. So if he's behind it—"

"He hired someone to kill you, yes," Chandler said. "And picked someone who looked somewhat convincingly like Alannah Greene to do it?"

"She passed, figure-wise," I said. "In the dark, in the heat of the fight, with the mask on, yeah. But she was a Hercules, so if Alannah is not a Hercules—"

"Alannah's not your killer," Chandler said, stroking his chin. "Unless—"

"She's a multi-power meta?" I drew the conclusion myself, then rubbed my skull. "Those are rare. Or at least the serum is. Doubt she came across it hiding out in the woods of East Tennessee."

"Don't discount it. I was raised there; you'd be amazed at the drugs you get offered in the woods of East Tennessee."

"That serum's not meth," I said, "and the girl's not been raised with lots of human contact. Plus, she's a natural born meta." I shook my head. "No, I'm 90/10 on that. It's not impossible, but it is unlikely. I think if she's not a Herc, she's probably not the one who tried to kill me the second time. Which puts the lens of suspicion squarely on—"

"The rich guy," Chandler sighed. "The big schemes always have a rich guy behind them, don't they? But what dirty deeds do you think he's getting up to out there in the woods?"

"Don't know," I said, decision made, and I started to head

for the back door. The dogs orbited around me as Chandler followed. "But I know this – there's always a paper trail, if someone's willing to look hard enough for it."

Chandler's face fell. "By someone, you mean 'me,' don't you?"

"You said you wanted to help," I said, giving him my best impish smile, "but you didn't want to drive to East Tennessee–"

"No, I said I have a full caseload here. That's not the same as–"

"Yes," I said with great patronization. "You have such a full caseload that you've come to my house at noon in order to feed my dogs and watch a Blu-Ray in my theater room."

Chandler made a whimpering noise. "It's *Seven*. David Fincher's masterpiece."

"So watch it tonight."

"I have a date with Shakti tonight."

"Duty calls, Chandler," I said, cracking open the door. "Work from your laptop and hang out here by the pool if you want." A blast of chilly air hit me in the face as I stepped onto the porch, much more of a November feel than I'd tasted thus far this year. "Brrrr. Or not."

He blanched at the rush of cold air. "Feels like it's dropped ten degrees since I got here."

"Maybe start up the fireplace," I said, waving vaguely at the one on the far end of the porch, under the TV. "You know, if you're going to work out here by the pool."

"Think I might work by the one inside, thanks," Chandler said. "But where are you going? First, I mean. I know you've got ideas or you wouldn't be striding all purposefully out of here, ready to take off into the heavens."

"Gonna get my car first," I said. "Then I'm going to Johnson City."

"That sounds so dirty, but you have my condolences for

having to go there." Chandler said. "And to a bar, no less." He frowned. "Hey, isn't that bad for an alcoholic?"

"I'll bring a friend to keep me steady in the face of temptation," I said and slipped out the porch door. Then I cut ties with gravity, rising a couple feet in the air. "Find me the paper trail, Chandler."

"Yeah, yeah." He waved me off. "I get to explore one of the deadly sins in less interesting and more sterile detail. Enjoy your trip to the bar."

"Enjoy your date," I said, and took off into the graying skies, heading east.

Because I had questions that needed answers. And maybe a little itch called closure that desperately needed scratching.

CHAPTER THIRTY-NINE

I landed by the motel and found half the officers that had been on scene when I left had already cleared out. The place wasn't buzzing anymore; forensics was finishing up, ordinary-looking people shedding their plastic suits and locking away samples and tools, laughing and talking like normal humans now that their job was done.

Also, I found AA standing by herself at the edge of the scene, deep in contemplation, the sheriff and any other company for her long gone.

"Hey," I said from about twenty feet up.

She jumped, throwing all the coffee out of the little white Styrofoam cup in her hand. The light brown liquid peppered the ground in a long stream, saturating it with enough cream and sugar to fatten the ants at the edge of this broken parking lot for quite some time. Her hand found her chest and her eyes found me hanging above her, and when she had settled down – no curses spat out, to my surprise – she said, "You're back."

I floated down beside her, not bothering to hide my chuckles at her hyper-reaction. "I'd say I'm sorry about your coffee, but based on what you just did, you've clearly had enough for today."

"It was only my second cup," she said, almost mournfully. "You here for your car?" She jerked her head toward the Explorer at the far edge of the parking lot.

"Yes and no," I said, settling down next to her on the cracked pavement. "I do need it. But I'm thinking I'm not quite done here, yet."

AA cocked her head, her wide braided ponytail hanging off-angle behind her narrow shoulders. "Okay. Why?"

"A friend pointed out to me that I've had two murder attempts on me since I arrived," I said, "and you don't typically pull out the murder card unless you've got a solid reason to play it. Now, I think we all understand what was going on with Alannah Greene—"

"Sure. Personal vendetta."

"—But if she wasn't responsible for the second attempt—"

AA's eyes lit up. "Something else is going on here."

"Got it in one," I said. "I'm going to take this opportunity before I leave town to dig a little. See what I might be missing."

She nodded slowly. "Makes sense. And personally, I hate to leave a thing unfinished or a question unanswered, so...what did you have in mind?"

Now that she was on board with my scheme, I couldn't help but smile a little. "Would you mind accompanying me to a bar?"

CHAPTER FORTY

The bar was called Antonio's and it was right on the outskirts of Johnson City. It took us about an hour to get there, a relatively quiet hour in which AA seemed to mostly stare off into space as we drove over the high hills (almost mountains) of the Smokies. The air had turned colder and the sky grayed with every hour that passed, and somehow temps were now already in the fifties when they'd been in the eighties just this morning.

"This your kind of place when you were drinking?" AA asked as we pulled into the dirt parking lot. No cop cars present; I guess they'd done their questioning of our missing persons and moved on. Hell, maybe our guys had moved on, too; I doubted it, though. AA had heard through the sheriff that our men in question were on a bender and barely willing to stop to answer anything when they'd been found.

"Any place with alcohol was my kind of place when I was drinking," I said, steeling myself to go in. The air had a cold, biting quality to it that suggested lower temps than the thermometer in my car did. A wind was blowing in off the hills, and it made me want to take some of the sting out of it with fire.

Or you could just think about me, Brianna said, so I did, and suddenly it didn't feel so cold anymore.

"I hate to go all *Game of Thrones*, given how badly it ended," AA said, shivering as we walked toward the bar's door, "but winter is definitely coming."

"Oh, you mean how the show came in like a lion and went out like a lamb being slaughtered by a toothless, knifeless, fingerless, angry hobo who was determined to get the job done no matter how much screaming and crying it took?" I asked.

"Yeah, and that's not even to mention how much screaming and crying the lamb did," AA deadpanned as we walked into Antonio's.

Antonio's seemed like it should have been a roadside bar without much flair.

Well...it was half that, because there was so. Much. Flair.

Road signs, real and fake, were covering every square inch of the walls. Stop signs rested off-axis next to a bizarre sign that warned of packages that were choking hazards next to ones that suggested the bearer supported single women (with a picture of an outline of a pole dancer on it). From the sedate to the bawdy, this place had wall decor to cover it all.

Also...it had karaoke.

A big redneck wearing jeans that wouldn't have been out of place on Andre the Giant was singing Darius Rucker's "Wagon Wheel" with quite a bit of gusto and pretty on-key, though without Rucker's trademark smoothness. The guy was wearing a baseball hat proclaiming that he'd been to Enchanted Rock, wherever that was – Texas somewhere, I thought – and a T-shirt with a band on it that was so faded I couldn't read it even with my metahuman eyesight.

He brought the Rucker song to a decent close and

launched right into a surprisingly decent rendition of Sarah McLachlan's "Angel".

AA, beside me, was frowning. "Okay. Based on the wall decor, I gotta believe everything after this is going to be downhill."

"Maybe so," I said, casting around for our boys. I found three guys in the corner who looked fairly blotto, and whose attention I'd caught the second I walked in. "Maybe not. Could be there's a surprise or two waiting for you yet in this place."

"I don't like surprises," AA said miserably. "Do you like surprises?"

"Only the pleasant kind," I said, shouldering my way through. We passed the bar, where stood an overweight man with an open two-liter bottle of Coke sitting in front of him. Nothing else.

"Welcome to diabeetustown, bro," I heard AA mutter under her breath as she went past. "Population: you."

I made it through a last throng of customers and to the corner table, where the three guys were looking up at me as a group. One stood, pulling out the last chair as I walked up, and offered it to me. I nodded in appreciation through the noise, and he hurried to grab another chair for AA, stumbling drunkenly to the next table and asking if they were using their spare chair.

The least drunk of the three guys piped up then: "Didn't know you were gonna be coming out here to talk to us," he said. He was tall, his legs comically stretched things barely covered over by the table, knees bumping the bottom of it. "You want anything?" He motioned to one of the waitresses, but she didn't notice him.

"No," I lied, smacking my lips as I caught the scent of the Jack and Coke in front of him. "Just wanted to ask you guys a couple questions. You're Andrew, right?"

Tall drink of Jack and Coke shook his head. "David Waverly." He pointed across the table at a shorter guy with rampant facial scruff and wild tufts of hair sticking out of his own trucker hat. "That's Andrew."

"And I'm Tyrese," the last guy said, sliding a seat up for AA, who took it, nodding her thanks. "You know, we already talked to the cops."

"I did hear that," I said, leaning forward now that they were all at the table. "I didn't hear what you told them, though – and I wanted to hear it for myself."

Sir David the Excessively Long-limbed looked furtively at the other two. "Look...we just didn't want to be on that job site anymore, that's all." He slurred his words as he talked, and he reeked of cheap, delicious liquor.

"That place was a prison, man," Tyrese said, almost giggling.

"On planet bullshit!" Andrew added, and they all three cracked up. "It's from *Stepbrothers*," he added.

"So you decided to bail and have your own Catalina effing Jack and Coke mixer," I said, nodding at David's drink. "I get that. I can almost respect it, even, given some of the workdays I've had." I leaned in a little more. "But we all know that's not the whole story."

Sarah McLachlan's big, redneck impersonator hit a bad note, and everyone in the bar cringed. It was decent cover for the bomb I'd just dropped on the three of them.

But not good enough. Or maybe their acting just wasn't. "The job sucked," David said, shrugging his wide shoulders. He was heavily tanned. "What else is there to say?"

"How about you just tell me the real reason you left," I said. "Then you can get back to drinking and I can get the hell out of here and leave you to whatever song that big guy sings next. My money's on Barbra Streisand's "Memory", in case we're putting money down on these things."

"God, please, let him go to the welcoming arms of Johnny Cash instead," Tyrese said.

"What makes you think there's anything more to this than what we already told you?" David asked.

"How long have you guys worked for Larry Benson's crew?" I asked, settling back in my chair and crossing one leg over the other.

Another uneasy glance exchanged between the three. "Four years," David admitted.

"Three," Tyrese said.

"Five," Briggs said.

"Okay," I said. "So you're all telling me you're walking off a job – not first day, not first week, but years later – and you're not even telling the boss? What?" I folded my arms in front of me. "Is the pay shit?"

"No." David focused all his attention on his drink. "The pay was good."

"Better than I ever made anywhere else," Tyrese said, looking at his own drink. There was a pained air about them.

"So you quit on the best paying jobs the three of you ever had," I said. "Did you have another lined up? Because I know you're not getting unemployment if you walked off. So...what? Was it a scam to try and make people think you'd been kidnapped?"

"We didn't tell anyone we were kidnapped," Briggs said angrily, leaning forward into the conversation. "We just left. They did that shit on their own."

"I believe you," I said. "But I also believe there's something you're not telling...well, anybody else." I leaned in again, dispensing with the cocky, knowing facade. "Something you think they won't believe. Something that spooked you so bad that you threw away the best jobs you three ever had. Now...you know me." I put a hand on my chest. "You know I've seen some things in my time, things no one would believe. So tell me, no shame, no judgment...what did you see that made you three run away and not tell a soul you were leaving?"

"Damn," David whispered, pulling off his hat to reveal mussed hair that hadn't been washed in days and smelled...well, about as you'd expect after a bender. "Yeah." He looked up at me, nowhere near clear-eyed, but seeing some truth nonetheless. "Okay." He nodded once, and took a drink, as if steeling himself. "I'll tell you what we saw."

CHAPTER FORTY-ONE

David Waverly

"Come on, we need to stake this over here," David said, measuring tape rolling out. "This tree, this tree, this–"

The screech of the measuring tape came to a halt as David paused. An explosive clap of bird wings bursting into motion some thirty yards away caught his attention. They shot through the dense canopy overhead, swaying the branches and sending a half dozen still-green leaves plummeting into the darkness.

Earthen smells filled the air, along with the faint reek of Andrew's Skoal can. With a spit, he sent a wash of snuff to the forest floor, and the minty scent joined with the dirt aroma.

"You hear that?" Tyrese was holding the other end of the measuring tape. It swayed slightly as he moved his hand, cupping it to his ear.

"I hear the damned dozer going in the distance," David

said quickly, pulling out a round of orange marking tape and tying it off around a massive old oak. The bark was course and rough and thick, the trunk and branches all bearing the character of a very old tree, something that almost looked alive enough to reach out and tap him on the head.

But David paused, listening.

"Do you?" Andrew asked, his voice higher than usual. "Because all the sudden...I don't."

"Shut up," David said, half-dismissively...and half-alarmed, because...no, he didn't hear them anymore.

There was no wind, just a feeling of close, warm air, not circulating or moving in this part of the forest. They'd only gone a couple hundred yards in, marking the path of the road for the trees to be harvested. It was shit work, they'd all rather be on pavement detail, surprisingly, but here they were in this cramped and weirdly claustrophobic wood.

"Ah...guys?" Tyrese asked, turning in a half-circle. "Is it my imagination or did the gap between the trees like...disappear?"

David did a quick glance around. They'd been walking in well-spaced woods, the tall trees around them providing a thick bed of old, rotting leaves that crinkled wherever they stepped, a rich and full sound.

But those spaces, almost lanes, between the old trees seemed to have...filled in. Branches hung low where before they'd stood tall and straight, heaven-reaching trees seemed to be stooped and twisted, the trunks gnarled and compact, barring their progress forward...

...Or back.

"Did we wander into a haunted swamp?" Andrew asked, looking around. "Because this looks like a haunted swamp. And it *feels* like a haunted swamp. And—"

"Shut up," David said without feeling. How did the woods change in a minute? The sky above had darkened, sure as shit, like the leaves had moved to squelch the light coming in. "Probably just clouds rolling over, that's all."

"And the paths?" Tyrese asked, gesturing around. "Cuz we walked in here, you know? But I don't see how we're walking out."

"Oh, we're walking out," David said, and moved toward the direction he was sure they'd come from. A stray branch, hanging low over the ground and burdened with more leaves than it rightly ought to have had, seemed to move to block his path. "Out of my way, you—"

A branch cracked him across the jaw.

Hard.

David took a staggering step back, dropping the tape, letting go of the measuring reel. His ass made solid contact with the ground, and the crunch of leaves was muffled by the shock of pain that ran through him from the tailbone on up.

"What the hell?" Andrew asked, there in a second. "That branch just shove you?"

"Punched me, more like," David said, taste of blood tingeing his tongue.

Get out.

A whisper, carried on the wind, rattling the branches and showering them with stray leaves, pushed through the forest.

"Uhm...whazzat?" Tyrese asked, now standing just over David's shoulder.

Get out.

The voice again, more insistent.

"Hey," Andrew said, "you guys know what I'm thinking? Antonio's. You know, the bar in Johnson City. Now, hear me out—"

"Oh, I am in," Tyrese said without hesitation.

"Yep," David said, letting Andrew help him to his feet.

As if the Red Sea were translated to branches and leaves, a path opened just for them. Branches moved aside, leaving nothing but drifting leaves in their wake, and a clear, leaf-lined road over the nearest hill, back where they'd come.

"First round's on me," David said, and he took off at a dead run, leaving the equipment behind them. For once he was glad of his long legs, because they carried him back to his truck before Andrew or Tyrese had barely made it out of the treeline.

CHAPTER FORTY-TWO

Sienna

David settled his long-limbed self back in his seat, looking at me with world-weary eyes over a domestic beer that had been dropped off for him by one of the waitresses during his story. He downed it quickly, then moved back to his Jack and Coke. "You believe me?" he asked, though by his haunted eyes it would have taken a harder heart than mine to tell him no.

"Of course I believe you," I said, settling back in my own seat. "Kinda kicking myself for not having put two and two together myself before now."

AA just stared at me blankly. "Two and two? What?"

"Their last name is 'Greene,'" I said "So of course they're Persephone types." That got a round of blank stares from everyone, and I remembered that oh, right, I was the only one who dealt in Greek myth for a living. And because it was my family history. "Persephone. Vegetation goddess.

Daughter of Zeus and Demeter, wife to Hades. Also: my great-grandmother."

"Ohhhhh," Andrew said, like he just got it.

"I think I heard that on the news once," Tyrese said.

"So either Brenda or Alannah decided to scare the shit out of them with their powers?" AA asked. "That's your working thesis?"

"Well, as a thesis," David said, raising his glass, "it worked. Cuz I wouldn't go back to that job site."

"Hell to the no," Andrew said.

"Yeah, I guess whichever one of them decided to scare these guys," I said, "went easier on them than they did on me."

AA thought about it a minute. "Okay. So Brenda or Alannah or both are a Persephone. Does that mean–?"

"Gentlemen, I appreciate your help," I said. "Thanks for your time and your candor." I gave each of them a nod, then headed for the door.

"You're welcome," David called to me. Halfhearted agreement came from the other two as well, but I barely noticed it as I burst out of the sweet, whiskey smelling bar just as the big redneck guy announced, "For my next song, I'm doing "Memory" by Barbra Streisand–"

"Ew," AA said as the door closed behind us. "How the hell did you call that one?"

"I might have been thinking about it in the back of my head while occasionally remembering my psychic-powered meta," I said, unsure if I'd actually had anything to do with that particular atrocity or not.

David burst forth from the bar, a disgusted look on his face as strains of the big fella's voice rang out in the parking lot. "That was dirty, Nealon. Real dirty."

"Sorry, sorry," I said. "But you guys needed to go home anyway."

David shook his head at me. "Just mean-spirited." And he walked away.

"Wait, where are Andrew and Tyrese?" AA called after him.

"Still drinking," he called back. "I guess they like Streisand." Then he disappeared around the corner of the bar; sounds of vomiting followed moments later, either from his drinking too much or the song choice. Hard to say which.

"If Brenda's a Persephone," AA said, in her own thoughts but spitting them out loud, "that doesn't rule out Alannah being a Hercules, right?"

"No," I said. "It'd probably come from her father's side, though. Or it could be a dormant power unlocked by that other serum." I shrugged. "Still...it makes it less likely."

AA nodded. "Okay. So...what do we do now?"

"Couple things," I said, and tossed her my keys. "One, you drive back to Fountain Run. Call in while you do it, see if you can get preliminary forensics on the hotel room attack. My attacker had to have an entry point to my room. Maybe it was the front door, maybe it wasn't. If it wasn't, perhaps she left footprints, bootprints, something we can use to track her."

"Got it," AA nodded. "What are you going to be doing?"

I lifted off, turning southwest, and shouted as I prepared to shoot off at high speed. "I'm going to go find Brenda Greene," I said, turning into the wind. "And we're going to have ourselves a little talk."

CHAPTER FORTY-THREE

Following my GPS over the woods and wilds and small towns of East Tennessee was surprisingly idyllic. The temperature continued to drop as I flew, and by the time I was descending into Fountain Run – name of the city and county, I realized belatedly – my GPS informed me it was forty-five degrees.

It appeared to me like the whole character of the Greene's woods had changed in the last day, maybe even the last hours. Red and brown leaves were starting to appear, mingled with shocks of gold and bright red. Autumn had begun, but crowds of eager city folk and newly-transplanted Californians had not made their way here for the requisite leaf-peeping – yet.

The Greene's valley appeared before I knew it, a wide swath of colored trees that sprawled between two low ridges, the gravel parking lot at the edge a dead giveaway telling me I'd arrived. I started high, circling as I looked for a disturbance in the boughs. Then I came in lower, conscious that maybe Alannah was lurking below the surface like a damned tree shark, ready for round two or possibly three.

Eventually a breeze washed over the canopy and I saw something white through the new reds and golds, and moved closer, lower. Branches parted and revealed a corrugated metal rooftop beneath a tall maple, scattered leaves peppering its top.

When I was fifty feet above the canopy, I took a hard, gulping breath. Bringing myself down slowly was a formula for ambush.

So I rocketed through the canopy and brought myself to an abrupt stop inches above the ground, the blur of the environs coming to a rocking stop as all the blood rushed to my brain.

A trailer house waited there, nestled between the trees. An old single wide with plenty of rust marking its sides, it was nonetheless situated in a great location, just atop a rise that led down to the creek. A clothesline waited, stretched between two tree trunks, and between the two posts Brenda Greene stood with an old, worn plastic laundry basket, staring at me with one eyebrow slightly higher than the other. "Just invite yourself right down, why don'tcha?" she asked with perfect acidity.

"Don't mind if I do," I said, settling on the ground, leaves crunching beneath my boots. "Sorry to interrupt your laundry."

"We call it warshin' round here," she said, really letting the East Tennessee accent unnaturally blend with her more Midwestern drawl. Tossing the basket down, she folded her arms across her broad chest. "What do you want? To talk to my daughter? Because that's a no; our lawyer said–"

"I don't want to talk to your daughter, no," I said. "I want to talk to you." I paused for dramatic effect. "They found those three missing workers."

Not a flicker of surprise creased her forehead; she maintained her suspicious look. "Oh? Good, I guess. Solves your problem, so maybe you can leave us alone now."

"See I would," I said, "except your daughter tried to kill me."

"She was just up to some good-natured fun," Brenda said. "Kids will be kids and all that."

"Yeah," I said, "there's a difference between spray-painting the school gym and snapping the neck of a TBI agent under your boot. Subtle, but it's there. Anyway, that's not what I'm here to talk about, either, really." I paused, trying to prep myself for what needed to come next. "So...you're a Persephone."

Brenda unfolded her arms, shifted her stance. "Who told you that?"

"The guys," I said. "The workers, you know? With the story they told."

"I didn't meet these guys you're talking about," Brenda said. "I was off in–" She paused, the realization cutting into her real quick. She exhaled under breath and said, meta-low, "I'ma kill that girl."

"So Alannah is a Persephone, too?" I asked, and saw the pained flash of expression on Brenda's face.

"I got nothing to say to that," Brenda said, once she got control of her face.

"That's a shame," I said. "Because a Hercules tried to choke the life out of me this afternoon in my motel room. And if Alannah's a Persephone, that kind of eliminates her from suspicion for the crime, see?"

Brenda's pained look tightened. "Anything happen to these worker fellows?"

"Nothing criminal," I said. "They just got scared by trees and voices, that's all. They were thinking 'ghosts' and felt the need to go off and drink."

"Yeah, my daughter is a Persephone," Brenda said, sullen,

looking away. "And before you ask, her daddy's a human, not a Hercules, so no, she didn't sneak any additional powers in on the sly."

"So she hasn't had the drug?" I asked, really watching Brenda's reaction.

Her slightly moon-face froze for a second, then a slow smile spread across it. "Well...not *that* kind."

"Nice," I said, looking away abruptly.

"We live in the woods. Plants grow – I'm just saying." She got all serious again. "Besides...do you really care about that?"

"Probably not," I said. "I'm a little more concerned about your daughter curb-stomping me. Minus the curb."

"She had her reason," Brenda said. "Your momma done my family a real wrong. My girl grew up on the stories of that. It's a surprise to you that she's mad when you show up out of the blue?"

"Getting launched at by a homicidal lunatic from out of the trees was a surprise to me," I said. "Almost getting my neck broken by her was a bit of a shocker, too."

"She's young, she's stupid," Brenda said, digging deep. "And now that you know that you got brought here by a thing we didn't even really do – nothing serious, anyway – you could just pull up stakes and leave, you know? Drop those charges." She let her palms drift upward at her sides. "Some might even say after what your momma did...you owe us one."

I snorted. "Do you actually expect me to feel guilt over something my mother did before I was even born? Because you can miss me with that shit. I don't even feel an ounce of it. Not a smidgen, not a scintilla."

Brenda reddened. "She stole my land."

"And if I were living on it, or had the proceeds in my personal bank account, you might have cause to be pissed," I said. "But I don't." I paused, looking up. "Oh, I wish I did. I could use some more dollars in that bank account. The three pennies in there are lonely. They don't get along, see. Irreconcilable differences, I guess—"

"Fine," Brenda said, crossing her arms in front of her wide body. "I get it. You don't care what your momma did."

"More like 'I am not *responsible*,'" I said. "Any more than you're responsible for any of the shit your parents get up to. See how this works? You can be responsible for the trouble your minor daughter gets up to, until she's of age, but not what your parents did in the distant past." I leaned in, covered my mouth as if whispering a secret. "Because you are not in charge of your parents. Besides – if my mom came after you, I'm sure she had a reason."

"Yeah, it's because she hated me," Brenda said, her eyes lit up and blazing. "And she always had."

"You were helping shelter a bank robber," I said, shaking my head. "It's not surprising she'd come after you—"

"You think your mom cared that my boyfriend robbed a bank?" Brenda let out a humorless cackle. "That was just the axe she wanted to grind. Nah, her problems with me stretched back decades."

"She knew you decades before she arrested you?" I shook my head. "That's before she was even in law enforcement. How would she have known you?"

"Because, my dear girl, me and her...and you and me, really..." Brenda's eyes showed the glint of self-satisfaction as she cracked a small smile. "...we're family."

CHAPTER FORTY-FOUR

"I'm gonna go ahead and say I'm basically an orphan at this point," I said, staring Brenda Greene right in the eye. "Just to head you off before you switch from the 'Your mom did me wrong and you owe me!' collective guilt track to the 'We're family and you owe me!' one."

We stood in the shelter of the trees outside the Greene family trailer, fresh laundry hanging on the line and the basket at Brenda Greene's feet. She was a husky woman, face like a bulldog, and her growling visage was turned my way, though a hint of triumph lit her eyes and the lines of her face. "Got no blood loyalty in you since your mom died?"

"Probably it died before her," I said. "You mentioned my aunt Charlie earlier?"

Brenda's face fell. "Crazy Charlie. Yeah...figures she'd screw us all over one last time before she went out."

"You make it sound like you really knew her," I said.

"I did know her," Brenda said. "Knew her as a kid when your grandmama would bring her to the family reunions. Oh, we only did 'em once every ten years or so, so I met her probably twice before she got out on her own, but she was hell in a handbasket back then. Came to this one reunion we had in this park in central Virginia. She was probably...sixteen? Seventeen at the time?" Her expression got hard, the lines of her face disappearing. "She half-absorbed one of our cousins from California, the Acheron branch of the family. Don't think we invited the Lethe crew again. Succubus/incubus prejudice finally sunk in."

I kept my face carefully neutral, trying to avoid digging into all the meat on the bone she'd just tossed in front of me. "Did you know Lethe?"

"I mean, I met her," Brenda said. "She was my aunt. Mom's sister, you know? Always real standoffish, though. Like her shit didn't stink." She paused, thinking about it. "You know, I never realized it at the time, but later, when I saw *Ghostbusters* for the first time, I thought–"

"She looked like Sigourney Weaver?" I kept my arms folded in front of me like a shield. "Yeah. I've heard that one before."

Brenda shrugged. "Only time I ever saw her was at the reunions."

I tried to keep my face from twitching. Neither my mother nor my grandmother had mentioned that they'd attended family reunions. Ever. "When was the last time you saw any of my family at a reunion?"

Brenda's face got screwed up as she contemplated this question deeply. "Right after the war, so...1955? Somewhere in there."

I made a mental note later to ask Lethe exactly when my mother had been born. Because I realized, maybe for the first time that the truth I'd always gone with, the one on her fake driver's license in Minnesota that said she was born in 1968, was possibly a *huge* lie. Given how slowly succubi aged, my mom could have been a hundred by the time she had me. Technically, she could have been *several* hundred years old, actually, though that seemed less probable. "What was your mom's name?"

"Styx," Brenda said. "Not the least known of Persephone and Hades's daughters, but maybe the least understood." She shook her head slowly. "Much as our family tree has thinned, hard to believe we're that closely related to ancient myth." She chuckled. "I met Persephone back then, you know? She used to come to reunions. Before she died during the war, you know – the Sovereign war."

"Yeah, she's not dead," I said, keeping my voice carefully neutral. Brenda frowned. "She lives in West Texas, though, so...close, I guess."

"What are you talking about?" Brenda's brow was thickly furrowed.

"She's alive and well," I said. "Mimaw, I mean. Just went into hiding. Anyway, about this Acheron branch of the family–"

"She *died*," Brenda said, staring at me in deep concentration. "Everyone said she died in the war, that Sovereign and his chumps got her outside Cleveland–"

"Well, I guess they're damned liars or just misinformed, then," I said. "Because I saw her a few months ago and she was fine. Also, I keep getting told to get my ass down to Texas for a visit, so..." I shrugged, then hoped I wasn't actively causing a family incident by allowing this information out. Would Persephone coldly deny her kin the knowledge of her survival?

Looking at Brenda and thinking of her rage-filled spawn...I could see an argument for letting them think she was dead.

"Huh. Well that's interesting." Brenda's face relaxed as she seemed to take my word for it. "You met Hades, too, didn't you?"

"Yeah," I said, debating whether to say it. "I did."

"What that must have been like," Brenda mused. "I never even knew he was alive until that Revelen business. Came as a real surprise. Never showed up to any of the reunions, obviously, because...well, the dead thing. Now I guess he is for real, though."

"No, he's in Central Florida," I said. "At the Villages. Playing golf, nailing old ladies." I frowned. "Kinda wish he was dead every time I have to speak that thought out loud to explain to people what he does with his days. Let's bring this around, though, because I could talk family history all day."

"All right, let's do that," Brenda said, and I could see the deadly serious tinge in her eyes. "Because maybe now you understand me, as blood alone can. I raised my daughter in this valley and I'll be damned if I let some penny-ante government shitbag take my home from me a second time." She looked me right in the eye. "You tell 'em that. That prissy tech boy. Anyone from the government that needs to hear it." She picked up her laundry basket and started to walk away. "You tell them they ain't getting me off this spread. Not unless they want to kill me to do it, in which case..." And she spoke so coldly I knew she was telling the truth, "...I won't be going alone."

CHAPTER FORTY-FIVE

My questions answered, I considered the conversation with Brenda over. After mumbling some sort of pleasantries, I jetted into the sky and left her behind, my head spinning and my fingers already dialing a contact in my cell phone.

"Ah, if it isn't my favorite great-granddaughter," Hades answered in his typically boisterous tone, the sound of fresh air behind him. "It's Sienna," he stage-whispered to whoever was with him. Someone answered back with a voice that reminded me of a thunderclap.

"Is that Odin?" I asked.

"Yes, we are playing golf," Hades said.

"I have a question for him, then, before I get into the reason I called," I said.

A mumbled answer behind him prompted Hades to say, "He is listening."

"Ask him how depth perception works with one eye. I'm genuinely curious."

"I have to turn my head very slightly, very quickly, changing the position of my eye so that it produces a similar result to having two eyes," Odin said, his voice strong and clear at last. I guess that wasn't the question he was anticipating from me.

"Cool," I said, rushing through the air toward Fountain Run. I overflew the construction equipment, already working again to clear Wil Waters's path through the Greenes' land. "Now, the reason I called: Styx."

Hades was quiet for a moment. "My daughter, Styx? Or the band? Because if you are asking my opinion of the latter, "Lady" is an enjoyable song."

"I'm dealing with a lady named Brenda Greene in East Tennessee," I said, "who tells me she's Styx's daughter. That she grew up with family reunions that included Persephone, Lethe...and my mom."

"O...kay," Hades said, his voice jarringly discomfited. "I was not involved with the family at that point in time, I imagine, having had no contact with them since...oh, 400's BC? So I am not sure what you would have me tell you about this 'Brenda' or any familial activities during that time."

"I suspect you know something of family reunions held during that time," I said, "and your lineage. Revelen's intelligence agency budget wasn't zero, after all. But that's not the primary thing I'm calling to ask." My voice softened. "What I want to know is...is Persephone a liar, to your knowledge?"

"Uhhhhh," Hades sounded almost pained. "She is as capable of lying as any of us, but...if you are asking my opinion as her very, very ex-husband...lying is not a go-to move for her. Why?"

"This is painful to listen to," Odin muttered in the background. "I'm going to go do something more fun, like aim for that sand trap."

"Use a three wood," Hades said without missing a beat.

"Because Persephone hasn't shared any family history with me," I said. "I had no idea this Brenda Greene was out here. And she's never mentioned the other branches of the family, either – Acheron, Styx – hell, I don't even know them all."

"Acheron, Styx, Lethe, Cocytus, and Phlegethon," Hades said. "But that's just the daughters. My little river goddesses."

"See, you clearly know the family history–"

"Yes, I know all my children. Because I am not Zeus."

"–But none of you seem keen to share it. Why is that?"

Hades chuckled lightly. "You know the history of our family in relation to metahumans as a whole. Does the question not answer itself?"

I paused, thinking. "Who was Janus married to?"

"Cocytus," Hades said. "And an instructive lesson, in fact, for Cocytus was killed herself by a group of angry metas in a manner not dissimilar to her daughter. Of course, I was 'dead' by then and could not go mad with fatherly rage across all of Greece...however much I might have wanted to." His voice sounded tight. "Why are you dredging all this up for me? Why not ask Persephone?"

"Because I'm trying to gauge whether I can trust her answers," I said. "This is your opportunity to shine, grandpapa."

"I will not trash your 'Mimaw,'" Hades said, a bit archly. "Other than perhaps for choosing that sobriquet. She is not a bad woman. A fearsome one, yes, but I think she would tell you the truth if you asked her about these family matters, and about this Brenda Greene. She was more connected to our offspring, being...well...alive to them. I expect I can be of little assistance to you in this, other than to answer your question about Persephone."

The sheriff's office was ahead, and I could see my Explorer parked in the lot outside. "Well...thank you for that," I said, beginning my descent. I hadn't been flying very fast, just milking the time for this conversation. "I appreciate your honesty."

"If you want to talk about something more interesting and less personally painful than the fact I'm cut off from most of the people I would consider family, I would relish the opportunity to speak further," Hades said, and there was a note of hope in his voice that made me squeamish.

"I'm working a case right now and trying to get to the bottom of this Brenda's story, but I'll reach out again soon," I said. "I promise."

"Then I will eagerly await your call," Hades said, about twenty percent brighter. There was, however, still a note of disappointment in his voice that I tried to ignore as I hung up and began dialing Persephone's number.

CHAPTER FORTY-SIX

Before I could hit the CALL button, the door to the sheriff's station opened and AA stepped out, waving me down. She even shouted, "Hey!" As if I didn't see her already.

I landed with a spring in my step on the cracked parking lot. "What's up?" The breeze kicked up, blowing a chill around me that might have made me shudder if Brianna hadn't been girding my loins. My skin still tingled, little goosebumps taking the opportunity to spring up all over my arms.

"Well, I found some things," she said, waving me inside. I followed, and she let the door swing shut behind her as we stepped into the dimmer light of the sheriff's station.

Sheriff Miles was sitting on the far side of the room, his feet up on his desk. He gave me a nod as I came in. "Saw you flying back and forth up there while you were on the phone. You ever consider learning ballet?"

I paused in the middle of the waiting area. "No. No, I have not. Why?"

He shrugged his broad shoulders, and a slow smile spread across his broad features. "I have a certain appreciation for the ballet. My daughter's at Julliard, see? And every time I see you fly I can't help but wonder how long it'll be before some enterprising soul at the Bolshoi recruits a team of classically trained metas who can fly and puts them out on stage doing a three-dimensional version of Swan Lake." His voice drifted off. "I bet it'd be mesmerizing."

"Right, so anyway," AA said, "forensics found footprints leading up to the window of your motel, which was forced open. Women's shoe, size 6–"

"Not exactly a Bigfoot," I said.

"Following them led to a set of tire tracks on a nearby road," AA said, "so one of the sheriff's deputies canvassed the neighboring houses." She grabbed a sheaf of papers off the desk. "Turns out one of the locals had a trail camera set up by the road because – and I'm quoting the report here – 'a monster buck tends to cross there–'"

"I assume you mean a male deer, but I have this sudden vision of a giant dollar bill just blowing across the road. Please don't ruin it for me."

AA lightly shook her head. "Anyway, this is what we got from it."

I took the pages and opened it to reveal a photo of a car – a white Hyundai sedan with a masked woman behind the wheel.

A masked, slightly swole woman.

"Tell me you can use this to ID her," I said, flipping the pages to see if there were any more photos.

There were.

"Front license plate is visible on that one," AA said with a satisfied smirk. "California tag, registered to a rental car company that says they rented it to a Lianne Terry just yesterday at Asheville Regional Airport."

"Nice work," I said, offering the papers back. "Now, if we can find this person via tracing any credit cards she has–"

"Already done," AA said, nodding at the sheaf. "The same credit card used to rent the car checked into a hotel in Asheville, North Carolina – about an hour from here – last night. And when I called the hotel..." Her eyes danced, almost playfully, "...they said she hasn't checked out yet."

"Guess I'm going to Asheville," I said, holding the papers in my hand.

"*We're* going to Asheville," AA said.

"*We* are," I said. "We are indeed."

CHAPTER FORTY-SEVEN

We were about forty-five minutes into our hour-long ride to Asheville when AA broke the blessed silence that had allowed me to cosset myself in my own thoughts. The mountain road had just taken a hard turn when she spoke, saying, "But the real question is, will this Lianne Terry go peacefully or are we going to have a problem in the middle of Asheville?"

I froze, hands on the wheel, wondering if she'd even meant to say that out loud. Turning to look at her in the passenger seat, fingers nervously playing with her braid, I found her looking right at me and had to wonder if she'd just invited me into a conversation she was already having in her own head.

"Seems likely, based on my experience," I said, "that we'll have a problem in Asheville. Why?"

"Because I need to know," AA said, "in order to inform TBI, who can inform NC State Police and have a couple of their troopers on hand in case things go sour."

"Probably ought to do that," I said, taking the turn a little faster than I probably should have. The Explorer's tires gripped the road, though, and we came out of the curve safely. Which was good, because I'd glanced below and estimated a couple hundred foot slope into a ravine. Sure, I probably could have put my hands on the roof and flown the car back to stable ground, but why chance it?

AA fidgeted for a minute or two with her phone, then announced, "My boss is taking care of North Carolina. He's got contacts in the state police over here." She looked up, straight ahead at the gray skies and mountain road that looped off behind another turn, and said, "Where are we at with this case? In your mind, I mean?"

"Uhm," I said, having just done that summation myself, internally, working through the problem. An earthy smell filled the air, like all my walking in the woods had left the scent of fresh dirt on my new boots. "Seems to me that this Lianne Terry tried to kill me for someone. We need to know who."

"Yeah, I worked that one out," AA said. "My question is – what's going on with the bigger case? You think this assassination attempt has to do with Wil Waters's land grab?"

"I don't know," I said, keeping my fingers tight to the wheel. "Brenda Greene had enough money to purchase her land and pay the property taxes each year, which are not small. Plus she was quite adamant when I talked to her about how she would not be leaving her land except feet-first. Could be she hired the assassin, thinking it'd get rid of me and the case."

"Because you're the star witness?"

"I'm the only witness against her daughter," I said. "Don't get me wrong, my word is worth a hell of a lot more than hers, but if I'm dead?"

"It's worth zero," AA said. "I got it. Still, does our meeting with Waters earlier stick in your craw? Because it's sticking in mine."

"He's an asshole, no doubt," I said. "And he's definitely working an angle, though I can't see what from here. Building a corporate HQ for a tech company in rural ass, BFE Tennessee?" I shook my head. "Something about that doesn't seem right, does it?"

"I don't know," AA said, shrugging. "I've given up trying to figure out why billionaires do what they do with their cash. They keep buying newspapers and launching themselves into space. Meanwhile, I'm wishing I had enough spare money to buy more yarn." I must have looked at her funny, because she added, "I like to knit."

"I thought about taking that up once, but decided there'd be too much temptation to stab people with the needles," I said. "Anyway, Waters is an asshole, no doubt. Probably even a greedy asshole. But we can't arrest people for being assholes, fortunately, or I'd be serving a life sentence by now."

"Damned right you would."

That answer came not from AA, but from a quiet voice, muffled, in the backseat, and it took every ounce of control I possessed not to scream and jerk the wheel, sending us plummeting off the road into a ditch.

AA, to her credit, had her duty weapon clear of the holster and around – without muzzling me, also a credit to her – and pointed into the backseat in about a half second. "What the hell?!" she shouted, the barrel clanging against the reinforced cage separating us from the backseat.

"Chill, lady," that same voice came again, and slowly, as I drifted the car off to the shoulder, a dark, frizzed head appeared from behind the seats, along with a pair of hands, dirty palms out to show us our inadvertent prisoner was unarmed and – presumably – peaceful.

A second later, the grinning face of Alannah Greene appeared, wide grin splitting her lips. She took us both in with something that looked like insufferable pride and said, "What's up again, bitches?"

CHAPTER FORTY-EIGHT

"The hell are you doing here?" I asked, the car safely at the side of the road and in park. Asheville, North Carolina lay spread before us, the hill we were parked on providing a great view of the town itself.

Also, a great view of the little shit that had stowed away in my back seat. Alannah Greene was clearly unrepentant, grinning at the two of us, her hands up and facing us. "What? I'm just a hitchhiker, taking a little ride with y'all."

"This is a police vehicle," AA said. She had not put her gun away, and it was pointed at Alannah's chest. "Breaking and entering is a serious charge."

"I didn't break nothing, it was open," Alannah said. "Maybe y'all should learn to hit that lock button as you walk away from your car."

"Guess I didn't think I needed to out here in the country," I said, squinting at her. "Point made. Why did you stow away in the back of my car?"

"I don't know if you noticed while we were talking earlier, but there ain't much to do around my ol' homestead that I ain't already done," she said. "So when I heard you talking to my momma, I followed you." She shrugged. "No big."

"This is a big," AA said. Still hadn't put her gun away, and I was beginning to get concerned. "Big."

"Okay," I said, and gently put my hand on her Glock, pushing the muzzle down so that it wasn't primed to blast Alannah Greene's heart out the back of her chest. "Let's just turn the temp down a few degrees."

"Yeah, let's not, it's already cold as a witch's teat in here," Alannah said, rubbing her bare arms. "You know it's like forty degrees out, right?"

"So put a sweater on," I said.

AA shifted uncomfortably, putting her gun back in the holster. "She's right, it's cold as hell in here."

"You can put on a sweater, too," I said. "It's forty outside. You people need to plan accordingly." Hands gripped firmly on the wheel, I grunted. "What the hell do we do now? We're five minutes from the hotel where this perp is staying and we find out we have an uninvited guest."

"North Carolina troopers are waiting for us about a block from the scene," AA said, checking her phone. "They'll technically have to make the arrest, and then we're dealing with extradition to Tennessee, so it's not like this Lianne Terry is riding home with us."

"Such a shame," Alannah said, leaning forward, wrapping her fingers around the cage wires. "I could have sat on your lap the whole way home, honey-pot."

AA grimaced slightly. "You're not my type."

Alannah grinned. "Because I have a vagina?"

"Also, you're like twelve," AA said, and that wiped the grin right off Alannah's face. "I say we park on the street and leave her here 'til we get back."

"I don't see anything wrong with that," I said. "Let's just make it quick so her mom doesn't accuse me of kidnapping or some such shit." I gave Alannah a glance as I pulled the car back on the road; she'd gone sullen. "How did you even make it to my car in time to grab a ride? I went straight from your place to the sheriff's office."

"Yeah, but you spent all that time on the phone circling," Alannah said. "And I hate to be the one to tell you, but I could see your ass – literally your ass – from miles away. Following you was easier than your mom after a near beer."

"I just found out we're related, something I think you already knew," I said. "Which means these 'ur mom' jokes are taking on a real Lannister-like quality now."

"Oh, gross," AA said, her normally staid disposition evaporating into something approaching horror. "God, could you be a more offensive stereotype?"

"Your mom's an offensive stereotype," Alannah said, and brought her forefinger and middle finger together on one hand, then thrust her tongue into it suggestively. "But I love her anyway."

"My mom's dead, so chalk another case of necrophilia up for you," AA said. "Unless you want to claim she's in hiding...?"

"Nah, I'm bored of that one," Alannah said, all the pretense dropping from her face as it returned to neutral, bordering on disinterested. "Who are we after here again?"

"*We* are after the person who tried to choke me out while possibly impersonating you," I said. "Were you not listening on the way up here?"

"Yeah, but I think I might have fallen asleep while y'all were talking," she said. "I'm not saying you're boring conversationalists, I'm just gonna say that I could eat some random mushrooms from the woods and it still wouldn't be enough to keep me awake for that car ride."

I shook my head, ignoring that. We were coming into Asheville now, a charming little town that wasn't quite as little as I might have thought, more like a mid-sized city in the mountains, vintage architecture interspersed with ten-story buildings. We passed a dozen charming restaurants as we drove down one of the side streets following AA's GPS.

Also...there were a lot of homeless here. Like San Francisco levels of people experiencing houselessness, or whatever the PC, feel-good bullshit term was these days.

AA shifted uncomfortably in her seat as we passed a white guy with an overgrown beard that was bigger than he was, bless his bony soul. He clearly had some sort of addiction, probably heroin, and his yellow muscle shirt was deeply stained.

And he had a twenty-four-inch machete strapped to his belt like it was no big deal, as if he were about to path-find his way through the nearby mountains to blaze a new hiking trail for the tourists.

In the next six blocks we passed probably thirty or forty homeless people, all of whom had massive knives strapped to their belts.

"What's up with all the bums carrying pig stickers?" Alannah asked with her customary tact. "Feels like every scary story my momma told about cities was underselling it now that I'm seeing this shit."

"I...don't know," I said, because honestly I was flummoxed. We stopped at a red light, and on the corner was a restaurant with a cutesie name, a menu posted out front that looked like it probably used the freshest farm-to-table ingredients, had its own mixologist on staff...

...and sitting on the concrete right there was a young lady, probably in her twenties, rolling a joint on the sidewalk, a dog attached to her belt by a leash, a cat riding on top of her boulder sized backpack, and the requisite Rambo knife dangling off her hip. She caught my eye as she lit up, taking a deep breath and exhaling a cloud of smoke. With a flick of the wrist she showed me a sign that had an Instaphoto account name written on it and a Cashfer address in case I wanted to make a donation to her...I don't even know what. Panhandling efforts? Public weed smoking? Whatever, I suppose.

"Shit, this ain't what the cities look like on TV," Alannah said, glued to the window like a sticky cat with suction cups.

"This is not what *all* cities look like," I said, cringing. "Nashville, for instance, has homeless but it's not, uh...quite like this." I'd seen more homeless in six blocks of Asheville than I had in all of Nashville the entire time I'd lived there. "How big is this city?"

"Ninety thousand people," AA said helpfully, her voice a little strained.

"It's like a little slice of San Fran closer to home," I muttered.

"Yes," she said, "that's what some of the locals call it. Little San Francisco."

We pulled up in front of the hotel and I parked right in the fire lane. I could see a North Carolina trooper car down the block, and I waved as I got out. A couple troopers stepped out a moment later and made their way over.

"Y'all ain't gonna really leave me in here while you do the fun stuff, are you?" Alannah asked.

"Yes," AA and I chorused, and then shut our doors.

"Y'all bitches!" Alannah pronounced from the back seat, then sat back, arms folded, the perfect image of teen sulking.

"Someone should tell her that calling us that only works if you don't use it casually in conversation as a greeting, too," AA said as we stepped up on the sidewalk to wait.

"Fine!" Alannah shouted, muffled, from within the Explorer, over the running engine. Then she called us something worse.

AA blanched. "That's just uncalled for."

I shrugged. "You sort of called for it, in her mind, I imagine."

Whatever response she had to that she stuffed down deep inside as the NC troopers came up. "Biggs," one of them announced himself, extending his hand to me.

"Tell me you're not Wedge," I said to the other when the time came to pump his hand.

He did not look amused. "Knox. Heard you had a perp you need picked up?"

"Yeah, and probably meta, too," I said. "Got your serum handy?"

Knox patted the dart gun on his waist that had become standard equipment for departments all across the US after the meta secret came to light. "We're set, but you want to take the lead on this, chit-chat-wise?"

"Yeah, I'll lead with my chin," I said. Better for me to take a meta-powered hit than any of these guys.

"Sounds like a plan," AA said, and in we went.

The hotel was nice, certainly nicer than the one I was staying in out in Fountain Run. It was a pretty standard modern American hotel, though, with a sunlit lobby and front desk space that expanded into a breakfast room/bar that was already seeing some action given the hour. A half dozen people lingered there, chatting or working on laptops, their heads down.

I started to head to the front desk but AA tugged on my shoulder. When I turned to give her a questioning look, she jerked her head toward the bar area, and one person in particular sitting off on her own.

It was a petite young lady, probably around my age, maybe a shade younger, wearing black clothes with hints of something that looked like dust all over them. She was typing furiously on a laptop that sat on the table in front of her, oblivious to anything happening in the world – like two TBI agents and two NC troopers walking into her hotel and pointing her out.

I held up a hand and made the 'shush' sign to Knox and Biggs, who nodded in understanding. Then I started toward Lianne Terry, who continued typing furiously, taking no notice of my approach as I circled around to the blind side of her. AA matched my move, very casually, from the other direction, and Biggs and Knox held position, just waiting and covering us.

When I was in the right place, I cut back, coming in on Terry from her five o'clock, just out of her peripheral vision. This gave me a solid view of her computer screen. She appeared to be in some sort of instant messenger app, and I caught a couple snatches of text:

should have finished the job, then.

Listen, asshole, I don't work for free, and I damned sure don't tangle with Sienna Nealon for no pay. Wire me half now, or we're going to have a problem.

That was as far as I got before my boot scuffed on the tile floor and Lianne Terry sat up and turned, taking notice of my smiling mug all of five feet from her.

"Hi," I said, watching the color drain out of her tanned face. "You wanted a do-over, didn't you?"

She was at least a couple inches shorter than me, and petite to the point of being a near stick figure compared to my, uh…robustness.

But then, in about a quarter second, that changed as Terry swelled to twice my width and backhanded her computer across the room as she kicked a chair squarely into my knees before I could dodge. A shock of pain right in the bone stunned me, but I managed to right myself in a hover as she snatched up her table and hurled it at me at about a hundred miles an hour.

CHAPTER FORTY-NINE

The thrown table missed my head by all of three inches as I turned a flip that sent my feet pointing toward the hotel bar ceiling and my stomach's near-empty contents plummeting and threatening to burst out of my mouth. I felt the wind of the table sailing past at what seemed like a hundred miles an hour and knew I'd just dodged a mighty headache by mere inches.

Lianne Terry, my perp du jour, didn't stop with the table throwing. She let out a shout of perfectly inchoate rage and charged me, slapping my head and causing me to go into a flat spin as she shot past me, leaping through the window her table throw had just shattered.

Shards of glass sprinkled across the hotel bar's floor, the crash still echoing among the high ceilings as Terry burst out onto the street. My head was spinning and so was I, but I managed to get control of myself and shoot after her in a feat of balletic acrobatics that would have thrilled Sheriff Miles.

I controlled my arc and ignored the ringing in my ears from that forceful slap to the head she'd delivered on her way out the door. The suddenly huge beast of a woman turned back at me, veins showing in her neck as she let out another furious roar.

"Whoa, girl," I said, hovering as I turned my body to put myself between her and the nearest pedestrian, that homeless girl with the cat on her backpack and the dog on her leash. The glint of the near-machete on her belt in the late-day sun through its cloth sheath was like someone winking at me out of the corner of my eye. "I know you're probably not a great thinker when you're that big, but this is no time to leave all reason behind."

A window shattered behind her, sending shards of safety glass pebbling into her hair. She didn't blanch from it; she turned, roaring toward the source of the disturbance—

Which was Alannah, her head and body half out the window of my Explorer, disappearing at the waist within. She seemed to realize she'd messed up in catching the attention of the angry beast in front of her before she was free of the car, because she froze, smiled sort of weakly and said, "'Sup, bitch?"

Lianne Terry reached out for her, grabbing Alannah by the head and neck, causing the girl to let out a scream of surprise.

With almost zero time to react, I did several things at once, none of which were optimal.

I shouted, "HEY!" at the top of my lungs, causing Terry to turn her head to look at me, and several windows to shatter in the immediate vicinity because I channeled more than a little Brance Venable entirely by accident. I also lunged at her, leading with my left shoulder in a sharp jab aimed at her jaw, fire springing up to cover my hand as I gave her a hard crack.

At the same time, my right hand thrust back and I reached out with my magnetic powers, seizing hold of the homeless girl's machete and yanking it out of her sheath. She didn't interrupt its short flight, which was fortunate because it was wobbling by the time it reached my hand and I secured it tightly in my grip–

And then brought it around and buried it into the center of Lianne Terry's chest just as she was trying to cement her killer grip on Alannah. The pointed knife went in through the ribs, producing a sickening crunch of bones.

Terry's eyes snapped wide in shock at having a damned-near-sword plunged into her heart. Before she could take any more action, I gave the knife a hard twist, cracking the bones further and ripping her heart completely asunder in her chest. With a hard shove from my left hand, I pushed her off the tip and she fell, her grip already slackening on Alannah such that she didn't even drag the girl down with her.

The *thwip!* of three darts going off was followed by bright fletchings appearing in Terry's neck, her left cheek, and her arm. AA and the two North Carolina troopers were arrayed around the wreckage of the hotel window, two still standing inside with weapons drawn, and Knox on the sidewalk, shoes crackling in the field of broken glass.

"Unhhh...unhhh," Lianne Terry said, coughing up blood. Apparently my vicious twist of the knife had gotten at least one lung, too. She was already shrinking back to miniature size.

I fell to my knees beside her, pressing her down as I landed. She didn't fight it; she didn't have much fight left in her by my reckoning. The sidewalk beneath her was already a small pond of crimson and it was expanding by the second. "Lianne," I said, "tell me who hired you."

Her face was small now, like she was, and her chin was covered with blood. As were her teeth, which she bared at me in a defiant grin. "Up yours," she whispered, and then she went slack beneath my hand.

I sagged and fell back on my haunches, seething as I

looked up at Alannah, who'd wriggled her way out of the back of my car and was looking at the dead body in front of me, all the jadedness gone from her eyes. I knew by the look that this was the first time she'd actually seen a person die.

Didn't matter, though. I sat in my stony silence, knowing that no matter what...I'd just lost the only real lead to whoever had tried to kill me.

CHAPTER FIFTY

Sorting things out with the North Carolina troopers had turned out to be a lot easier than making things right with the city of Asheville.

"How dare you," a sanctimonious detective with the Asheville PD asked me, her bright eyes flashing, long blond hair swinging over her shoulder as she stuck a thin, perfectly-manicured finger in my face. She wore zero makeup, like I used to, and her suit was a fashion reject like most of mine.

"With the greatest ease, that's how I dare," I said, because I'd been chewed out by way scarier people than some glorified bureaucrat in a town where they probably spent most of their time on cases involving the local homeless carving each other up like Sunday roasts. "Also: with aplomb. And the help of the North Carolina state troopers, so..." I flipped her a bird, and it was not subtle. "Sorry things went sideways on your street."

She gritted her teeth, eyes flaring like her soul was burning and her ass was next to catch. "Get. Out."

"Okay, but only because I'm really intimidated by you right now," I said. "I mean...just terrifying, that visage. I'm definitely not ever going to cause problems for you here in this little hobo mecca ever again. Unless I'm passing through and want an artisanal dinner and some homeless knife-fight theater."

She spun and stormed off, a sound deep in her throat like a tea kettle preparing to squeal trailing after her, but quietly. It wasn't thirty seconds after she left that AA sauntered up to me and said, "I see you're forging diplomatic relations everywhere you go."

I grimaced, then cursed under my breath. "You know, I generally do a better job than that, but she really got my goat."

"Yeah, I kinda noticed her coming at you full throttle," AA said. "What was up with that?"

I glanced up and the down the Asheville street. Things had quieted; it was only a town of 90,000, after all, it was Monday night, and almost all the action had moved indoors. A couple of the restaurants down the way had small crowds out front taking regular, surreptitious looks at us, and a scattering of homeless were watching us from their various perches along the street. "Probably just sore that I killed a person on the street of her tourist town."

"I've seen the Asheville crime rate," AA said, looking for all the world like someone who needed a cup of coffee in her hand. "She can't be that upset about one little righteous kill among the dozens of shootings."

"Hm." My eyebrows rose. "Is it that bad here?"

"Oh, it's in the top ten percent for violence nationwide." She cast a knowing eye up and down the street. "So, if I were you, I might write that one off as a cop just frustrated about her job and taking it out on whoever was convenient."

"If I'd known that, I might have taken my chastening with more grace," I said, rubbing my eyes. It had been a long day; I made a mental note to reach out to Asheville PD and offer some sort of concession, like my help on a community policing project or something. I sighed. Maybe after I'd gotten East and West Tennessee a little more in order.

"We good, here?" AA asked, chucking a thumb at my Explorer parked in the middle of the scene, which was nearly cleared. Alannah Green was leaned against the hood, watching everything going on around us on the street with fresh interest, a kid in the candy store.

"No 'we' are not," I said, narrowing my eyes as I looked at Alannah. "But we can talk about that little problem when we bring that girl home."

CHAPTER FIFTY-ONE

The phone call I'd been dreading hit as we were passing through a mountain gap on the way back to Fountain Run. I would have thought cell phone service would have been spotty as hell in these environs, but when I answered the phone and announced, "Hello," the voice of Ileona Marsh came in absolutely free of crackling over the Explorer's Bluetooth connection.

"So," Marsh said, "what are you up to out east?"

"I feel I should warn you that I've got a local TBI agent and a troublesome pest in the car with me," I said, and heard Alannah grunt in the cage behind me. AA just frowned lightly.

"Thanks for the added context," Marsh said, her voice still even. "But the question stands."

"Well," I said, "I went to pick up a murder suspect across the line in Asheville – with the aid of North Carolina troopers – and things kinda took a turn. Had to put the suspect down to prevent a, uhm...hitchhiker...from getting murdered in front of me."

"That the same 'hitchhiker' that tried to murder you in

the woods yesterday?" Marsh sounded unimpressed. For some reason.

"She's a mischievous scamp, that one," I said, not bothering to look back at Alannah, who chortled under her breath. "Gets up to all manner of trouble."

"What I'm not clear on," Marsh said, "is how someone who gets the drop on you to the point of nearly being able to deliver the coup de grace...somehow goes helpless against what Chandler describes as the 'Meta that drops common loot.'" She paused. "Whatever that means."

"Hey, you try and fight a double jumbo steroidal freak when there ain't a tree handy to work with," Alannah said. "I was in the forest when I beat Nealon's ass–"

"Please stop before your lawyer tries to rip the souls out of our bodies for this," I said, holding up a hand to stay her big mouth.

"Why?" Alannah asked. "You feel like him doing that is stepping on your toes?"

"Lawyers have been stealing souls since long before I was born. If anything, I'm stepping on their territory," I said. "Anyway, uhm...it is what it is, boss. Pretty sure we'll tie the body we have to the attack on me in the motel room, but she's dead and didn't talk about who hired her before she kicked off the mortal coil."

"You sure she was working for someone?" Marsh asked.

"Pretty sure based on the tiny amount of conversation I saw on her computer before she smashed it to block us," I said. "Unfortunately, I didn't get any more than the very basics."

"We'll take a peek deeper into her background," Marsh said. "Where's the computer?"

"Asheville PD grabbed it," I said, and once more, cringed. "I'm not sure we're going to get much cooperation from them. At the very least, it probably won't be expedient."

"Oh, you know that, do you?" Marsh asked, voice thick with sarcasm. "Well, good, I'm glad you realize how pissed they are at you right now. I was afraid I'd have to explain it to you as one explains the feelings of others to a toddler."

"No, I was aware I was pissing them off," I said. "Bummed that it happened, but the detective came at me pretty hard out there and I, uh..."

"What happened?" Alannah asked. "Did you actually feel something for a quarter second down in that icy heart of yours?"

That produced a moment of silence in the Explorer. "I can tell you got your hands full right now," Marsh said. "Why don't you call me back once you get that trouble dropped off?"

"Roger that," I said, and ended the call.

"Thank God," Alannah said. "Rather have my nips hooked up to a car battery than listen to you debase yourself to some weak-teated boss about getting in a brawl on a city street."

I tried to find my level, but it was a rising level, like water coming over a road in a flood. "I wouldn't have gotten in nearly so bad of a brawl if I hadn't had to save your ass by killing my only lead."

"Don't do me no favors," Alannah said. In the rearview I could see her dirty cheeks reddening. "You know I wouldn't do none for you."

"You just broke a car window and tried to shimmy out in the middle of a fight to help her," AA said, spinning around to fix her with an exasperated glare. "What was that, if not a favor?"

"I saw a fight, I just wanted to get a piece of it, that's all," Alannah said, arms folded across her thin mint self. "Like she ain't done the same before." She nodded at me. "At least, before she got her clitoridectomy and lost all feeling down there."

"What the f–" AA started to say.

"Settle down," I said, shaking off the urge to answer fast and hostile. "She's just trying to rile you."

"Nah, I'm trying to rile *you*," Alannah said. "But it ain't working because the clitoris has 7,000 nerves and you have zero of them left, 'parently."

"You're really gonna let her talk that shit to you?" AA asked, sotto voce.

"Yes," I said, "because it's better than her doing murderous shit to me. Listen, Alannah–"

"You can call me 'Ms. Greene,'" Alannah said snootily. "Don't be acting like you know me."

"Well, I just killed a woman for you," I said, "so I must know you at least a little."

"Hey, did you notice her last words were 'up yours?'" Alannah chuckled. "You know, I can respect that level of commitment to being obtuse."

"It was a very 'you' thing to say, wasn't it?" I asked.

I could see the storm cloud descend over Alannah's face in the rearview, shadows lengthening as the sun fell behind a mountain to our left. "Up yours," she said, and clammed up for the rest of the ride.

CHAPTER FIFTY-TWO

We stopped off at the sheriff's station outside town because AA was "about to burst." She didn't have the mom vibe, but clearly had the bladder of one, so I obliged her rather than just driving out to the forest's edge to turn loose Alannah like the wild animal she was.

I didn't feel like waiting in the car with her, so as soon as AA scrambled for the front door of the sheriff's station, desperately trying to keep her legs together and bladder's seal in place, I got out of the car and started to stretch. Figured I'd go inside, see if Sheriff Miles had anything for me of note.

The sound of a faint grunt made me turn, and when I did I found Alannah trying to squeeze out the open window again. She had only made it to just below her sternum when I reached out and grabbed the door handle, pulling it open and throwing her off balance. She tumbled out like a stretched-out worm, still half-hanging on the door.

"Leave it to the simple minds to figure out the simple solutions," she said, picking herself up and giving herself a good dusting off.

I rolled my eyes and left her to that, heading for the sheriff's station. Once inside I found a pleasant, warm aura in the building that made me realize just how chilly it had been outside.

Alannah's entrance reinforced that feeling. "Ah, warmth. I was beginning to worry I wouldn't ever feel that again."

"Maybe if you hadn't broken the window we wouldn't have had to drive with the air blowing in the whole way back."

"Maybe if you hadn't gotten yourself damned near decapitated by a powerlifter with a table, I wouldn't have thought, 'Huh. That girl needs some help,'" she fired back.

The sheriff was watching us with his feet up on the desk. "I heard y'all had a little kerfuffle out in Asheville."

"Do 'kerfuffles' usually end with someone getting their heart cut out?" Alannah asked. "Cuz if so, it was, straight-up."

"Things went a little off the rails with our sole lead," I said. "On the plus side, I pioneered some of that in-air ballet that you were thrilling to earlier."

"Y'all are so damned soft," Alannah muttered. "I don't know how you win any fights."

"Through sheer, utter savagery, duh," I said, not giving her a look. "This one stowed away in my car, gotta bring her back to momma once AA is done using the little girl's wee wee room."

Miles looked at me funny, but didn't comment on that. "You heading out to their homestead anyway, I got something you can deliver."

"I hope it's a pizza," Alannah said. "If so, it's the only useful thing to come out of this office since I met y'all idiots."

The sheriff shook his head, then picked up an envelope from the desktop. "Nah, it's official paperwork related to your property. County clerk threw it at me this afternoon, but I ain't much up for hiking in the dark to deliver it." He looked at me. "If you wouldn't mind seeing her ma gets it..."

"Sure," I said, and received the envelope. It was fresh,

crisp, and unopened. "Might as well hand her mom some legal docs that'll piss her off at the same time as I bring her truant daughter home."

"That's the team spirit," the sheriff said, settling back in his chair. "So...you really cut the heart out of the Hercules that came after you at the motel?" He looked somewhat suspiciously at Alannah as he said this, and the subtext was plain: *Or did you get the wrong one?*

"Pretty sure I got her, yeah," I said, pocketing the thick envelope. The toilet flushed in the next room, and I could hear AA fumbling with the knob. "You get anything back from forensics?"

"Just what Ashley in there already told you," he said with a shrug.

"Who the eff is Ashl – oh. AA."

She emerged just then, frowning and wiping her hands with a paper towel. "Yes. Ashley. A remarkably simple name that most people can remember without resorting to calling me 'AA.'"

"Take it easy on the old lady," Alannah said, not quite keeping a straight face. "She's been hit in the head a lot in her life. It ain't the years, it's city miles, you know."

"Come on," I said, heading for the door. "Let's get this over with. I didn't get much sleep last night for some reason, and I don't want to be stuck in the woods at midnight trying to find a gingerbread house among the trees." And I stalked off for the door.

CHAPTER FIFTY-THREE

"You want to wait here while I fly in?" I asked, as I parked at the edge of the woods by the construction site. All the equipment was dead and silent, not even a gate or fence up for the night because all that was here to be stolen was the heavy excavation equipment, and presumably they'd taken the keys for those.

AA was sitting stonily in the passenger seat, and I wasn't even really certain why she hadn't gotten off this ride at the sheriff's office and just gone home. "No," she said, stirring, "I'll wait for you here. How are you gonna get her back home?"

"Don't you worry about me, *Ashley*," Alannah said, putting a particularly snarky emphasis on her name. "I can glide over the treetops as easily as you can surf a condom."

"Okay, sewer mouth, let's go," I said, taking Alannah by the arm and tugging her toward the edge of the woods. It was pitch black, only a half moon overhead for guidance now that my headlights had cut off and the car's dome light shed barely any glow. "Before you outstay your welcome and convince everyone your manners are bad."

"Just send me off to Europe like Daisy Miller, why don'tcha?" Alannah tore her arm out of my grasp.

"I could only hope you catch the 'Roman fever,'" I said. "Come on."

She flipped me the bird. "Think you can keep up with me?" A tree branch reached down and wrapped itself around her waist with stunning alacrity. It had her up and in the air, riding the treetops almost before I got off the ground.

"In terms of the slutting around you're going to do the moment you're out of your mom's sight? No, I'll pass," I said, but she was already a hundred yards ahead of me and I had to pour on the speed to try and catch up.

She moved across the canopy like she was crowd surfing at a rock concert, only faster and in a straight line. The rustle of branches and the fall of leaves being jarred by the movement of the trees was the soundtrack of this dark night, along with the blowing of a cold wind. I heard Alannah's teeth chatter about twenty yards ahead and matched my pace to it as we rolled toward a light in the distance.

Alannah vanished into the canopy just as we were coming up on the glow, and I followed the noise of her movement through the branches. Soon I came to that gap in the boughs and saw the trailer house aglow. Darting down beneath the surface of the canopy, I came to a landing just as a long branch released Alannah only a few feet from her door–

Where waited Brenda, her face umbered against the glow behind her, and her whole body looking like she was a stone wall barring her daughter's entrance back into the trailer.

"So, your daughter followed me back to my car earlier and snuck into it," I said, before she could lay into me for fraternizing with her underage criminal of a kid. "I was almost to Asheville to arrest a suspect, and was forced to cart her along–"

"You did what now?" Brenda asked, looking right at me, though I couldn't quite see her eyes.

"I had to take her with," I said. "And then, as I'm about to arrest the lady who just about killed me earlier–"

"You took my daughter along on an arrest?" Brenda asked, steely and cold. "You weren't supposed to have any contact with her."

"Maybe you missed the part where *she* followed *me* and snuck into my car?"

"Yeah, well, she and I'll have words about that later." Brenda wagged a thick finger at me. "You took her along on an arrest? What were you thinking?"

"I was thinking 'It's a long drive to Asheville and back, and gosh I really want to get my perp before she flees back wherever she came from,'" I said. "Also, I assumed a minimum standard of behavior from Alannah, like she could follow the simple instructions such as, 'Wait in the car.' Clearly, I overestimated her."

"So damned much gratitude," Alannah said. "I saved your life, didn't I?"

"I remember it differently," I said, "and I bet the body camera footage of the North Carolina troopers would back me up on my version of events."

"Hush up, both of y'all!" Brenda's voice split the night. "I'm gonna talk to our lawyer about this, you know?"

"Yeah, I don't care," I said, shaking my head. "Far as I'm concerned, your daughter probably walks for what happened yesterday and good riddance." I shuffled over to her, brandishing the envelope. "The sheriff asked me to deliver this to you and then, as far as I'm concerned, we're done. I won't be showing back up to testify against Alannah – not because she doesn't deserve a little time in jail, but because I'm frankly sick of dealing with the problems that she's caused me." I slapped the envelope squarely into Brenda's outstretched hands. "I just wanted to make sure she got back to you safe and sound so that she is your problem once more."

"Bitch, I'm everybody's problem," Alannah announced. "You done opened the door on that one."

"Don't be that way," I said. "Nobody wants you as a problem. Don't make yourself one and life will return to a pleasant normal around here."

"I doubt that," Brenda said, voice full of spite. She had opened the envelope, and was holding the enclosed pages up so she could read them in the light emanating from the trailer. She turned one around to me, and the look on her face was pure venom. "See this shit you just handed me? It's an eviction notice. Like we're squatters on someone else's property." Her eyes blazed in the darkness. "I told you – I wasn't gonna let your family take my land again." And she raised up, ready to strike at me.

CHAPTER FIFTY-FOUR

"That frigging sheriff," I gasped through gritted teeth, striking a defensive stance and preparing to blast off into the heavens. "I didn't know what it was." My words were crisp and clear in the dark of the woods, but echoed.

So did Brenda's, but they were harder, like knives to the ears. "The hell you didn't." She stepped forward, and I felt branches rustle around me, in the distance.

"Momma, no!" Alannah thrust herself between us, holding her hands up. I paused, listening for motion behind me, half-convinced her move was just a feint to get me to look at them while she split my skull with a tree branch from the back. "I was there when she got it handed to her, he just said it was legal papers. Didn't say nothing about heaving us off."

"Well, that's what it is, daughter of mine," Brenda said, and she crumpled the pages and threw them in the dirt with meta-strength.

"I don't understand," Alannah said, a hand pressed against her mother's gut. She was looking at me, though, in something approaching bewilderment. "Doesn't it take time for them to toss us off of here? Years and lawyers and motions and hearings and all that shit?"

"I'm not a legal expert, but I would have thought so, yes," I said. In terms of those feelings Alannah claimed I'd lost...well, I was feeling some now. Pity and regret, mostly.

"That's not what this says," Brenda spat on the discarded papers. "This says we are to clear out by tomorrow at noon – or we'll be *removed*."

"Pffft!" Alannah did a quick spit of her own. "Who do they think they're going to send out here to get us, huh? Who have they got that has the sand to kick us off our land?"

They both slowly looked up at me, and I felt compelled to answer, and swiftly: "Uh, no, I don't do evictions. Also, I'm probably headed home. I think my boss is pissed about the whole Asheville thing. Even more so about dragging her into it."

"I don't blame her. But they're gonna call you back here," Brenda said. "We're gonna make a stink, they're gonna have to."

I sighed. "Or, alternatively...you could not make a stink."

Brenda took a step closer to me, and Alannah no longer held her back. "I didn't have a chance to fight for myself and my home last time someone took it from me. If you think I'm just gonna bend like a willow...you got another thing coming."

I looked past her, at Alannah. "That go for you, too?"

Alannah's face was shadowed in the dim, single source of light coming out of the trailer. "You know I don't shy away from a fight." There was no wicked grin now, though, no devil-may-care temptation playing across her face. Just an angry determination not to be pushed around.

"Well, for my part, I hope you manage it," I said, lifting off. "I wouldn't want a piece of either of you. Try and be a little gentle, though; surely you can stop these folks without killing anyone."

"I ain't making no promises," Brenda said.

"Best of luck," I said, giving each of them one last look.

"This is what you can do with your luck," Alannah said, giving me the bird.

"Why am I not surprised?" I muttered, heading off into the chilly night air. I was already pulling out my phone, because I had a call to return.

CHAPTER FIFTY-FIVE

"Glad you called me back," Ileona Marsh said upon answering. I could hear the sounds of the road behind her, which meant she was finally calling it a day. She kept late hours and early hours, all part of the job. "I figured you might duck me and keep going."

"Well, there is still an open murder investigation on who tried to whack me," I said. "Thanks to the whole Asheville clusterbump."

"I know," she said and sighed. "Sometimes a case just goes off the rails, and you need to put some fresh eyes on it. That particular branch of evidence appears to be salted and dead. I'll assign someone else to it. Maybe they can sort things out."

"This whole thing stinks, Marsh," I said. "There's something going on here. Something dirty. I can feel it."

"You mean there's something unpleasant happening to the people who already tried to kill you once? That's such a shame."

"I know this is going to sound patently insane," I said, "but...I kind of feel for the girl."

I could imagine the look on Marsh's face, pity mixed with

dark amusement. "The one who tried to kill you? Pity for people who would happily murder you is not a trait one finds in those who long survive in this business."

"There's history there, though," I said. "My mom did her mom wrong, we're related – it's a whole thing."

"Then you *really* don't need to be on this case if it's a family feud," Marsh said. "Sorry, but my decision is sounding better and better all the time."

"Distant relations," I said. "I'd never even met them before. Mom's cousins sort of thing."

"Still...better to keep your investigations impersonal, yourself detached."

I laughed. "I think I might have become a little too detached of late, boss."

"If detachment means you can keep bringing in the collars like you have, then by all means, stay detached." She cleared her throat uncomfortably. "And to that end, I've had some talks up the chain, and...we think it's best if you start working your magic in West Tennessee before returning to the east. Memphis could use your help–"

"I'm being booted?" I asked.

"It's a temporary thing," she said. "You knew you were going to start working to clean up the rest of the state the way you have the middle. It was inevitable. We're just changing things up a little bit given the trouble you've had out east."

"Just feels like I'm leaving something unfinished," I said.

"Because you are," Marsh said with some small reassurance in her voice. "We all have cases that we don't feel get properly put to bed. That's police work. Surely you've run across a few unsolved mysteries by now."

"One or two," I whispered, the wind whipping by my face, stirring my hair. I was treading air now, and could see AA waiting in my Explorer in the distance, but I didn't want to approach until I finished my talk with Marsh.

"Let us handle this one from here. We'll get someone else on it, have your local agent bring in a partner. They'll finish the job – if it can be."

"Copy that," I said, a strange, non-elemental chill emanating from the depths of my very being. "I'll, uh...see you tomorrow, I guess."

"Sounds good. Rest easy. You've earned it." And with that, she hung up.

I stayed there in the air for a few more minutes, trying to chew through what was going on in my head. But it was all frustration boiling beneath the surface – way beneath the surface – about leaving the thing undone, and finally I put it aside and jetted back down to AA waiting in my car.

CHAPTER FIFTY-SIX

"How'd that go?" AA asked, putting aside the phone she'd been looking at when I entered the car.

"Just dandy," I said, shifting it into gear. I'd left it running so she wouldn't freeze. "Turns out the sheriff handed me an eviction notice to serve without letting me know what I was giving Brenda."

AA grimaced. "I bet that went well."

"Yeah, they're gonna fight it," I said, backing up the Explorer. "And really...I can't blame them."

"I don't blame them, either," AA said. "I bet they'll have some success in court, too."

"No – the notice is for them to vacate by tomorrow," I said. "They're going to fight it. Fight-fight, not courtroom-fight."

"Oh – oh!" AA's eyes flashed as she realized what I meant. "How are they getting booted tomorrow? Those sort of procedures take months, even years, and it's not like they didn't own the land to start with."

"I guess they don't anymore, so one would question how

much standing they have to protest," I said, white-knuckling the wheel. "Whatever. Not my problem anymore."

AA shook her head at this. "Wait...were you yanked from the case?"

"Gently, but yes," I said. "I've being recalled and reassigned. Turns out they think West Tennessee needs me more than the east right now."

"They're probably right," AA said, "but we could have used you, too. Lots of towns in East Tennessee could use a hand like yours. Athens. Sweetwater. Crossville."

"And they'll get it – eventually," I said. "But that's the problem with working for the government. Any government, really. They provide me shelter from the storm that is the laws of other states and maybe the feds, and in return I take the hit to the ego and discipline myself not to just go out and deliver my conception of justice to every soul I meet who deserves it." I felt my jaw tighten. "You'll get another partner to help you finish this one off."

"I can appreciate the desire to put someone who doesn't have a murder attempt on them into this case, but," AA shook her head again, "it seems to me I'm not going to get another metahuman, and this is a meta case through and through."

"Well, don't get yourself killed," I said.

"It's uppermost on my mind, I assure you."

"I'll be back this way in a few months," I said, "once I've made a dent in West Tennessee and things have a chance to cool down. Maybe we'll get to work together again." I shrugged. "Who knows how these things work?"

"Internal politics of the TBI? No one knows how they work, not even the brass."

We both got a chuckle out of that, and lapsed into a silence as we approached the sheriff's station.

AA broke it. "You driving back tonight, then?"

I felt a tiredness deep in my soul. "No...I'll leave my car here and fly it. Come back tomorrow morning and pick it up for the drive." I rubbed my eyes; I really didn't have four hours on the road left in me after the events of the day. "That'll give me a little windshield time tomorrow."

"And more crash time tonight. Makes sense." AA thrust out her hand as I pulled into a parking place. "Well...nice working with you, I guess."

"You guess?" I smirked and took her hand. "Same."

"Even if you can't remember my name?"

"What's in a name?" I asked, getting out of the car and locking it. I looked at her over the top of the Explorer. "See you later...Ashley."

"So long, Sienna." And she gave me a half salute as I streaked off into the night, heading west for Nashville.

And home.

CHAPTER FIFTY-SEVEN

I made it home in minutes, made sure the dogs were taken care of (they didn't need to be fed, though they whined that they did, though Emma didn't), and had almost made it to bed when my phone rang. The caller ID displayed the name I least wanted to see right now, the one I'd let myself avoid calling all day:

Mimaw

"Hey," I said, because I couldn't bring myself to dodge my great-grandmother's call. There was a considerable amount of static on the line, and somehow I knew that the fault lay in New Asgard, Texas and not on my end. "Who told you?"

"I had to have a conversation today with your great-grandfather," Persephone said, mincing no words in that acquired drawl of hers. "You know how much it pains me to talk to him at this point?"

"Because you hate him so much?"

"I don't hate him so much, actually," she said, some of the sting coming out of her words. "Which may be the problem."

"Well, maybe he should have kept his big, soul-sucking mouth shut."

"He's worried," Persephone said. "Or he was trying to curry favor with me. Could be either of those."

"He's doing that with everyone nowadays," I said. "Guess he's feeling the prick of old age. Kinda like how those old ladies in the Villages are feeling—"

"You don't need to be finishing that sentence; I don't care to hear it," she snapped. "He told me you're having a head-to-head with your own kinfolk?"

"No, I'm not," I said. "I had a squabble with Brenda Greene and her daughter Alannah, but it's done now. Sorted."

"And they ain't dead or in jail?"

"Neither...for now." I clenched my phone tight and pushed the loose hair back over my head, missing my ponytail that I'd just unbound. "I can't speak to what will happen tomorrow."

Persephone had lived a year or two. "What's that supposed to mean?"

"Their locality has decided to sell their land and move 'em off it," I said. "Gears have been in motion for a while, I guess, though they didn't realize it. Anyway, the sheriff is enforcing the legal...whatever, framework. Nothing to do with me, I'm out of this one. No war between us."

"Well, it ain't exactly ending in peace if you're going to let them twist under the auspices of the law!"

"I'm not...letting them twist," I said. "I'm just not going to fight a war against the local politicos. Besides, it's got nothing to do with me."

"They're family," Persephone said, coming in hot. "That means—"

"Means nothing to me," I said, and I regretted it after I did, though I went on. "Look, I don't know them. Alannah tried to kill me right off because of the beef her mom and mine had, which tells me a lot about how our so-called family operates."

"Wasn't always the case," Persephone said. "We used to look out for each other, because, especially in the succubus and incubus branch of our family...no one else would."

"Those days are gone," I said. "I have meta friends who watch my back. Maybe Brenda should have found some of those, the kind that don't rob banks and let you take the fall for their idiot decisions."

"We ain't all as fortunate in our choice of friends as you are," Persephone said. "And we get no choice on family. That's ties of blood, you know. Thicker than–"

"Thieves?" I offered, settling back on the bed. I had no energy for this conversation, and little emotion.

"Ain't a one of us in this family ain't done some thieving in our time, Sienna."

"Yeah, well I'm not really allowed to do that anymore." I looked at the bedside table, where my TBI badge rested. "I have an obligation to the people who are giving me a place to live, and to me it seems a lot bigger than any I have to cousins I've never met, who were perfectly willing to kill me only a couple days ago."

"So that's it?" I could hear the disappointment in her voice. "You're just going to walk away?"

"I don't think even you'd want to get involved in what they're planning out there, Mimaw. They're going to go hard against the law. I don't know how well you know her, but Brenda doesn't seem like a shrinking violet, and her underage daughter is stone cold." I sighed. "Doubt she'll come to a good end."

"Someone might have said the same about you, once upon a time," Persephone said. "Two men bust open your door, you came at 'em like a cat on a couple mice, beat the living hell out of them as I recall."

I remembered that day so well, kicking the crap out of Zack and Kurt Hannegan. Then I'd met Reed, and Wolfe, and... "I guess now she's going to come up against an unstoppable force."

"It's unlikely the local government is just going to bend over and relent," Persephone said. "They're going to call you, you know. My question is...what are you going to do then?"

"I don't know," I whispered, knowing she'd hear it.

"Well, you might want to figure it out," she said, and boy did her voice drip disappointment. "Because you may think you're out of this one, but I expect you are about to get dragged back in." And she hung up on me.

I looked at the phone, then tossed it aside. It clattered on the nightstand table as I took a deep breath.

Cali and Jack snuggled against me, having taken no notice of my conversation. I clicked the remote that controlled the lights and stared into the dark. Emma scratched against something in her baby cage, then meowed into the quiet, rustling as she tried to get comfortable.

How the hell was I supposed to handle this, I wondered, my brain locked in a spin-cycle of questions. It seemed an obvious, binary question: get involved on the side of my family and put myself in opposition to the law and my bosses at TBI, or wait for the law to either wipe out Brenda and Alannah, or be foiled by them and call me in to intercede.

Two choices, ultimately: for or against, and I was going to be stuck no matter what.

I thought about calling Reed, or Augustus, or Jamal, or even Dr. Zollers. But it was late, and I was tired. I thought of my grandmother as I started to drift off, wondering why she hadn't been in the background of my conversation with Persephone. And then, as I felt myself slip into unconsciousness, I remembered – she'd been visiting Odin, hadn't she?

And that thought carried me off into dreams.

CHAPTER FIFTY-EIGHT

He really did only have the one eye, and I realized my error almost as soon as I recognized him standing there before me in the dreamwalk. He was tall and forbidding, solidly built, his long, gray hair slicked back in a man-bun, an appalling synthesis of old-world legend and new-world awful aesthetics.

I didn't call him out on it, though, because the scowl on his face told me everything I needed to know about how he felt about being here.

"Did your brother not tell you of my warning?" Odin said, the walls of the dreamwalk shaking with a raw mental power that was a hell of a lot more forceful than my meager Warmind. "Of what would happen if you sought me?"

"Chill out, One-Eyed Willie," I said, ignoring the quaking feeling in my stomach. "I didn't mean to bring you here. I was stuck in a brain-fried loop in which I remembered my grandmother talking about how she was 'visiting' you," I gave him the finger quotes with an appropriate amount of sarcasm, "and I think we all know what *that* means."

Odin's anger faded by a matter of degrees, turning into an

uncertainty that would have been hilarious in almost any other circumstances. "What...what do you mean?"

"Oh, fuck you, Step-All-Grandfather," I said, shooting him a bird in a style very reminiscent of Alannah's. "Don't make me say it out loud, it's bad enough when your buddy Hades shares his escapades with me."

"I am sorry." Odin looked really, truly abashed. "I did not know you were here by...accident."

"Yeah, well, since I got you here," I said, "best of luck with Lethe. She seemed happy to..." My eyes rolled back in my head involuntarily. "...whatever. Hang out with you."

"I...enjoy her company as well," Odin said. "And always have, though perhaps in different ways." A flash of lightning in his eyes washed away his shame. "This still does not make me want to converse with you."

"I. Didn't. *Try*," I said, squeezing out every word with a force that shook my dreamwalk and made Odin take a step back. "I know you don't want to see me. I'm sure you still hold me responsible for Bjorn and Loki–"

"Yes," he said quietly. "But...as you say, since you are here, can you tell about...how they died?"

"Sure," I sighed. "Why not? Loki and I fought in a casino in Vegas," I said, averting my eyes from him. "He was stuck with Century, tasked by them to kill me. We talked before he made a move, like reaching for a gun, that required my partner to shoot him."

"You didn't kill him yourself?" Odin's eye was narrowed, thinking.

"No," I said. "He didn't have a gun, either. He made the move so we would kill him, to free him from Sovereign, from Century." I took a deep breath. "I felt like I understood him better than...well, most of the foes I face. He didn't want to be there, but he had little choice."

Odin took it all in, and finally nodded. "And my boy Bjorn?"

"He died twice, I think you know," I said. "Once when I absorbed him against my will…" The scene shifted to the vision of me being held by Clyde Clary as Old Man Winter pushed Bjorn, that giant Norseman, against my outstretched hands. Our screams, his and mine, filled the dreamwalk, making me cringe even now, after all this time.

"And the other death?" Odin asked quietly.

"He gave his life to save me," I said. Once more the scene shifted, this time to the end, to the last whispers of Bjorn in my mind, his grin plastered on his face: "I hated you. But not as much as I hate this c—"

Odin watched the end unfold in mute silence, and nodded again. "In truth, he died for you. I see that now." Looking at his feet, he said, "I cannot fault you for any of this, then."

"You can if you want to," I said. "I certainly do, and there's no lack of people looking to, and with a hell of a lot less reason than you've got."

"No," Odin said, and now the scene shifted of his accord. We stood on snowy ground, blood tingeing the white. "Long have I blamed you, blamed others, for what has happened in this world while I was absent. But the acts of my children, the acts of my sons and daughters…they are not on you. Nor on me, save for as I have abdicated any responsibility for walking in this world."

"Yeah, that's sort of my guiding philosophy, too," I said, "and the reason I can't really just disappear to an island in the Caribbean for the rest of my life." I frowned. "That and my waistline. I spent a month on St. Thomas one time, and it was just…" I mimicked a balloon blowing up.

Odin took no notice of my babbling, but turned to look back at me with that lone, crackling eye. "You are in another storm now, are you not?"

"Always," I said, starting to turn away. "But that's nothing you need to worry about. I got into it, and I'll get myself ou—"

"Hold," he said, and suddenly he wasn't wearing a slicked-back man bun anymore, nor a Polo shirt and khaki shorts.

Suddenly...he was *Odin*.

Bright armor covered him over, a sharp and terrifying helm making him seem more wolfish and less human. His gray hair was pulled back, and an eyepatch replaced that blank, glass atrocity. He towered over me, and his spear was like the staff of a monarch. When he spoke, it resonated, not in a fearful way, but in one that made me feel like I should take a knee and bow before my true and wrathful king.

I didn't, though. Because I'm an American, and we don't have kings. We damned sure don't bow.

"You have had motherly advice," Odin said, "I know. And your great-grandfather, though he might have heard your problems, dared not to say to you what he truly felt for fear of alienating your heart from him. So," and here his eye sparkled brightly, "I give you this, in repayment for what you have shown me."

"Is it your spear?" I asked. "Because Reed told me about it and the no-miss targeting thing? Seems really cool."

He laughed. "No, don't be a jackass. Gungnir is mine. I give you the wisdom of the All-Father, because no one else will set you straight."

"I think Persephone just tried, but give it a go," I said. "Maybe you'll make a point she missed."

"The people you serve will not always be right," Odin said. "The people you dislike are not always wrong. And the bonds of blood, however strained, should not be cut without ample reason. Certainly not over a foolish grudge or a blind mistake."

"So you're on Team: Family is All," I said, nodding along.

"Makes sense. You're from the times of tribal people. Loyalty is important."

"Is not loyalty important to you?" Odin asked. "Is that not what you have shown time and again in your willingness to break laws to help the people you care about?"

"People who have shown me loyalty, sure," I said. "I'd go to the ends of the earth – to orbit, I guess – for them. But for some family that's supposedly related but has caused me nothing but headaches?" I shook my head. "What, I'm supposed to give up my whole life and stand with them as they throw themselves into the gears of modernity?"

"You have thrown yourself into the gears for much less, have you not?" Odin asked. "Faced down enemies across the globe for less reason…because it was *right*."

"Oh my gosh, I hate you for saying that," I said, the slow, creaking realization coming over me that yeah, I was refusing to get involved in what was obviously a tilted situation because a) I'd had a bad experience with the family in trouble, and b)…

I had a sweet deal going with the State of Tennessee, and was terrified of doing something that would cause *Minnesota, Part 2: More Minnesotan* to happen. You betcha.

Letting that steep for about twenty seconds in silence, I opened my mouth and shouted into the black abyss that the dreamwalk had become. "SHIIIIIIIIIIIIT!"

Because hell if I wasn't about to stand on principle and cause myself a mighty headache.

A string of muted, near-whispered curses followed as I realized what I was going to have to do here. "Dammit," I finished, and it was nearly a whimper. "And things were going so well here, too."

"Things will only go well for you so long as you don't cross that line in your head," Odin said, "the one that tells you...'this is right and this is wrong.' Let yourself become imprisoned by law over right...and it costs you your soul."

"Dammit, guy who has literally gone a-viking and killed thousands," I pointed a finger at him, "you're getting away with turning my world upside-down because you are right in this case. But I don't have to like the fact that my moral instruction is coming from you, he who has so much frigging blood on his hands."

"You should not take advice from one who knows by experience?" Odin looked right at me. "Who would you take advice from, then? Someone innocent as a babe? For how could they truly counsel you on the cost of blood on your conscience unless they had felt it themselves?"

"Sonofabitch," I muttered. "Fine. You win." I shook my head, and in the process, started to shake myself out of sleep. "I won't let it stand. Thanks for screwing everything up."

"It may yet work out in your favor," Odin said, his voice fading as I started to jar awake, darkness surrounding him. "If you hold to doing what is right over what is law."

I sat bolt upright in my bed, covered in a cold sweat, the first light of dawn bleeding in through the blinds. "I don't think I'm walking out of this one with anything other than abject disaster on my hands," I said to the surprise of my dogs, who both jerked away with me. "But," and here I felt a true regret, and perhaps a hint of longing for what Odin had said, "I'd sure like to be pleasantly surprised for once."

CHAPTER FIFTY-NINE

I was out the door and on the phone before I even hit cruising altitude, cursing the fact I'd never bothered to collect Brenda or Alannah's cell phone numbers. Sure, the sheriff probably had them, but hell if I'd call and give him the courtesy of a heads up that I was coming in hot to (possibly, probably) interfere with his eviction proceedings.

"AA," I said as soon as she picked up and before she could even get out a greeting. "I'm heading your way."

"Oh?" she sounded slightly surprised, and maybe a touch sleepy. "To pick up your car?"

"Noooooooooot reallllllly," I said, grinding the words out. "I think this land seizure thing is wrong, and I can't just stand aside and let it happen, regardless of how aggravating and murderous I find the Greenes."

AA was quiet for a long moment. "I'm glad to hear you say that, actually."

That made me blink. "Why?"

"Because I did a little digging last night," AA said, "just from the internet, some public records searches on Fountain Run's property records and...I'm not entirely sure that the

Greenes' land was properly handled in their eminent domain case."

"Huh, what?" I was already over Crossville, the lights winking out as the first strains of daylight were appearing over the eastern horizon.

"The minutes of the meetings where the land sale was supposed to be handled? They're not online. Neither is the sale record, which is weird." She seemed to be checking something. "Fountain Run County has *all* their transaction records online, and it looks to me that they post about a month or two behind the transaction. But I can't find the record of sale for the Greenes' land even though it apparently happened over a year ago. Based on the zoning changes for the project."

"Maybe a function of the eminent domain factor?" I asked. "Because of the special nature of the sale?"

"Maybe," AA said, "but that's kinda convenient for them, isn't it? Not the Greenes, but rather Waters and the county?"

"There is a lot of money in it for Fountain Run in terms of tax revenue and the development from Waters," I said. "I just struggle with the idea that they could...y'know...?"

"Be blatantly corrupt in welcoming their new tech oligarch overlord?" AA asked. "Don't be. That town is a lot like the one I grew up in. If someone showed up with Wil Waters's money and offered to buy the place, they'd bend over forwards prostituting themselves however he wanted in order to get some of that sweet, sweet corporate cash."

I grimaced at the analogy. "Did you just channel Alannah Greene there?"

"Maybe a little. But the point stands – I look at Fountain Run, I see people willing to make a deal to claw out of their town's economic downward spiral."

"You may be right," I said, "and if so, there's a crucial component in their plan. A weak link, if you will."

I could practically hear her nod over the phone. "Without enforcement, government decisions are just words."

"That's right," I said, a little smirk appearing on my face as I saw the sheriff's station appear in the haze of the early morning, the first rays of the sun shining over the horizon. "Think I'll go have a talk with our missing link...see just how weak he is."

CHAPTER SIXTY

I swaggered into the sheriff's office, my boot heels clopping against the tile. The place was empty save for the man himself, scrolling on a computer. He looked up as I entered, raising an eyebrow and taking me in with a quick look before turning back to the screen. "Come back for your car?"

"Who told you I was leaving?" I asked, walking over the waist-high wood counter that separated their work area from the waiting area. I stair stepped up and over it casually, taking my time as I made my way toward him.

"Heard you got recalled, sent west," he said, now looking up with definite interest. "Something about Memphis needing your very particular set of talents."

"I'm sure they do," I said, not taking my eyes off him. "But a thing you should know about me by now – I don't leave a job unfinished, and I don't leave town when there's a nasty mystery still waiting to be turned over."

His face froze for a second like a record skipping, then he forced a smile that looked in no way natural. "Well, I can't say

I blame you for that. Having that murder thing hanging out there–"

"I'm not talking about Alannah Greene," I said, finally reaching his desk and just standing there. I'm a little too short to loom ominously, so I subtly added a couple inches to my height by floating off the ground. "I'm talking about someone hiring a contract killer to murder me in my motel room. I'm talking about the dirty dealings going on around here with that eviction notice you handed me last night."

"Why, that's all aboveboard," he said, and I could practically hear him starting to sweat. "County council made it official." He laughed weakly. "I mean, I'm sorry for 'em – sorry as I can be given their rather obvious predilection toward hating the law – but it's a fact that the property is no longer theirs."

"Seems to me they should have some legal recourse," I said, "seeing as they were not informed that their land was being sold. Yet for some reason you're trying to boot them off *today*." I put my knuckles on the desk and leaned toward him. "Why the hurry?"

"The land's been sold," he said, shrugging rather exaggeratedly. There was a hitch in his voice, though, as it cracked, and I could feel myself getting to him. "Development plans are proceeding."

Or maybe he just had a guilty conscience.

"Wil Waters is a wealthy man," I said. "Getting tied up in court for a few months or years must be a normal occurrence for him, something he could almost plan for. Why, I'm shocked the Sierra Club or some other organization hasn't already sued him to stop development. We're not talking about some small parcel in the middle of Knoxville, after all. This is big. Two thousand acres of prime woodland, a pristine valley."

"A little less pristine with that trailer in the middle of it,"

Sheriff Miles said with another weak chuckle that died on his lips. "I – I don't know what to tell you. I'm just doing my j–"

"No, you're not." I brought my face to within inches of his, and it was then that I realized I'd forgotten to brush my teeth this morning. How embarrassing. "You're doing something else entirely. Tell me something – your daughter that's going to Julliard? Expensive school, am I right?"

"Sh – she's on scholarship," he said, but the way he blanched told me I had my finger on a pressure point.

"Who funded it?" I asked, voice like iron.

I'd seen men crack before, but not like this. Tears welled up in his eyes, and it was as if he couldn't look away from me. "Okay...okay...please." They coursed down his cheeks. "Waters paid for it. Paid for it all, through one of his foundations."

A squeak behind me didn't even make me turn, but I heard the familiar strides of AA's heels clicking across the tile. "You get that?" I asked.

"Witnessed," she said. "Scholarship, huh? What was in it for the county board?"

"Lots of things," the sheriff said quietly. "Business loans for any that are struggling – or even those that aren't. Zero interest, forgivable. Jobs for their kids, spouses. Donations to made-up charities. A whole web of generosity for us."

"Damn," AA whispered. "And all they had to do was get the title to the property away from its true owners?"

"Through use of the eminent domain power, yeah," he said. "Just hand it over, zone it however he wanted, and the rest was...well, money in the bank." He bowed his head. "Please...please, my daughter..."

"You might want to tell her goodbye while you have a chance," I said, straightening up. It took no effort to look down on him, because he looked so...small. "I'm no prosecutor, but I think you and your county cronies are going to be going away for a while. Almost certainly until after she graduates."

"I'm cooperating," he said in a broken voice. "Ain't that worth anything?"

"Depends," AA said. "Can you give us anything useful beyond the roots of the scheme?"

"Yeah." He sniffled. "That paper I had you deliver yesterday? Wil Waters himself brought it over."

"The eviction notice?" I asked. "So he's taking control?"

The sheriff nodded his gray head. "Told me I didn't need to bother showing up for the removal, that he'd take care of everything. Hired some folks from out of town that specialized in these sort of...situations. Far as I know..." he chewed his lip. "...they're already there, setting up and getting ready to do...whatever they're gonna do."

AA and I exchanged a look. "What does that even mean?" she asked.

"If I had to guess?" My mind was racing. "Mercenaries. Quick on the trigger and slow on the mercy. Cleans the whole problem right up in no time at all. Sanctify and sanitize."

Her eyes widened. "You're kidding, right? This is the United States, not some third world country. You can't get away with that kind of thing here."

"Something I've learned," I said, giving the sheriff one last look on the way out the door. "The idea we live in a civilized society is a fiction we comfort ourselves with. Because you can get away with almost anything if you've got the money and others are willing to look away." We left him crying silently, contemplating his future.

CHAPTER SIXTY-ONE

"So what do we do?" AA asked as we hit the parking lot. "I mean, if what you're saying is right, and Waters is sending in professional killers to take out the Greenes?"

That was a good question, and one I was asking myself as my breath fogged in the light of the morning sun. "I hit the weapons locker in the back of my vehicle for some choice armaments and fly ahead, you follow behind in the Explorer."

"Why don't we just go together, now?" AA asked as I unlocked the back of my vehicle and sprung the weapons locker open with a fast-dial of the electronic keypad.

It popped open, and AA's eyes widened as she took in my beautiful armament.

"While you're gawking, the answer is 'because the enemy is already on site and I feel like the Greenes deserve a warning,'" I said, grabbing the AR out of the locker along with the black kevlar vest. I put it on, tightening it around me. It read TBI and POLICE in bold letters across front and back. Slinging my AR-15 over one shoulder and following with my custom-modded Mossberg shotgun over the other, I finished by strapping extra mag pouches on my MOLLE webbing and a belt with shotgun shells around my waist.

AA watched, eyeing the other weapons in the locker. "Mind if I borrow that rifle?" She pointed at my FN SCAR 20S, the sniping wonder the TBI had given me.

"Not sure how much use I'll have for something that long range in the depths of the woods," I said, working to snug a loose first aid kit to my back. I also strapped a Gerber survival knife to my upper thigh. "Knock yourself out."

"It's only a .308, right?" AA asked, picking it up and checking the chamber. There was a round in, of course. She put it to her shoulder, pointing it in a safe direction as she looked through the scope. "This won't knock me out."

"See you at the party," I said, tossing her the keys as I slipped a couple extra mag pockets for my pistol on my belt and jetted into the air. I heard her run for the car as I shot into the sky, turning already toward the lonely stretch of woods where the Greenes – and trouble – waited.

CHAPTER SIXTY-TWO

I didn't intend to do a close flyby of the construction site, but it was in my way as I headed for the Greenes' trailer home. I could have veered around the desolate strip of dirt road and gravel parking lots with all the heavy machinery, but I didn't.

Whoops.

The first clue I'd screwed up in my flight plan was the series of SUVs and vans all strewn in a line, their direction a map of their intent: forward, not sideways, all pointed toward the forest. They were grouped in formations, squads of men in camo, fireteam size, weapons on clear display.

And when I got close...they opened fire.

The rounds hissed over my head and I upped the speed, catching a stray round at my right elbow. A small graze, but it stung like a big, nasty bee. The full-auto chatter of their weapons told me they had more than just your average, civilian ARs at their disposal.

They had big guns. M249 SAWs (Squad Automatic Weapon), and M2 Browning machine guns. The kind that only the military was really allowed to have, in spite of the party line about weapons of war being in civilian hands in the US.

And they poured the fire on at me. I dove for the deck and hit the afterburners, making the tree line and cracking out a sonic boom as I did so. I thought I caught a glimpse of Wil Waters watching me as I disappeared over the fields of green boughs.

Cranking down the speed once I was clear of the free-fire zone, I skimmed the treetops, listening to the crack of the weapons still going in the distance. Maybe they thought there was still a chance to bring me down. Maybe they were being overcautious.

Either way, I went for my phone, figuring I'd call AA and warn her off; there was no point in sending her into an army with that kind of weaponry.

No sooner had I gotten it in my hand than a tree limb reached up and thrust itself squarely in my path. It smacked me firmly across the face and something cracked, either in me, in it, or both.

I spun out, my body flaring in a wide circle like a helicopter that lost its propeller control. I slammed sideways into a tree and felt all the ribs on my left side break like a candy cane under a hammer blow. I bounced sideways and caught another branch on my right arm that crushed my humerus and sent a wave of pain followed by numbness all the way to my hand.

My landing was not the sort you walk away from, even as a metahuman. It broke things, things I needed in order to walk, in order to have a functioning brain. Blood rolled into my eyes in a steady flow, and my left hip came so hard out of its joint that I couldn't tell whether the ball had shattered or the joint had. Either way, my leg bent in a way that shouldn't have been possible for anything other than a Play-Doh figure.

I rolled to a stop, covered in dead leaves and dirt, blood

and earth filling my nostrils, the pain present but at some remove...as was the world. For I was no longer in it, and death was no longer my profession but rather my fate...

...And the darkness started to close in my helpless body as I faded into oblivion, unable to muster even enough of a thought to cry *Wolfe!* and save myself.

CHAPTER SIXTY-THREE

"...The hell are you doing?"

The angry words stirred me into consciousness. Blood filled my mouth and I gagged it out in a sputter. Slick and warm, it fell down my cheek and my chin, like spittle but with a thicker consistency and metallic smell.

"You damned near killed her," came a second voice. "I'm trying to not tack on a murder charge." A moment's hesitation, and then, "Again."

"Oh, now you want to save her?" came the first voice again. Older. Angrier, maybe. "Look at how she's armed. We're going to have to kill her. This is a reprieve. A stay of execution."

Light began to enter my eyes, pain began to recede from my body – after flooding back in for a brief moment that made me gasp – and a thin shadow hovered over me, looking down disapproving, a hand on my cheek. She pulled it away just then, and the pain came back in full force.

"Damn, that shit burns," Alannah Greene said, falling back on her haunches as she dragged her hand off my cheek. "That what an STD feels like?"

"Don't know, never had one," Brenda said sourly, watching me from farther back. She made a motion with her hand, and strong roots reached from the earth and bound me tight around the arms and legs. I felt a rock stabbing me in the kidney, as if trying to remind me I was alive, if only barely.

"Wolfe," I whispered, and the pain started again to recede. Within a few seconds, I managed a groan that got the attention of both of them. "Gah. You two really do have...the worst welcoming parties."

"Because you ain't welcome," Brenda said.

"What are you even doing here?" Alannah said, looking pale after her lifesaving measures. She watched me carefully, too, but with none of the murderous malice present at our first encounter. "I thought you said goodbye?"

"You've got some nasty mercenaries coming for you," I said, squinting against the blood in my eye. I tried to conjure some water with my Scott Byerly power, but it squirted out of my bound hands, wetting nothing but the earth, so I stopped. "Turns out Wil Waters bribed everybody in this town's government to seize your land. There's some arrests coming, but unfortunately he's moving rather hastily to wipe you out. Figured I'd help save your lives before I go start bagging all the bad guys."

"By 'bagging' you mean slutting with, right?" Alannah gave me a toothy grin. "You ho."

"I'm here to help you," I said with a sigh. I rattled against the greenery that had me affixed to the ground, my own weapons pinching against my arms where they were pinned between me and the earth. "You know...if you want that sort of thing."

Brenda was looking at me suspiciously. "Why would you help us? You got nothing but disdain for us, from the way we dress to our trailer house."

I blinked at that. "Have you seen the way I dress? You

think I'm judging you for your attire?" I looked at each in turn. "Lady, I have no shoes that don't include a steel toe. Most of my wardrobe is T-shirts. A fashionista I am not. And as to your house..." I tried to look around, but was swallowed by the small indentation in the earth where I lay, quite against my will. "Well, I've stayed in worse places. I don't know who you think I am, but if I'm judging you for anything, it's whacking me out of the sky with a tree branch when I was coming to help you."

"You're really gonna help us against those guys?" Alannah asked.

"Shush," Brenda said. "Who you even talking about? Who's coming for us? That sheriff?"

"Nope, he folded like he had a spine made of wet cardboard," I said. "Turns out Waters – our bad guy in this equation – told him to steer clear of this place this morning. Had his own people coming in to evict you. From the planet. I saw 'em on the way in. You may have heard how they greeted me."

"That's what that gunfire was," Alannah said, looking at her mom with something similar to hope.

"Maybe," Brenda allowed, narrowed eyes considering me.

"Momma, come on," Alannah said. "I know you can feel 'em. Coming into the woods right now–"

Brenda raised her eyes in alarm toward Alannah. "You can feel that?"

Alannah nodded. "In the crunch of the dead leaves against the earth, carried through the roots." Her eyes had a far-off quality. "Half a hundred footfalls, marching in."

Brenda stared at her. "I can't feel that far out...but I believe you." She looked right at me. "They armed, then?"

"With big guns," I said "Military weapons. And since they showed zero reticence at firing 'em off at me, flying overhead..." I left that one to her imagination.

She got there quick. "They're not coming to ask us politely."

"Fewer complications," I said.

"That's murder," Alannah said, blinking. "I mean...I know I'm the last person to maybe lecture on that, but...they're gonna straight up kill us?"

"I believe so," I said.

"Over an office park?" Brenda asked, disgust turning up her thick lips.

"Over something," I said. "I feel there's more going on here than we've unearthed thus far. But I figure saving you was more important than digging for the last grains of truth right now, y'know?"

The bonds around my hands and feet slackened. "You're really gonna help us, then?" Brenda asked.

"If you want," I said.

"Uh, I want," Alannah said, raising a hand. "I'm all for killing these bastards, but I wouldn't say no to some help given how many there are."

"Why would you help us?" Brenda asked, easing a little closer to me, casting those suspicious eyes upon me.

"Because I talked to Hades, to Persephone," I said, just omitting Odin entirely, "...and they reminded me of something." I looked from Brenda to Alannah. "I don't have much in the way of family left, so...I figured I'd give you the benefit of the doubt on the whole 'killing me' thing. You're up to two strikes, though, so probably don't push it again." I flexed my wrists, and ice ran through the roots against my flesh, shattering them as I sat up.

Brenda stared at me for a second, taking in the fact I hadn't been at her mercy, not really, for a while. Finally, she nodded. "All right, then. What do we do?"

"Thought you'd never ask," I said, getting to my feet and unslinging my AR. I checked the barrel; it was surprisingly undamaged. A similar glance at my shotgun found the same, and I chucked it at her. She caught it just fine, and like someone who knew exactly what to do with it. "I say we have a family reunion, right here and now...and anyone that ain't family..." I just grinned.

Brenda slammed the shotgun into a beefy hand. "...we know what to do with uninvited guests around here."

Alannah couldn't contain herself anymore. "Hell yeah! Let's skin 'em all alive." We both looked at her maybe a little different than she expected, because she blushed, then shrugged. "Or just kill 'em. We could just kill 'em, I guess."

CHAPTER SIXTY-FOUR

We had a solid half hour to prepare before the first mercenary reached us, and even with all three of us working full tilt-meta the whole time, we still could have used hours more.

"First one's a hundred yards out," Alannah announced, ending the frenzied pace of preparation we'd engaged in. Dirt had flown everywhere. Between me using a shovel and the two of them moving tree roots, we'd created a trench some fifty yards long stretching in front of the trailer, all the way to the creek in the distance.

A front line, some four feet deep. Just high enough I could stick my head over the top and fire with most of my body under cover.

"Any of you seen my phone?" I asked, patting myself down for the tenth time as I discarded the old, worn shovel I'd been using to furiously dig between the tree root-dug entrenchments. "Think I lost it in the crash."

A shrug from Brenda dashed my hopes for finding it in a jiffy. "Guess we'll just have to hope AA doesn't come blundering into the middle of the battlefield to get herself killed," I said.

"Probably ought to lower our voices until the shooting starts," Brenda said, hopping into the trench and tossing my shotgun back to me.

"Uh, aren't you gonna need that?" I asked.

She frowned at it for a second, then shook her head. "I got one of my own." Alannah appeared just then and tossed it to her, a decent one with wood furniture and a long barrel. A second later Brenda caught a box of ammo, then another. "You gettin' the rifle?"

"Gettin' both of them," Alannah said, and disappeared back toward the trailer.

I glanced – just glanced – at Brenda. "What?" she asked. "What do you think we eat out here? Ain't no supermarket close at hand, and I wouldn't waste the money anyhow when there's deer and turkey and squirrels aplenty."

"Didn't say anything." I looked down at my weapon.

"You ain't one of them vegans, are you?" Brenda looked me over. "I mean, I wouldn't guess so by your physique, but–"

"No, I'm not," I said, checking the chamber of my AR. "I just...don't kill animals, that's all."

"You don't kill animals *yourself*, you mean," Brenda said with a sly grin. "Because if you eat meat, you're killing animals. You're just outsourcing the murder, that's all."

"I have no problems with killing, clearly," I said, letting the bolt slap back into place.

"Clearly." Alannah jumped back into the trench next to me, arms full with three long guns. Another shotgun similar to Brenda's, and two rifles. I couldn't tell the caliber, but they didn't look like piddly .22's. She stood the shotgun up against the side of the trench, then said to her mother, "You want the .243 or the .270?"

"Don't rightly care," Brenda said, propping up her own shotgun against the trench wall but hanging onto the shell box. She filled her windbreaker's pockets with spare shells as she waited.

Alannah tossed one of the rifles to her, then pulled a big box of ammo out of her pocket and tossed that, too. It jangled like keys, and I could tell by the sound it wasn't full.

Brenda must have read my expression, because she smiled. "We don't miss much, so this ought to be enough."

"Think you mean *I* don't miss much," Alannah said, sliding back the bolt on her rifle. It was scoped, a simple bolt action hunting rifle. She pushed down the shells within and quick-loaded two more rounds before apparently satisfying herself she was full up. Then she racked the bolt forward and put the sling over her shoulder, raising it up to rest on the ground in front of the trench. Squinting through the scope, she scanned the field of battle. "I can feel 'em coming."

"Long as you can't feel their bullets yet," Brenda said. She, too, had her eye to her scope and was looking ahead. "Reckon they'll hit our first surprise pretty quick here."

I so badly wished I could fly up and scout, see for myself the action that was happening. But that'd have been foolish, exposing me to the same volumes of enemy fire I'd caught on the way in. Instead I waited, my AR-15 in hand, the 3x magnifier snapped in front of the holographic sight, a red dot signifying where my bullets would impact when I stroked the trigger.

My field of vision was surprisingly good. It felt a little like the shrubs and low-to-the-ground foliage had pulled back, and I could hear rustling in the distance as the mercenary team hacked their way through the thick, unspoiled woods that filled this area. For a moment I had a vision of what this region must have been like before the settlers came in and cut roads into the landscape and cleared fields for farms and then towns and cities. Wild, unspoiled.

And, as I heard the first distinct mercenary footfall find a pit in the distance, murderous.

"Got one," Alannah said with a huge grin as a scream echoed in the valley. With their root-digging powers, they'd hollowed pits some hundred yards out along the most likely approach to our position. Another scream echoed as I heard the ground give way once more. The depth was only a few feet, but roots waited to greet – and crush – the mercenaries within. The sound of weapons fire popping off heralded a brief rush of panic, then began to subside.

"I got three of 'em," Alannah said, concentrating, like she was listening to something in the distance. Besides the screaming. Some cue I couldn't hear.

"Let's just bind 'em up tight for now," Brenda said. She jerked. "What'd you do?"

"I bound 'em up tight," Alannah said.

"You're choking 'em to death," Brenda said, and concentrated. "Don't be doing that."

"If they get out, they're going to come kill us," Alannah said, looking to me for support.

I couldn't really argue with that. "Can you keep them bound up tight, no chance of escape until we finish with their pals?"

Brenda hesitated, but that was an answer unto itself. "No. We lose concentration while we're shooting, they could get out."

I shrugged. "I can't tell you what to do, but..."

Brenda nodded, and I saw her squeeze her hand like it was on an invisible neck.

"Hey," Alannah said, looking all pissed off. "I wanted to do it!"

"You're going to have no shortage of chances," I said, peering into the forest ahead. At the edge of my vision, moving between the trunks of trees in short runs, taking advantage of the woods for cover, I saw camo-clad men in motion. "Here they come."

CHAPTER SIXTY-FIVE

"Make sure and hold your fire until you can see the whites of their eyes," I said, watching the forms of men wearing digital camo slowly break out of patterns of leaves and boughs that made up the forest ahead. The whisper and squeak and crack of a branch that came from their footfalls against dry leaves and fallen twigs were like a rising chorus.

"Yes, momma," Alannah said with withering sarcasm. "I'll be holding." She leaned in, pushing her shoulder against the buttstock of her hunting rifle, drawing slow and easy breaths.

I watched through the 3x magnifier as a man in camo slowed his pace, probably sure that he was safe behind cover. But concealment was not the same as cover, and I lifted my targeting reticle to rest just above the front plate of his plate carrier, and fired.

Bristol Harbin, the TBI armorer, had installed a little something special in my AR-15. A binary firing trigger that let my weapon fire once upon pressing the trigger, and another shot came as I let it loose back to the reset position. Every time I pulled, I shot twice.

My target took two rounds of 5.56 just below the neck, and his reaction was immediate. He wasn't knocked off his feet, but he did stagger to his knees, dropping his weapon as he stumbled forward.

A flurry of movement behind him heralded the flight of the other mercs who weren't behind cover, and a shot rang out to my right as Alannah loosed her first round, the thundering crack of the .270 splitting the air.

I shot her a glance, and she didn't look up before chambering another round and blasting away again. "Oh, look," she said. "White-ass eyes."

I took a few more potshots – catching the leg of one merc who hadn't quite gotten his thigh behind cover, and drilling a round through another's weapon, rendering his rifle (hopefully) useless – then ceased fire. I needed to wait for a target, and I suspected a return volley of suppressing fire was going to follow shortly.

It did, and boy did it light up the woods. Forty or fifty guys fired blind at us, or near enough to it as not to matter. Bullets winged overhead, and I lost all ability to hear movement and motion in the thundering crack of branches snapping from stray shots and the hiss of lead flying over my head.

"Got a group breaking off and coming left," Alannah announced, pointing toward her mother.

Brenda did not reply; she had yet to make a single shot, and was huddled with her rifle across her body. A pained look painted her broad face, but she acknowledged this detail with a nod and said, "Why don't you start whipping them boys out of cover while I deal with the flanking attack?"

"A-yup," Alannah said, then, to me, "I'll drive 'em, you rope 'em."

It took me a second to work out what she meant, and by then the first shouts of panic broke through over the flurry of bullets. I lifted my head – barely – over the trench lip, just enough to see to shoot, and realized half the gunfire had died down and the other half was pointed about thirty yards to my right.

All the mercs that had been hiding behind trees were being forced out from behind them now, branches bending low and whipping them furiously. They were finding little unguarded flesh on the armed and armored mercs but still, the military men were shouting in a babel of native languages I didn't recognize and retreating into the open spaces between the trees.

I shot them down every time they gave me a chance. I'd met a few private military contractors in my time that I could respect. Men taking contract work for the CIA, for the government, providing private security. Some of the stories they told me painted a class of warriors that had a code yet still fought for a paycheck. Admirable, even.

These guys...were not them. This was a different class than a PMC, just a straight-up mercenary. I'd encountered their like before in the employ of cartels, working for dirty corporations in the third world where maybe a village that sat on top of an oil deposit needed to be moved and someone had to do it.

My mercy for men who took jobs like this was zero, especially after they'd already shot at me. I had a feeling TBI might not appreciate my fast and loose play with the laws of the State of Tennessee, but by my reckoning they'd see a mercenary army of foreign nationals using illegal weapons trying to kill a TBI agent as a fairly clear-cut thing...probably.

Which was why I pegged these assholes in the chest, in the head, in the legs, with shot after shot, without worry or concern. Cleanup could come later. For now, I blasted clouds of pink mist into the air, watching the bullets drop, pierced through legs and sent men staggering to be finished off with a head or a neck shot, whatever I could manage. With steady hands I reloaded, dropping one mag and slamming another home before hitting the bolt catch and listening to it ram closed.

A steady cadence of gunfire came from my left and right, a dull booming roar every few seconds as Alannah and Brenda hit their stride, running their bolt action rifles faster than most humans could operate an AR-15. "I'm down to ten shots!" Alannah declared after we'd downed twenty, thirty guys. Half as many remained, I thought, but it was hard to tell because they were running in and out of cover, plagued by the relentless whip of angry tree branches of varying thicknesses. I saw one thick branch rain down on a man's head just as he was drawing a bead on us. It split his skull and sent him to the ground insensate.

"You saw us, but did you see that coming?" I heard Alannah chortle before loosing another .270 round. It skimmed a tree trunk just as a merc dodged behind it, and I heard her swear. "Sorry! I didn't mean to do that to you, baby!"

"You're apologizing to the tree?" I asked, and felt a round impact a foot or so to my left, spraying dirt at me. I quickly adjusted my aim, putting my red, glowing reticle on the throat of a merc wearing camo fatigues and wife-beater, and opened up the jugular with a double shot. He dropped his weapon and clawed at his throat before keeling over. "Where was that sense of decency when you almost curb-stomped me?"

"I didn't mean to shoot the tree," she said, then grinned.

About to respond, I stopped myself when something changed in the air. Like a shift in the wind, there was a rippling in the forest that heralded something...

...Bad.

A glare of red caught my eye slashing through the treetops some ten feet above the ground. It glowed bright and moved fast, like a flyer crashing through the canopy, but without the sound of something real in motion.

It was a beam of energy, and of a kind I was familiar with.

Eyebeams. Of the sort I possessed thanks to Amanda Gustafson.

But this was so much more than I could have summoned. It was a blast some ten feet in diameter, and it shredded and destroyed the treetops, blowing them away and scattering the leaves in a tornado of bright crimson energy. When it ceased, Alannah stood a few feet to my right, gasping, holding a hand to her chest...

...Because where the forest had stood at her command only seconds earlier, now all that remained was the trunks of trees that had been sheered of all branches and leaves, smoking like thick, burnt matchsticks, signaling the beginning of a new phase in the battle.

Metas had entered the field.

CHAPTER SIXTY-SIX

"Change up!" I shouted, searching for a target. I couldn't see the origin of the eyebeam blast that had cleared the treetops and left a hundred square yards of the woods into a sheered tableau, nothing remaining of the forest canopy save for the drifting, smoking remains of a thousand leaves.

The smell of scorched chlorophyll was an odd one and made me want to cover my nose. Visibility had gone hazy from the falling detritus of leaf and branch. Still, I could see shadows moving in the haze, and I picked out a target. Hoping it wasn't AA coming through the enemy lines, I opened fire.

It wasn't.

But the bullets didn't make the normal wet smack as they carved through flesh. Instead, the sound was a *spanging* noise, as though they'd encountered metal and ricocheted off.

From the smoke I saw a shadowed figure emerging. Shaped different than a human, it almost looked like a teardrop walking out of the haze. Black texture like snakeskin rippled as I fired, bullets impacting across it and bouncing off as I walked my shots up the thing.

"What is that?" Brenda asked, firing a round into it with just as little luck as I experienced.

I stared, squinting, and the realization came to me.

"It's hair," I said, lowering my aim, trying to find feet below. "A shield of hair. It's a Medusa."

"And you say my hair's oily," Alannah said to her mom. She fired a round, too, but it did nothing against the solid shield of follicles.

"Because it is!" Brenda shouted back as the slippery, writhing mass kept coming toward us. "I buy you shampoo for a reason!"

"Yeah, to get out of here and leave me behind by my lonesome," Alannah muttered.

I ignored the odd rhyming between their past and my own as shots blazed through an opening in the shield of hair. A gun barrel stuck out at us, firing blind. It wasn't in great danger of hitting us – the shots landed between Alannah and me – but forced us to duck out of caution.

"How do we get through that thing?" Brenda asked.

Alannah was concentrating. "Gimme a sec."

I stared at her. "Those trees are cinders out there. You cannot be feeling anything from them."

"Yeah, they got scalped good," Alannah said, "but the roots run deep." A wicked smile crossed her face. "And all I need is a root to do some shit they won't see coming."

The ground shook slightly, jarring me forward. I caught myself on the side of the trench, staring at Alannah, who looked just as alarmed. "Wasn't me," she said quickly.

"Nor I," Brenda said, and looked up over the trench lip.

I did the same, and found more figures advancing through the mist. Not nearly as many as before, but moving swifter, mostly. A few human merc stragglers joined them, darting between the scalped trunks of the trees. The scorched leaves had almost entirely reached the ground, leaving nothing but the thin haze of smoke to obscure our view.

The source of the vibrations was obvious. A man with way too many teeth for his mouth was striding across the field, grinning, hands extended as he made zero effort to find cover. The ground pitched and yawed, the dirt walls of the trench threatening to collapse.

"That's enough of that shit," Alannah said, and she stood, rifle aimed without a rest. In spite of the jarring of the earth, she stood there like that for a second, the earth rising and falling a foot at a time beneath us before she went sprawling sideways. "I can't do it!"

"Leave it to me," I said, and lifted a few inches off the ground as I took a knee in midair. The earth moving all herky jerky didn't bother me a bit; I knelt above its most spasmodic motions, leveling my reticle on the face of the grinning earth-mover. Arrogance bled off him such that he didn't even see my rifle barrel pointing at him–

Until his head exploded in a shower of brains, and his corpse pitched over. That prompted a cascade of shouts across the field, and an increased volume of fire coming our way. One of those belt-fed machine guns had been emplaced by one of the smarter mercs, and he was pumping lead in our direction, forcing me to drop below the edge of the trench once more.

"Thanks for restoring some equilibrium," Brenda said. "Still got a couple of them flankers coming at us from my side, though."

"One thing at a time," I said, catching a breath and running through my options. Using fire or ice while blind was a bad idea. Same with my sonic voice, or magnetics. Warmind was similarly out, and I couldn't see how animal control or my weak tea eyebeams were going to do anything more effective than a 5.56 round at this point.

"You wanna go full dragon?" Alannah asked, as if reading my mind. "Be cool to see you go full dragon."

"Pretty sure I'd get chopped in half by that eyebeam guy," I said. "Or strangled by the Medusa." I glanced up over the edge and ducked back down because a round impacted a few inches from my head, sending a piece of gravel skimming across my scalp and drawing a little blood, which I quickly staunched with my Wolfe healing. "We need to thin their numbers some more or they're going to plow over us in the next couple minutes."

"That Medusa's coming up on us," Brenda said, nodding toward me. "Slow and steady, she means to win the race."

"When she jumps down in the trench, I'll take care of her," I said, because I already had a plan.

"Down to my last seven rifle rounds," Alannah announced. "Then it's shotgun time, I suppose."

"Like Christmas, it'll be here before you know it," I said, trying to remember how many rounds I had before needing a mag change. It wasn't many, so I ejected and replaced it with a fresh one, pocketing the near empty behind one of my full mags in one of my pouches. Probably a soldierly no-no, but I wasn't a soldier and I might need it later, given the limits of my ammo supply.

Alannah popped her head up and fired twice, and between the booms I heard the bullets bouncing off something solid and unyielding, and I knew the Medusa was closing in fast. A couple of shots rang out very nearby, and I ducked, preparing myself. If I could place a couple rounds in the Medusa's feet before they got over the trench lip...

I didn't even get a chance to make that shot, though. The hum of something obnoxiously loud seared my ears, then my eyes, as the space a mere six inches from my face dissolved in a burst of light and crackling energy.

The eye beam.

It cut into the space before me, bisecting the trench all the way through, like a train was suddenly appearing out of a tunnel to my left and burning straight through to my right...

And when it cut out a moment later, the whining scream of the energy dispersing into the sound of ordinary gunshots rattling around us...

...Alannah Greene was gone as if she'd never even existed.

CHAPTER SIXTY-SEVEN

Brenda let out a howl of inarticulate rage that chilled my bones and rose to her feet, throwing herself open to gunfire, head and shoulders sticking out of the top of the trench. She fired her .243 almost from the hip, letting it roar along with her screams, firing ineffectually at some unseen assailant until a splash of blood burst out of her shoulder and she dropped, rifle clattering out of her hands.

"Damn you!" she howled, sprawled against the side of the trench, shoulder pumping blood out in bursts that corresponded with the beating of her heart. A little pond of crimson was already forming beneath her, staining her jeans as she lay there, a pained look on her broad face.

"You all right?" I asked, starting to move toward her.

Didn't get a chance to finish the thought. Or the move.

A raven-colored teardrop the size of a human dropped into the trench at the intersection that had formed where the eyebeam had gouged a perpendicular line into the earth. It writhed and undulated, like an ocean of black sliding across the ground. Amused eyes watched me between the gaps. A swirl in the hair produced a motion, and I knew what was about to follow.

Hair like a sword, coming to carve my heart out.

"Lemme stop you right there, Locks of Hate," I said, and thrust out a hand that shoved hard against the shield of hair, thinking of Brianna Glover all the way. "Here, have a cold rinse." I blasted her with ice, a hard, flurrying storm raining forth from my palm and sending the Medusa back a step.

A step was not enough, though, and after a solid three seconds I heard the click of the Medusa trying their gun. It piffed, the hammer failing to break through the ice forming on the primer. I could have sworn I heard the whole gun break internally, but it was impossible to tell from behind the veil of cold that separated us.

A hard frost had formed over the shield of hair, and I whipped my rifle butt around with metahuman force. The locks shattered like safety glass and I was left staring at a very abashed young lady who held what looked like an old, Gangsta Ingram M-10 and was furiously pulling the trigger with no results.

"Oh mah gawd," I said, "look at this dandruff beneath your hair!" Then I shot her in the face. Twice, because that's how many bullets came out when I pulled the trigger. "Oops, I guess that was just you."

I watched her drop, then took a quick look above the trench. There was still motion out there, and I sent a few bullets down range to let them know we weren't dead, and to keep them from rushing the trench while I moved quickly to help Brenda.

"They got my daughter," she choked out as I took a knee beside her.

"We don't know that for sure," I said, glancing at the giant cross trench that the eyebeams had cut in ours. Probably we'd have enemies coming in from that direction, and soon, but seeing as my only remaining (visible) ally was down, I needed to staunch the bleeding if I wanted any hope of having someone to watch my back as this fight proceeded on its downward spiral. "She could have run in the opposite direction, toward the creek."

"She was there before the laser, and gone after," Brenda said through gritted, bloody teeth. Looked like the bullet had done some internal damage. "You tell me what that means."

"It means that wherever she is, she ain't here right now," I said, and grabbed Brenda's hand, shoving it against the bloody wound. "Hold pressure here, okay? And if you feel like helping me out by pumping a round or twelve into anyone that tries to get behind me, that'd be great."

"I'm checking out here," she said woozy from the blood loss. "Don't know how much use I'll be."

"A lot, I dearly hope," I said, as a rifle barrel emerged over the edge of the trench, pointed toward my previous position. I brought up my own, waiting as the owner's head appeared at the edge. I pumped a double shot into it and watched the merc tip over into the trench, boneless and planting himself exploded-skull-first into the ground. "I'm gonna need some help to finish this off without, y'know...dying."

"You look like you're doing okay," Brenda said, but then she snapped to, lifting her rifle with her uninjured arm and blasting a round squarely into the throat of an oncoming mercenary. He made the most sickening guttural noises in his quest not to choke to death on his own blood, then fell on the edge of the trench, boots hanging over and twitching madly as he went through the throes of expiration. "Heads up," she said weakly, dropping her weapon and reaching for her shotgun, which was knocked over about five feet away. "Gimme that, will you?"

I fetched it for her, keeping low beneath the edge of the trench. A machine gun was still thundering away, sweeping the air above us sporadically, raking from one end of the trench to the other. It was meant to keep my head down, to keep me from returning fire on them, and it would work because I probably couldn't survive a bullet to the brain.

Which meant I was going to have to deal with whatever came my way right here in the trench...with absolutely no warning.

CHAPTER SIXTY-EIGHT

"Ideas, ideas," I muttered to myself, scanning the lip of the trench with my weapon. The blue sky was slightly hazy above, an artifact of the powerful eyebeam blast churning up scorched trees, and now dirt from the cut the shooter had just carved in the earth.

I was outnumbered and my allies were in short supply. Alannah was gone, maybe – probably – dead, and Brenda was bleeding out with no one to heal her. Another merc popped his weapon over the edge of the trench and fired down blind.

With careful aim, I blasted his hand, sending two fingers flying off and making him scream. He lifted his head, mouth open wide, and I put two bullets into his cramhole, causing him to slump forward, dead.

Overhead two different machine guns raked past, concentrating their fire in a thirty-foot span to either side of me. The gunners had dialed in well on my position, and getting out of this trench was becoming increasingly improbable. Alive, at least.

"Here's an idea," Brenda said, words starting to slur, "you go kill 'em all, and I'll wait for you here."

"Brilliant," I said, trying to decide if the moment had come to swap out my AR-15 for my Mossberg shotgun. Yeah. Yeah, it was, and I let the AR down gently, slinging it back behind me as I took up the shotgun and did a quick chamber check. A round of double ought buck was waiting to be unleashed, which meant a slug was probably queued up to follow. A devastating combo, those two; a huge, angry wad of leaden pellets followed by a giant ball bearing. Perfect for blasting a head off and then...uh...shooting through the empty space remaining, really.

Whatever. I held the stock against my shoulder, hand tight to the pistol grip. Movement at my eleven o'clock coincided with Brenda murmuring, "Look out!"

I swung the barrel around and fired at the neck of a merc in body-armor. Some of the buckshot caught the upper edge of his armor plate carrier.

Most...did not.

He was toddling on unsteady legs, his jaw hanging loose, when I finished him with the slug. It made a hell of a mess and sent him over backward, boots dangling over the edge of the trench.

"You're a fine one to be all bent out of shape at Alannah about killing," Brenda said. "Look at what you're doing."

"I don't object to killing," I said, bringing my gun around and popping the top off another mercenary. The buckshot caught him just beneath his helmet and sent that sucker flying off, along with a significant geyser of red. "It's the target I'm particular about. When it's me, I don't like it. When it's guys like this?" I fired again, hitting a merc who was trying to sneak up on my left, just outside the streams of machine gun fire. My shot sent him tumbling into the trench, dead. "Knock yourself out, I say."

"I got another idea for you, then," Brenda said, looking like she was about to finally pass out. "You can't keep hoping you're gonna kill 'em all when they pop their dumb heads up. They're gonna get smart and bum rush you sooner or later."

"I'm getting that feeling, yes," I said, trying to think how I could counteract that. Back in the day, when I was part of a burgeoning government agency, fighting a war against Sovereign, I'd had a drone operator on my side, able to give me some insight into trouble when it was coming my way.

That was a long time ago, though, having an eye in the sky. Would have been nice right about now, I thought, having someone watching overhead–

"Sonofa," I muttered as an idea presently hit me.

Drones weren't the only eyes in the sky.

"Hey," I shouted, channeling my animal-talking power, "anybody up there? Birds, I mean?"

"The hell are you doing?" Brenda asked, looking at me like I'd lost my damned mind. "Squeaking and squawking like a parakeet? You lost your damned mind?"

"Anybody?" I shouted again, hoping for some brave little bird to be sitting nearby, able to just give me a little heads up over the chatter of machine gun fire.

What I got instead...was a very different animal noise.

A bear roared and was in the trench before I could swing my shotgun around. He clamped his jaw down on my arm, on the barrel, and I heard metal give way as it sheared off.

"You're not a bird!" I shouted, punching the bear in the face.

It made a distinctly human noise as it let loose of my arm, blood dripping down its lips. If it was possible for a bear to smile, this one was. Then it spat, and the first ten inches of my shotgun clanked at my feet. The bear came at me again, and I knew this was no ordinary animal.

I barely got my arm up in time to absorb the blow. The weight of the bear pitched me back, and sharp teeth tore into my arm, breaking bones and dislocating joints. Something gave behind me as I hit the ground hard, my AR not exactly cushioning my fall as it rammed into my spine and lower back.

The remains of my shotgun were still clutched in my left hand, and I rammed the severed barrel between the bear's teeth, which were being held just barely open by my arm stuck in its mouth. With the damage it had taken, all I had was a hope it would still work. "I'd say 'bite me,' but you already have."

That bear's eyes got wide and started to shift into human ones as I pulled the trigger. It didn't stop a metric ton of buckshot from blasting out, though the receiver split in my hand from the partial barrel obstruction. It blew up, taking three of my fingers with it.

But it also took most of the top of the bear-human's skull, killing him as he was shifting. He finished his transition back to human, and a naked one at that, and I threw his lifeless corpse off of me as I triggered my Wolfe powers to heal.

"I honestly thought for second I was hallucinating," Brenda said slowly, still propped against the wall of the trench. The blood had completely soaked her shirt. "A bear jumping down in here right then. But now I see…he was a man." She turned up her nose at the corpse. "Not much of one, though."

"You're noticing *that* right now?" I asked through gritted teeth as new bones pushed forth out of my wounded handed, and tissues and muscle and skin latticed its way back into the form of fingers, pasty and new. I really ought to make videos of this and sell them to science teachers or something. Or make the sickest OnlyFans of all time, I dunno.

"I'm dying, it focuses the mind on the shit you miss," Brenda said, coughing up blood.

I kicked aside the remains of my shotgun. Machine gun bullets continued to sweep overhead, forcing me to keep my head down. Sliding my rifle off my back, I gave it a quick look.

The barrel tilted off noticeably at a nearly forty-five-degree angle from the receiver. Trying to fire it would probably result in an explosion in my face. I swore under my breath, casting it aside. "Bristol Harbin is going to kill me for effing up his weapons."

"He's going to have some competition for that," Brenda said, raising her fingers to point.

I spun around in time to see a hugely swole Hercules come around the corner of the burned-out trench. His eyes alighted on mine and his grin became feral. He was big enough that I knew from experience he wasn't firing on all cylinders.

He didn't need to be, though. My hand was not yet fully formed, and the teeth marks from my right arm were still ironing themselves out of my forearm.

Didn't matter, though. I pulled my pistol and shot him once, twice, three times–

"A lady," he said, ignoring the hollow points ripping through his ginormous chest and came charging at me, the bullets not doing a thing to slow him down.

CHAPTER SIXTY-NINE

Bullets did nothing to the Hercules coming at me. He was over six feet tall, seemed to be almost again as wide, and the glint of pure malice in his eyes told me that he had plans for when he got his hands on me, and none of them were good.

I fired twice more as he got closer, and little spots of red appeared around his muscled chest, like pinpricks on a normal person, telling me that this strategy was worse than useless.

Raising my hand to fire at his face, I got there too late. He swept a hand around and knocked the gun right out of mine as if batting away a rolled-up newspaper.

I spun and kicked, landing a solid blow on his chest that did...absolutely nothing.

By then...he'd snatched me up like he was picking up a burrito, then grabbed me in a bear hug that left only my recently-healed hand free.

"Girlllllllll," he growled, more animal at this point than the bear I'd just tangled with. He tightened his grip around my ribcage, and I felt five, six of them pop in that second.

They bit into my side like teeth, fiery teeth finding every nerve.

"Use...your...words...big...guy," I said, and channeled the spirit of Aleksandr Gavrikov.

My right arm, trapped in his squeeze, burst into flame, bright and hot, searing his wrist and filling the air with a barbecue smell. My left also burst into flames, but it was waving and free, like a cell phone light at a concert, and I reached back with it, ramming it toward his face with fingers extended–

My fist slid into his face like it was Jello, and he screamed for a few seconds and then stopped as his mouth dissolved into scorched meat.

He dropped me, new face-hole smoking like it was fresh off the grill, and I landed next to Brenda, who was slumped over, finally unconscious but still breathing – barely.

"Shit," I said, but it sounded like thunder in a sudden silence.

Because the noise of the machine guns had stopped.

I crouched, my hand smoking, my gun nowhere in sight. Brenda's shotgun was just over there, though, and I started to reach for it when laughter split the hair, cruel and loud, rattling my bones.

A face that appeared to be the size of the Statue of Liberty's appeared over my trench, leering down at me. As large as it was, it took me a moment to process what I was seeing.

An Atlas-type meta, a human grown to massive proportions. Though the trench obscured it, I felt sure a body to match that huge face waited just outside my vision.

A body that probably looked different than when last I'd seen it, because the face it was attached to had the slightly swole look of a Hercules.

Wil Waters was huge, and his face was hovering over me, looking down on me in my trench.

And as I stared at him, contemplating just turning to fire and blazing into his eyehole, his face burst into a blue, superheated plasma.

"Someone took all their serums," I said, trying not to gulp in the face of what was – no shit – the direst threat I'd faced in a long time.

He didn't answer...except to laugh in the way of a man who was sure he'd already won.

CHAPTER SEVENTY

"Do you get it now?" Waters asked, and his eyes glowed with a red tinge. No figment of my imagination, it was instead that massive eyebeam that had scorched the treetops and cut the new trench into ours. He let the light fade, still guffawing at my miniature discomfiture, his face glowing blue with swirling, white-hot plasma. The heat coming off him was intense, if localized, and I felt a little like I had been left out in the sun too long.

"You're the big man on this future campus, I guess." I brushed myself off and got to my knees, afraid to stick my head up. Yes, I was in danger of being vaporized by his eyes, but I was still worried about getting my head shot off by the machine guns triangulated on my position.

His eye twinkled again, this time nothing to do with the energy beam. "It was never going to be a campus."

"Oh, really?" I stared up at him. "All that trouble, all that corruption, my murder...and you don't actually want it for a corporate HQ?"

"Like I'd build my HQ out in this shithole jerkwater,"

Waters scoffed. "That was just the excuse to get things rolling."

I brushed off my sleeve, making a show of it to keep him talking. "And then, after you had things going, a road in, you were going to...what? Call it good?" I stared up at him. "Was the point the murder and mayhem and bribery?"

"No," he said, laughing as though I'd just told him the best joke of all time. "The point is the rare earth minerals under your feet. A couple billion dollars' worth, to be precise. But mining's not so easy in the US these days. Regulatory hoops to jump through, state, federal, and local. Now, I can leap most of them – with a little help – but this place – even a shit county like this – was not going to fall over themselves approving a mine. Certainly not enough to take it away from the current owners." He sneered down at Brenda, unconscious a few feet away from me. "Even as worthless as they are."

"You really are the big man, aren't you?" I said. "We little people...you barely notice us at all. Which makes me question why, if you were going to bribe everyone in the county council, you couldn't just square with them about the mine?"

"Because they needed a story they could tell themselves about why this is the virtuous thing to do," Waters said. "And me saying, 'It's for processors and car batteries that will forge the future'? Wouldn't play, even here. So instead: a corporate headquarters. Jobs. Economic relief." His voice was high and mocking. "I know the call of their hearts, and saving the world doesn't factor in. So I made them the heroes of their own story, and bribed them to do it. What a win, huh?" He sighed. "Of course, now that I've finished my evil monologue and you know the details of my evil plan–"

"I have to die, naturally," I said. "Quick question, though, first – are you just so detached from reality that you have never seen a movie in your entire life?"

He cocked his head at me, and I let him have it.

From the depths of my soul, I screamed like the damsel in distress I actually kind of was at the moment.

Oh, and I used the power of Brance Venable with it.

The plasma dancing across the surface of his face rippled as the sonic wave hit him, and he jerked his head back in pain. Blood hissed out of his enormous ear canals as it made contact with the plasma wreathing his skin. His mouth stood open, and within I could see not the black void I expected, but gum tissue, pink and moist, and I had a vision of being devoured whole, mashed up by teeth the height of me situated behind burning lips that would cook me almost to a crisp before he took the first bite.

"Oh, hell no," I whispered, and jetted into the sky.

I didn't get far, because I didn't really want to escape. I wanted to fight, to beat him, to take this so-called big man and cut him back down to appropriate size. Hopefully he didn't realize his power could render him microscopic, which carried with it a whole raft of problems I was unable to contend with at present. Him being the size of a building and burning at a hotter temperature than I could manage on my best day was trouble enough.

So, Brianna said in my head, *do we just hit him with the sonic blast until his brain turns to jelly?*

I tried again, almost experimentally, but I wasn't mere feet from his face, and the plasma currents on his face barely stirred at my effort. His ears were still steaming from the blood loss of the last try, and he squinted at me with dark eyes, then lifted his hand to swat me.

In movies, immensely enlarged characters move with a placid slowness, as if to make their movements comprehensible to the human eye. Whether it's Ant-Man or a *Pacific Rim* robot or Godzilla, giant characters on a screen don't move like a human – and certainly not like a metahuman.

Wil Waters snapped his hands together as fast as he would have if he'd been his normal height, and the wind his motion generated sent me tumbling back, his sweeping blow missing me by *inches*. I almost thought Reed had bowled me over with a full force wind blast, and when he clapped his hands together, the shock of the waves coming off it rattled my joints like a hard landing. My ears might even have started bleeding like his.

"Take her down!" Waters said, sounding like he was underwater to me. I shot sideways as I regained control of myself, and felt blood drip from my ear canals. Yep, bleeding.

I didn't realize what he meant at first, and then bullets whiffed across the small of my back as the machine guns roared to life again, cutting through the hum in my ears to inform me something very bad was happening around me.

Bullets fenced me in, coming hard from the left, and then from the right, leaving me staring into the face of a man ten times my size, consumed with a plasma heat I couldn't pierce with ice or flame.

And he grinned at me, knowing that he had me utterly in his power.

CHAPTER SEVENTY-ONE

You could rocket to the side at near-sonic speed, Brianna said. *Past the bullets–*

Maybe, I thought back, the world humming around me, death staring me in the eye. *Or maybe I catch one, go flipping out of control, and before I can recover he burns me to a crisp. Also, if I leave? Brenda's dead.*

You don't leave, Brenda's dead anyway, she said. *Just a little slower.*

Dammit.

No good choices here, Brianna said. *You die, no one ever learns the truth of what Waters has done. Discretion is the better part of valor.*

A fleeting glance at Brenda was all I allowed myself. With Alannah maybe dead, my bid to help my extended family, to do the right thing?

It had really turned to shit.

I can't run, I thought, looking death right in the face, grinning and blue and burning. Time had slowed for a few beats as I escaped into my head, but my time was now almost up, and Waters was moving, bringing his hands up to clap me into oblivion once more. *I know it sounds stupid, but it's against everything I tried to do here – for family and decency and all that.*

Brianna sighed. *If anyone understands fighting for family well past the time you should quit...I do. It's been an honor and all that.*

Thanks, I said, and prepared to leave this small oasis of time and thought, where reality would intrude momentarily and I would be smited by an angry, burning god among men. *Thanks for keeping me company in my mind–*

My mind.

Yes, Brianna said. *Your mind. What about – oh.*

I couldn't touch this guy with a single physical power I had. I stared into those eyes, that glowing face. Even turning into a huge, flaming dragon I'd get burned through in seconds.

But I didn't just have physical powers, did I?

Reality snapped back to normal speed, and Wil Waters raised his hands with lightning quickness, preparing to clap them together once more with me as the (rather meager) meat to his Sienna sandwich.

But I thought of Bjorn Odin-son, and stared into the dark, wicked eyes of Waters–

And watched him jerk away in pain.

It was called the Warmind by Bjorn, and having been on the receiving end of it, I knew it hurt like hell – for a few seconds, at least. But Reed had told me his experience with it, fresh from Odin, and it had potential for more, for the manipulation of reality, for the instilling of pure terror.

I needed a little terror on my side right then. Needed it bad.

Waters's head snapped back like he'd been punched by someone his own size, and I knew this was the only opening I was going to get. I started to dart down, figuring I'd grab Brenda, do that strategic retreat we'd planned–

The first .50 cal machine round clipped me in the left

thigh when I was still ten feet off the ground. Another got my knee, and one more took off my foot as I pinwheeled into the earth some ten feet shy of the trench, crashing into the ground. It was not a gentle landing, but it was lighter than almost any I'd experienced in the last few days, and if I hadn't just had my left leg chewed up by a flotilla of bullets, I would have been able to walk it off.

Not so, now. I bled out in the dirt, hot sprays of crimson saucing the ground as the machine gun operator walked his aim down until a steady stream of rounds the size of my middle finger was churning through the air six inches above my nose.

Wil Waters roared into the mountain air and turned his angry eyes to me as I lay there, bleeding, imprisoned by his machine gunners, waiting for him to deliver the finishing blow.

CHAPTER SEVENTY-TWO

The bullets humming over my nose stopped after a discordant shot in the middle of the chattering, angry machine gun. It was the punctuation at the end of a sentence of gunfire, the end, period, and with it, a cessation of hostilities.

But Wil Waters didn't stop being hostile, and he didn't look up from his sole, total focus:

Destroying me.

Half-missing a left leg, I had no time to quibble about his priorities. Nor any to worry about why the gunfire stopped, or growing my leg back to its usual, stubby imperfection.

Jet the eff out of here, Brianna said.

I did.

Rocketing over the trench and into the air, well outside Waters's reach, I trailed the blood spraying from my femoral artery, my heart weakening with each feeble pump. It sluiced less with each beat as I contemplated the rugged face of Wolfe and his powers coursed through my veins, stopping the blood loss as I paused some hundred feet above Waters's reach.

His eyes glowed, and I knew trouble was coming my way. A blast of violent red burst forth, half the diameter of a skyscraper and pushing its way toward low earth orbit with a crackle of energy and fury. If it kept going and by some chance hit the moon, I had a feeling there'd be a new crater visible to the naked eye.

"You can't stand in the way of progress, Sienna!" Waters intoned, chasing me around the sky with his eyebeams. I wondered if they could see them in Knoxville. Probably.

"Can't stand at all after you dicks shot my leg," I muttered, trying to keep one step ahead of my own death. I looped around him at subsonic speed, looking for an opening and unable to take the smart course and abandon the battlefield. For two reasons, now.

One was still Brenda, alone and bleeding in the trench.

The other was Alannah, who waved at me, rifle slung over her shoulder as she hauled ass across the scorched landscape of the battlefield, skirting between decapitated trees and hiding from the sight of the oversized Waters. I hadn't heard the chatter of the other machine gun position in a while, and I had a feeling that, too, was because of her efforts.

I flew halfway around Waters's head, and he paused, turning quickly in the opposite direction, singeing me as he brought his devastating blast around almost quicker than I could avoid it. My newly healed left leg was gone again a second later, my jeans on that leg turned from bloody, ripped, and vaguely fashionable to *gone*.

Fashion was (probably) the least of my problems at that point; lightheadedness hit me in a hard wave, and I wobbled in the sky, about to lose control before I managed to steady myself. The trauma of losing limbs might have hit me less hard, but it was still no walk in the park.

Because I didn't have a leg, you insensitive asshole. How

can I walk with one leg? God, I can't even with you right now.

Kidding. ANYWAY.

"I'll take you one piece at a time if I have to, Sienna," Waters said as I dipped low behind his back, whizzing between his legs as he turned around, and then disappearing as I flew behind a matchstick of a tree not far from where I'd last seen Alannah.

She popped her head out from about three trees away. "Whatcha doing?" she mouthed at me.

I shrugged expansively. My left leg had almost finished growing back, and I gave it a glance. "Nothing much. You?" I mouthed in return, afraid to even go meta low for fear Waters could hear us ants muttering at his ankles.

She shrugged, pointing at her rifle. "Killing dudes. Waiting for you to take out that big bastard."

"I'd love to," I said. "Got any ideas?"

"This ain't really my thing," she said. "You got nothing?"

I shook my head. "Less than nothing. No power I have can burn through that plasma shield."

Alannah gave that a moment's consideration as Waters stomped off to our left, and thankfully away from Brenda. "Maybe ask the girl who took out the other machine gunner?"

I blinked. "Other...girl?" I mouthed.

She pointed at the other end of the battlefield, and I looked.

AA was crouching in the shadow of a tree that hadn't been scalped, barely visible and looking like she'd recede into the dark the moment Waters turned her way. She caught me looking, though, and gave me a nod.

"She popped that guy with the smaller MG," Alannah said, hissing just enough to draw my attention back to her. "From across the damned field. Hell of a shot."

"Easier than bagging a squirrel, I guess." I gave AA a look.

She had my SCAR 20S clutched in her hands, but didn't have it pointed at Waters or anywhere else, really. She'd clearly come to the same conclusion I had: guns were useless in this particular fight.

I frowned, putting together a couple pieces, and looking over at AA to check something. "Or are they...?"

"What are you talking about?" Alannah whispered, just loud enough to get my attention.

Apparently it got Waters's, too, because he came stomping our way. "I hear you!" he crowed, enjoying this way too much. I guess when all your joy in life comes from figuratively conquering people in the boardroom, getting out of the office to crush your enemies the old-fashioned way has a certain appeal.

"Stand by, help if you can!" I shouted, and darted into the air at near-sonic speed. I felt the blaze of Waters's eyebeams coming after me and hoped that if they hit a satellite in orbit, it was a Chinese government one, preferably with no nuclear material onboard.

Ducking behind a cloud, I turned back to the battlefield, coming in low behind AA, who jerked in surprise as I suddenly seemed to appear behind her.

"Hey, nice shooting, I hear," I said and she just about threw my (expensive) SCAR into the air. I caught the barrel and aimed it back down, keeping it pointed safely before she could do something that would land me even more solidly on Bristol Harbin's shit list. "Can you do me a favor?"

Her face barely had time to settle down from the last panic attack I'd pulled on her before it twisted into a suspicious look. "What...did you have in mind?"

I grinned, and told her. Honestly, it felt like the least little thing I'd asked of anyone all day.

CHAPTER SEVENTY-THREE

"I'm gonna kill this old broad, Nealon!" Wil Waters shouted to the heavens, as if asking permission before putting a giant-sized foot on Brenda. I could hear him, of course, huddled as I was some hundred yards away in the shadow of the surviving trees, their boughs rustling in the chill wind.

AA was staring at me in mild disbelief, but had already agreed to what I'd asked of her. She didn't look pleased, a condition which I understood completely. Killing and maiming and destroying one's enemies was not for the faint of heart, which was why I was going to step out onto that battlefield to face the seemingly invincible Wil Waters alone.

"Don't you touch her, you prick," I said, buzzing out of cover and heading right for Waters. "I surrender."

Waters covered the ground getting to me with his same astonishing quickness, strides the length of tennis courts chewing up the distance as he moved at a trot and violated every human land speed record doing so. I stayed as still as I could, and he reached for me with much less than the slap of hands that would have dispelled my body across the landscape. The blue plasma faded around it as he reached to scoop me up.

So I let him. I let him grab me and lift me to his face like a damned doll or insect in his hand.

His laugh was bitter and his breath smelled of terrible, rancid coffee, flooding out like a noxious gas escaping a mine. "I win," he said, squeezing me tight enough that things ruptured and burst within me, almost forcing me to lose concentration.

"Yeah," I said, dripping blood out of the corner of my mouth, barely able to speak. "Sort of."

He looked at me, and his plasma-burning brow furrowed in a shadowy blue line. "What the hell is that supposed to mean?"

I coughed up blood, spraying it everywhere, choking, and it colored the bare part of his hand he'd de-plasma'd to grab me. I made a motion as if trying to speak, but nothing came out.

"You scream again, I crush you," he said in warning, and I felt his grip slacken ever-so-little.

I nodded and let the healing power of Wolfe course through me. My mind got crisper, clearer, and I knew what I had to do.

A glimpse of AA sneaking behind him across the battlefield was all the warning I got, and then the sight of something black and small as she tossed it toward me.

That newfound clarity in my mind really helped as I channeled the power of Chad Goodwin and dragged the metal object from the ground up to me, from where it had been safe into the most dangerous of territory.

"You remember when we talked before?" I asked, the object rising slowly, just a few feet from the surface of his skin. It passed his belly button, his chest, and I held it in place below his chin, readying myself, steadying myself, for what I knew had to happen next. "I realized something."

He peered at me through dark eyes. "What? That you were going to lose?"

"That you're an arrogant prick," I said, and I creeped that metal just a couple feet higher as it hovered just off his chin. "And that your mouth is not *en fuego*."

He cocked his head at me, and opened his mouth to say, "Huh?"

At which point I tripped the trigger of AA's suppressant dart gun, and it sailed right in and implanted itself in the roof of his mouth.

It was so tiny and he was so large, I worried it wouldn't work, that such a small quantity of suppressant spread out over so large a body would just...dissipate.

But it didn't do that at all.

Waters jerked in pain as part of his mouth started to shrink. It was almost comical to watch, as his head became small and his body remained large, the plasma guttering out to reveal a shocked look on his distorted face.

It spread across his body in a wave, snuffing the plasma, dousing the glow of embers as he tried his eyebeams and they failed before he could do anything about it. We seemed to rocket toward the ground and suddenly his hand exploded open, his fingers and wrist bent back as the full size and weight of my body burst free of his grip.

By the time he hit his knees he was ten feet tall; by the time he was on all fours, he was back to usual size. He pulled the dart out of his mouth and gagged. Then he clutched his hand, looking up at me in obvious pain; his wrist was clearly broken. "So...arrogant, huh?" he asked, wincing.

I hovered over him, leering down. "Little bit."

He let out a slow breath. "Like...fatally?" Gauging my reaction.

I drifted down, retrieving my cuffs from my belt. Surprisingly, they'd survived where my pants leg had not. "Could be. But not today." I clicked the handcuffs on, pulling his hands behind him. "Wil Waters, you have the right to remain silent. But then...you've said enough already to get yourself in plenty of trouble, so feel free to keep going."

CHAPTER SEVENTY-FOUR

Getting the Tennessee Bureau of Investigation mobilized and swarming the scene took a couple hours, but swarm they did, and on the whole of Fountain Run County. The sheriff was under arrest, I was informed within an hour, and so were the county council within two.

"Make sure Wil Waters gets another dose of suppressant?" I said to AA at about the four-hour mark, just as a familiar but unmarked SUV was pulling up to the entry road to the valley, where the fleet of government cars stretched for what seemed like a mile, lights all flashing and interspersed with the fleet of vans the ill-fated mercenaries had arrived in.

"Yep yep," AA said, technically supervising but in reality at just about as loose ends as I was.

Ileona Marsh stepped out of her car, sunglasses perched on her nose. She picked me out of the crowd immediately and cut toward me like a shark. Cruising up and taking in the chaos, she asked, "So...how many dead?"

I leaned into the cringe, saying, oh-so-tentatively, "A lot."

Marsh nodded slowly. "Must be, if I'm here, right?" She

cracked a smile. "Heard you unearthed a real ring of corruption."

"Yeah," I said. "You mad?"

She shrugged. "Was at first, when I thought you were just being defiant. Now that I heard the story, and that you got a whole mercenary army called down on you...less so. Why don't you tell me what happened yourself?"

I did. Good thing she was wearing sunglasses, because even beneath them I could see she was blinking like a fiend as I went through the story bit by bit.

"All this for a mine?" she asked at the end, once I'd spat it all out. "A 'dig in the ground, pull out metals' mine?"

"He mentioned something about rare earth elements," I said. "I think those are kind of expensive. Like...billions. Also..." I frowned, "...I think I read they're just about completely owned by China, so maybe not a bad play on his part."

Her eyebrows, a perfect line, rose in concert. "Billion with a b?" I nodded. "Well...I guess that's worth a little bribery and murder. Uh, to some at least."

I shook my head. "Y'know, boss, first you might be willing to date a convict if he's hot enough, now you seem to be endorsing murder if the price is right...should I be worried about you?"

"Probably," she said. "But don't worry about yourself." She glanced out at the chaotic scene before us, all the TBI agents heading into the woods, others coming back out again after a long hike to the Greenes' trailer. "Looks to me like you did the right thing here." An approving nod followed. "You're suspended pending investigation—"

"Finally? How big a body count does it take to get you guys to sit up and take notice?"

She cocked an eyebrow at me. "More than you laid out in

that parking lot, less than this. You know you get a special kind of slack because you're a meta."

"Finally, someone recognizes my downright queenliness," I said.

Marsh just shook her head. "Good work, Nealon."

"Thanks," I said, with a warm little feeling in my soul.

"And don't get too comfortable with your vacation while we're picking through the remains of this," she said, giving me a solid finger wag as she moved off, probably looking for the agent in charge of this mess. "West Tennessee is still waiting for you to give 'em a hand."

CHAPTER SEVENTY-FIVE

I caught up to AA when she came trudging out of the woods a little while later after a long break. Her braid looked like it was coming loose, and she had that tired aura about her that comes after a long day. Sure, it was barely noon, but any day when you blow someone's head off is a taxing one, and I could see in her eyes and by the slowness of her steps that a nap would not be out of order.

"You look like you're ready to sit in a quiet room for a while with the shades closed and the lights off," I said as she forced one foot in front of the other in the last dozen steps to bring her to me.

"I don't know if you know this," she said, breaths coming with irregularity, "being as you can fly, but it's a bit of a hike to the trailer and back from here. The ground's not super even, and my time on the treadmill has been curtailed of late by work, by life, and by a desire to...well, turn on my TV and veg out when I'm done for the day."

I chuckled. "Well, you made it out to the war zone when it mattered, so you can probably take your time on the trip home."

"I think I'm done at this point," she said with a sigh. "I just walked the investigators through my part in the scene, and they told me I'm free to go. I've got to show up in a couple days with my union rep to answer questions, but otherwise..." She rubbed a smudge of dirt over her eye, only spreading it further. "...I'm going to go collapse for a while."

"Drink plenty of fluids," I said with a knowing smile. I'd been on these sorts of suspensions before. They were not relaxing, because even if you knew the shooting was justified, you were always waiting on tenterhooks to see if the investigators agreed, or whether they were going to fire you and then charge you with murder. Good times. "Maybe hit that treadmill."

She shook her head. "You look so calm about this."

"I've been through this a couple hundred times or so," I said. "I wouldn't say you get used to it, but..." I shrugged. "...Maybe I'm used to it."

"Don't know if I could handle that," she said, shaking her head slowly.

"That's a real shame," I said. "Because...I'll be back. And I could use some help when I come to clean house."

She paused, cocked her head, and a slow, savage smile creased her thin lips. "Maybe when you do, pick someone whose name you remember to help you?"

I laughed. "Haha...Ashley Aylor."

Her smile twisted into pure amusement, and only a moment of pensiveness. "I suppose I could get used to AA. And...maybe the occasional shooting investigation, if necessary."

"It's necessary if you're backing me up," I said. "And I could definitely get used to having a stone cold sniper at my back. I saw that dead man with the near-missing head. Like a squirrel, huh?"

"Almost no different." Her smile faded a bit. "Almost."

"Good," I said, giving her a nod. "I can see it's going to sit with you. And that's fortunate. Because if you ever get to the point where it doesn't bother you afterward...you might be in real trouble." I started to turn to walk away.

"So it still bothers you?" she called after me.

"A little bit," I said. Because it did. I'd left a number of bodies on the field, and I didn't know any of them, or anything about them except that they'd come to kill me on Wil Waters's orders. But I'd killed them, and it'd be with me for a good, long while.

But not as much as I tried to let on to her. I'd think about them here and there for the next few days; the things I remembered. The look on the face of that Hercules as I took it off. The way that bear shifted back to a scrawny, pathetic human after I blew his head off.

I would have been lying to say that it didn't get to me at all, massacring these men the way I had. It was like a stomach ache, low and growling, like something sat wrong with me.

And then in a few days it'd clear, and I'd get right back to doing whatever it took to do the job...and survive.

Because there was no way I could if I didn't.

And that was probably something that should worry me...eventually.

CHAPTER SEVENTY-SIX

"You get your interviews out of the way?" I asked as Brenda and Alannah came trudging out of the woods. Well...not trudging, exactly, as they didn't look quite as worn as AA had. But close; Brenda was still pretty wan, though I could see the spot where her gunshot wound was crusted over, already healed.

And Alannah was looking tired from the healing, which I'd seen her administer to her mother just after I'd cuffed and planted Wil Waters facedown in the dirt to wait for backup. She'd already healed me earlier, so I imagined she was just about tapped out. She looked it, too, pale beneath the dirt, as if the color had been leached out of her by her efforts.

"I'm sick of talking to law dogs," Alannah said, and she looked not just sick, but tired of it as well. Her eyes looked ready to shut, and when they reached me her mom plopped her ass against the car. Alannah put herself right next to Brenda, leaning against her. The two of them were a perfect image of what I'd always imagined a non-dysfunctional, non-succubus mother/daughter team would look like.

"That include me, too?" I asked.

She cracked one eye open. "You gonna ask me about killing those men?"

"Do you want to talk about it?" I asked.

"Maybe later," she said, and closed her eye again.

"They gonna let us sleep in our own beds tonight?" Brenda asked, finger probing at the bloody hole in her shirt.

"I wouldn't count on it," I said. "It's a complex scene, lot of dead bodies. They'll probably be working it for a couple days. I can recommend a motel nearby if you're interested. Just don't damage the place. They're touchy about that."

"Well, I'll try not to shit in the sheets," Alannah said, "but I can't make any promises. I'm powerful tired." Her stomach let loose a mild grumble. "And hungry, too."

"Hey, Nealon?" A uniformed cop trotted over to me. "We got a couple ladies that drove up to the perimeter asking for you."

"Names?" I asked.

"Uh," he blushed, "'Penny' and 'Sigourney.' Or that's what they said."

I chuckled. "Let 'em through."

"Who the hell is that?" Brenda asked once the officer had trotted away.

"Persephone and Lethe, I think."

"Turning it into a real family matter, huh?" Brenda brushed her daughter's dirty hair away from her face. "Well...I guess it might be nice to see relations again." She gave herself a once-over. "Would have prettied myself up if I knew company was coming."

"You ready to exit your long period of social isolation?" I asked. Alannah's eye perked open again.

Brenda sighed. "I could be persuaded." She looked down at her daughter's head, resting on her, and caught her looking. "You ready to get out in the world a little?"

"Hell yes I am," Alannah said, suddenly wide awake. "You gonna let me wander about the countryside?"

"Maybe," Brenda said. "I just worry about you, that's all. You watch too much of that *Beyond Human* shitshow. I'm worried you think that's real life."

"Wait," I said, squinting at that revelation, "you're a fan of *Kat?*"

Alannah bristled. "She's elegant and graceful and all the things you'll never be."

I blinked. "Was that supposed to be an insult? Like, you think that comes as a surprise to me?"

Alannah grinned. "Told you that you feel nuthin'." She hesitated. "Well...maybe not...nuthin'. Anymore." She glanced with great significance toward the woods, and the battlefield that rested beyond the autumn-tinged trees.

A car rolled to a slow stop about twenty feet from us, and I could see my grandmother in the driver's seat and great-grandmother in the passenger seat. Persephone was the first out, and she came over to her granddaughter and great-granddaughter with quite a spring in her step. "You made it through," she said with that drawl, fussing over Brenda's bloody shirt. "I was worried when I heard from our girl here that you were in for it. Got here as quick as we could." She gave me a sidelong glance. "Guess you didn't need our help."

"It was a close thing," Brenda said, looking at me. "But...it's good to know that there's still family in this world you can count on when things get rough."

"Always," Lethe said, and to my surprise, gave her niece a hug, too. "You must be Alannah." Her, she didn't hug.

Alannah took her in with one look. "What in the *Ghostbusters 3* development hell is this?" She looked at Brenda. "This your sister?"

"Aunt," Brenda said.

Alannah looked at me. "Grandmother," I said.

"You're well-preserved," Alannah said, looking Lethe over once, real good. Then she shifted attention to Penny. "And you're great-grandma? Damn, I hope I age like y'all. All the drugs I'm gonna do in college, though, I probably won't. Probably look like Hag-atha over here, crow's feet everywhere by the time I'm twenty-one." She pointed at me.

"Hey, you'd have looked a lot worse without my help," I sniped back, smirking.

Alannah's lips twisted puckishly. "Same goes, girl."

I nodded, and the war of insults ended right there. For now.

"So..." Persephone said, still standing close to Brenda, as if unable to keep herself from hovering, "...where's Styx?"

"Dunno," Brenda said. "Haven't heard from her in a good while. Thought maybe you knew what she was up to."

Persephone shook her head slowly, sadly. "No. I haven't heard from her in a while, either."

"Well...that's worrisome," Brenda said. "Wish we knew someone that could help with missing persons." She looked very suggestively at me.

"I'll...look into it," I said, feeling very resigned to the whole thing. Why wouldn't I look? She was my great aunt, after all. "But later. Right now...I'm suspended. And starving. Anyone want to get some lunch? There's a diner back in town."

"What?" Brenda asked. "You mean, as a...family? Feels weird to say that."

Alannah didn't mince words. "I could go for some frigging pancakes right now." Note: she did not say 'frigging.'

"I could eat," Persephone said, smiling first at them, then at me. She hooked her arm in mine, and her other in Alannah's, and I could feel the pride radiating off her. "If you think they can spare you here?"

I took one last look at the scene, the police buzzing

about. "They won't miss me here," I said, and felt a slow smile creep across my lips. "Let's go."

CHAPTER SEVENTY-SEVEN

I didn't make it home until well after nightfall, and the dogs didn't bark when I came in. The TV was on upstairs, and I could hear someone moving around in the kitchen, talking softly to Cali, Jack, and Emma as I floated up the stairs.

"...no, you can't have any more treats," the soft male voice said over the sound of a news program in the background. "I already gave you each one – well, except the kitten."

Not enough, Cali barked.

If we push at him enough he'll give us more, Jack said.

"He doesn't understand you," I said, coming around the corner and just about giving my brother a heart attack. Reed jerked like I'd fired a taser at the tramp stamp area of his back, turning around at me and twitching as he started to settle down. "And you don't need any more treats."

Aw, man, Cali said, and trudged away, her wildly fuzzy head hung low. Jack followed, albeit with slightly less shame.

"You're back," I said.

"Same to you," he said, giving me a quick hug. "Chandler had a date tonight. Texted asking if I could feed the animals, and Isabella is out of town, so..." He shrugged. "Chandler said you, uh...had a little incident in East Tennessee." He cocked an eyebrow at me. "I heard there was a body count."

"Little bit," I said, trying to decide how much to sugarcoat it. "How was Atlanta?"

"Wish all our cases were that quick and easy," my brother said. My half cut-off pants caught his raised eyebrow, which raised a little further. I could feel him trying to decide how hard to press. "What happened with yours?"

"Oh, just a slightly bigger-than-usual corruption-slash-land grab conspiracy with some murder and a family reunion thrown in," I said, checking the fridge. Yes, I'd just been at a diner with my extended family for several hours, but I felt a small need to hide my face from Reed, so I looked anyway.

"Whose family reunited?"

"Mine," I said, closing the door without taking anything out. "Persephone and Lethe showed up, because a couple of the principals in the case were Lethe's niece and her daughter."

"Wow, look at you, all this family coming out of the woodwork," Reed said, and shifted his balance, looking at his shoes.

"You're still my closest family, you know," I said to him, giving him a (very) light punch to the arm. He still winced. "And in that spirit, I feel like I should tell you...the body count on this one was very high."

He stared at me. "How high?"

"Like Willy Nelson and Snoop Dogg combined."

"Ouch," he said, turning back to the TV. "That's bad. But...if you want a little good news." And he gestured to the screen.

"Oh," I said, because the election results were coming in. I'd forgotten there was an election today. I peered at the TV. "Does that say...?"

"Sarah Barbour is getting her ass handed to her by Charlotte Mitchell," Reed said with a small smile. "Not that we're definitely Team Mitchell or anything, but I know how you feel about Barbour."

"That she's a hell beast released directly from the seventh circle and sent here to inflict herself upon me?"

"You might be taking her a little too personally," Reed said. "But in any case..." He glanced back at the TV. "...it sure looks like Mitchell's going to win, so let's hope she's a little more pro-meta than Barbour."

"She'd have to work hard to be worse," I said. "I do have to say, though – I'm glad Gondry lasted as long as he did. Can you imagine how we'd be feeling right now if he'd had to bow out before the primaries, and someone else – like say Bridget Shipley – had taken his place?"

"The entire US becoming like Minnesota is a thought that gives me nightmares," Reed said, cringing. But he slung an arm around my shoulder.

"Yeah, and who wants that?" I asked. Other than, apparently, Minnesota. Which was no longer my problem.

I smiled as I watched the results come in, and confirm the good news. Still, some stray thoughts about Shipley and Minnesota lingered like a bad aftertaste, soiling – just a little – what should have been a perfectly fine night.

CHAPTER SEVENTY-EIGHT

Wil Waters

The flights were murder, the injections were constant, and Wil Waters had had enough by the time he was pulled from the back of a police van and marched toward the Cube, the federal prison and jailhouse for metahumans.

He'd seen the pictures. The next phase of his life...was not one he was looking forward to. No more private jets to wherever. No more chefs stepping out of the kitchen to explain their most delectable creations to him personally. No more pretty girls sitting across from him for a meal and then slipping into his bed afterward, their dull, plasticine expressions barely changing.

No more freedom. For now, at least.

News cameras were positioned at the entrance to the Cube building, and someone was giving an interview under the bright lights. He caught a bit of it as the procession of officers slowed to rubberneck themselves.

"...what we have here is a prison that is filling up with people sent to our state from other places, without regard for us at all," the woman said. Waters recognized her after a few seconds – Bridget Shipley, Governor of Minnesota. Her pinched face and haughty demeanor gave her away. She reminded him of that friend's mom that everyone had, the one that made it unbearable to go to their house because you couldn't so much as disturb a sofa cushion without her losing it. "Most of these prisoners are coming from Sienna Nealon or her private detective agency, and who knows if they even deserve to be here?"

"I definitely don't," Waters announced as he was paraded by. "I was framed – by Sienna Nealon."

"See?" Shipley told the camera, as if that proved anything. Waters hid his grin and listened to the governor's diatribe until he was ushered inside, the doors hissing shut behind him.

Processing took a bit. He was issued a jumpsuit, shoes, bedsheets – all the necessities a man would need in prison. When he was finally let into the giant, open area from whence the place had received its name, he found himself almost disappointed. Orange prison jumpsuits were visible from one side to another, and cells ringed the open courtyard. Some of the prisoners looked mean, some looked extra-mean.

A guard with a name tag stitched into his shirt reading "Kennebec" went through the rules with Waters. He barely listened until one thing caught his interest, and he sat up straighter, and asked to hear it again.

"When the suppressant wears off," Kennebec said wearily, "you will not be given another dose. Under current federal laws, we will only chemically suppress you if you make trouble. So stay out of trouble and you'll avoid the dart, okay?"

Waters could only hide his reaction because of long years

at the negotiating table. "That's really a thing? You can't suppress unless we get out of line?"

Kennebec's jaw moved subtly, revealing what the guard thought of that policy: stupid, of course. Because it was. Waters couldn't agree more. "Those are the rules," was all Kennebec said before launching back into the canned speech.

But Waters had heard all he needed to. This was going to be a short stay, and then he'd be off to a place where these idiots – these absolute morons – couldn't touch him.

It was only a matter of time.

EPILOGUE

Beijing, China

"We lost the potential mine in Fountain Run, Tennessee."

The admission was stark, and Minister Fen Liu of the People's Republic of China felt it strike without any cushion for the blow. She sat at her desk, looking at the hung head of the messenger in this case, Jiahao Sung.

She shuffled two reports before replying. "What of Waters?" He was their man on this, after all. The American billionaire class was so pliable in carrying out party dictates in their own country. It was no shock to her that they were able to be bought. She'd bought enough of them over the years to know that they were all whores for their precious money and little else.

The shock was how little they could be bought for. Sometimes she wondered if she told a western billionaire there was a two-quarter profit increase in murdering their own grandmother, how many of them would have done it. All that she'd met, that seemed certain.

Waters was no different. Just another American whore she could buy and discard when he was no longer of use.

She considered her response before speaking. "Where is he now? At risk?"

"In the Cube." A simple answer, but one filled with rich possibility.

She didn't laugh. But not because she didn't want to. "He won't want to stay long, I imagine." She was not prone to smiling.

But if she had been...this would have definitely prompted one. So many birds could be killed by this one single stone...

...and Fen Liu would happily be the one to throw it, provided she could ensure that no one – especially not Sienna Nealon, or the US government – could see her do it.

Sienna Nealon Will Return in

HOME
The Girl in the Box, Book 48
Coming December 2021!

AUTHOR'S NOTE

Thanks for reading! If you want to know immediately when future books become available, take sixty seconds and sign up for my NEW RELEASE EMAIL ALERTS at my website, www.robertjcrane.com. I don't sell your information and I only send out emails when I have a new book out. The reason you should sign up for this is because I don't always set release dates, and even if you're following me on Facebook (robertJcrane (Author)) or Twitter (@robertJcrane), or part of my Facebook fan page (Team RJC), it's easy to miss my book announcements because … well, because social media is an imprecise thing.

Find listings for all my books plus some more behind-the-scenes info on my website: http://www.robertjcrane.com!

Cheers,
Robert J. Crane

Other Works by Robert J. Crane

The Girl in the Box
(and Out of the Box)
Contemporary Urban Fantasy

1. Alone
2. Untouched
3. Soulless
4. Family
5. Omega
6. Broken
7. Enemies
8. Legacy
9. Destiny
10. Power
11. Limitless
12. In the Wind
13. Ruthless
14. Grounded
15. Tormented
16. Vengeful
17. Sea Change
18. Painkiller
19. Masks
20. Prisoners
21. Unyielding
22. Hollow
23. Toxicity

24. Small Things
25. Hunters
26. Badder
27. Nemesis
28. Apex
29. Time
30. Driven
31. Remember
32. Hero
33. Flashback
34. Cold
35. Blood Ties
36. Music
37. Dragon
38. Control
39. Second Guess
40. Powerless
41. Meltdown
42. True North
43. Innocence
44. Southern Comfort
45. Underground
46. Silver Tongue
47. Backwoods
48. Home*

World of Sanctuary
Epic Fantasy
(in best reading order)

1. Defender (Volume 1)
2. Avenger (Volume 2)
3. Champion (Volume 3)
4. Crusader (Volume 4)

5. Sanctuary Tales (Volume 4.25)
6. Thy Father's Shadow (Volume 4.5)
7. Master (Volume 5)
8. Fated in Darkness (Volume 5.5)
9. Warlord (Volume 6)
10. Heretic (Volume 7)
11. Legend (Volume 8)
12. Ghosts of Sanctuary (Volume 9)
13. Call of the Hero (Volume 10)
14. The Scourge of Despair (Volume 11)* Coming in Late 2021/Early 2022!

Ashes of Luukessia
A Sanctuary Trilogy
(with Michael Winstone)
(Trilogy Complete)

1. A Haven in Ash (Ashes of Luukessia #1)
2. A Respite From Storms (Ashes of Luukessia #2)
3. A Home in the Hills (Ashes of Luukessia #3)

Liars and Vampires
YA Urban Fantasy
(with Lauren Harper)

1. No One Will Believe You
2. Someone Should Save Her
3. You Can't Go Home Again
4. Lies in the Dark
5. Her Lying Days Are Done
6. Heir of the Dog
7. Hit You Where You Live

8. Her Endless Night*
9. Burned Me*
10. Something In That Vein*

Southern Watch
Dark Contemporary Fantasy/Horror

1. Called
2. Depths
3. Corrupted
4. Unearthed
5. Legion
6. Starling
7. Forsaken
8. Hallowed* (Coming in 2022!)

The Mira Brand Adventures
YA Modern Fantasy
(Series Complete)

1. The World Beneath
2. The Tide of Ages
3. The City of Lies
4. The King of the Skies
5. The Best of Us
6. We Aimless Few
7. The Gang of Legend
8. The Antecessor Conundrum

*Forthcoming, title subject to change

ACKNOWLEDGMENTS

Thanks to Lewis Moore for the edits, Jeff Bryan, for the proofing, and Lillie of https://lilliesls.wordpress.com for her work proofing and compiling my series bible.

Thanks also to Karri Klawiter of artbykarri.com for the cover.

Thanks, too, to my family for making this all possible.

Printed in Great Britain
by Amazon